A NEBRASKA MYSTERY

THROUGH A
SHOT GLASS
DARKLY

SIOBHAN KELLY

CAT'S PAW PRESS

LONG BRANCH, NJ

This novel is a work of fiction. Names, characters, places and incidents are either the product of the author's imagination, or, if real, used fictitiously.

Printed in the United States
Library of Congress Cataloging-in-Publication Data

Designed by Robert L. Lascaro
www.LascaroDesign.com

Text set in ITC Stone Serif,
Cover title set in Mailart Rubberstamp

ISBN 978-09887090-2-7

Cat's Paw Press
Long Branch, New Jersey

For Mom and Dad

For now we see through a glass, darkly;
but then face to face:
now I know in part; but then shall I know
even as also I am known.

1 Corinthians 13:12

PROLOGUE

Nothing burns faster than paper. An old wooden building full of books was like a fireplace waiting to be lit. The store looked like a giant melting jack o' lantern, its upper and lower windows engulfed in flames. Fire trucks had arrived quickly but rivers of water couldn't save the store. Now it was about saving the buildings on either side.

It was beautiful, the tower of flames shooting up into the cold October night. Better than the Fourth of July, bigger than the Homecoming bonfire. For the town of Sherman, Nebraska, this was an unscheduled spectacle.

Amid the large crowd that had followed the sound of the fire trucks to Main Street, some were anxious. Was the owner inside? But everyone, whether they admitted it or not, felt a primal excitement.

One spectator felt powerful. And increasingly certain, as the flames rose high in the air, that justice had been done.

CHAPTER ONE

Alex Fitzpatrick, according to her friends, was the queen of tunnel vision. She preferred to call it focus. Alex ploughed ahead, looking straight at what she wanted. Gossip and personal politics and petty machinations—those irritants—were a blur in her peripheral vision field.

And that, she later realized, is why she never saw it coming: the grief, the loss, the sudden feeling of being unmoored in a place where she'd finally hoped to drop anchor.

But up until that October, tunnel vision had been Alex's secret weapon. What Alex had wanted for a long time was her own pub. She'd never expected that it would be in rural Nebraska.

Standing behind the bar, Alex surveyed the packed crowd that filled Fitzpatrick's that second Saturday night in October. It was a microcosm of the population of Sherman, Nebraska: farmers, townies, students, and professors. Admittedly, an odd place for a liberal lesbian to put down roots.

"You're not from around here, are you?" The old guy sitting at the bar peered at Alex. A rhetorical question.

Alex grinned. "Now why would you say that?"

"East Coast?" He twinkled at her from behind coke-bottle glasses.

"New Jersey."

Time for the big question. He leaned forward, the buttons on his bib overalls scraping the bar. "What are you doing *out here,* missy?" As if Alex might have lost her way en route to a Broadway play.

He wasn't the only one who wanted to know. Her Jersey friends who believed in karma figured she was being punished for sins in a former life. That, or she was living out some long-closeted *Little House on the Prairie* fantasy. They asked if there was indoor plumbing. Alex laughed at their snobbery though Sherman certainly had its *Little House* features: the crawling, covered-wagon pace of life, the friendly natives who smiled and waved at you for no apparent reason and never locked their doors at night. People, it seemed, as sunny and open as the land around them.

She had a lot to learn.

The old guy seemed to be expecting an answer. Alex gave him the Cliff Notes version. "Family."

"You related to Bill Fitzpatrick?"

"He's my cousin. Betsy Fitzpatrick was my great-aunt."

Suddenly a man's loud, angry voice cut through the bar. "Hey, we need some drinks here!"

What the hell? A few people sitting at the bar turned in the direction of the fireplace, where a group of men had pushed two tables together. Lauren was on the other side of the room and Annette had disappeared. Alex lifted the bar flap and walked over, scanning the table in hopes she'd recognize one of them. She did. Paul Nielson owned the farm supply store where she'd bought seedlings and garden implements for her kitchen garden back in June. Chuck Bauer, sitting next to him, was a manager at Bag 'n Go. The others looked familiar, too.

But there was a bad vibe coming off the whole group and this clearly wouldn't be their first drink of the night. Several were trying to wave down Lauren.

"Hey, Sarah Palin!" one of them called across the room. "We're thirsty!" They all laughed. Poor Lauren. People used to tell her she looked like Tina Fey. Lauren was a non-trad student at Sherman State, divorced, with two small kids to support. She had never voted in her life. Lauren was ignoring them and Alex couldn't blame her.

"Hi. Can I get you guys a drink?" She approached the table wearing her friendly barkeep face. Her friend Kathy had told her open confrontation was considered the height of rudeness in the Midwest. Looked like these guys hadn't gotten the memo. "Sorry you had to wait a few minutes."

"Oh, hi Alex," Paul Nielson said. "Guys, do you know Alex?" The table lit up with the fake smiles that she was getting used to in Sherman—almost.

The fat guy who'd called across the room scowled at her. "But we came to get a beer from Sarah," he slurred. He was hammered.

They ordered a round of draft Bud pints. Big spenders. Did they know Alex was the owner? If they didn't, they soon would. As she drew their pints, Don Roberts, owner of Huskers, the grubby sports bar on Main Street, came through the door. He made a slow progress through the room, greeting various tables as he headed towards the Sarah Palin Fan Club.

One of the first things Alex had discovered when she moved to Sherman this summer is that every other thing in Nebraska is called Husker-something. But for Don, she learned, it had a special resonance: he'd been a linebacker for the Cornhuskers back in the glory days of the 80s. At Huskers you got bad food, watered down drinks, and terrible service. But before Alex opened Fitzpatrick's, Huskers was the only game in town for grown-ups, the only alternative to the sticky-floored student bars. She'd gone to Huskers a couple times in the summer for a beer. Don had been all over her, asking how the renovation was going, promising to come by as soon as she opened. He hadn't. This was his first time at Fitzpatrick's.

"Hi, Don. Get you a drink?"

He flashed Alex a big smile. Don had the craggy-hand-some-cowboy thing going and he worked it, oblivious to her dyke indifference. "Busy, I see."

She nodded and fake-smiled back as she put the pints down. Did the sight of her busy pub make Don happy? Not likely.

Seems he read her mind. "Well," he smirked, "people are always interested in a new place. But you know, eventually it wears off." His buddies chuckled appreciatively.

"But Don," Alex leant on the table, feigning chumminess, "isn't Huskers the 'Cheers' of Sherman? I'm surprised you could get away on a Friday night!"

The table went silent as Don scrambled for a rejoinder. "Get you a drink?" she repeated.

The fat, drunk guy pointed to their mugs. "You're gonna have to get a pint." He frowned. "Place is too fancy for pitchers."

Don's face lit up. "Oh, I see, Alex is going for a classier crowd here! Look, there's a table of professors!" Belly laughs all around.

At the bar, Lauren and Annette were waiting for her, empty drink trays up on the station. "Gotta run, fellas. I'll send over a Bud for you, Don."

Alex slipped back under the bar flap and placed their tab on Annette's tray. "Tables two and three. They're all drinking Bud drafts," she said, pulling a pint. "This is for the guy in the red sweat shirt. Go slow on the refills, okay?"

"But they're in your station!" Annette protested, turning to Lauren. Annette was a Biology/pre-med major at Sherman State, five foot one, African-American, and built like a fire hydrant. All determination and no bullshit.

"You can trade it for a table in Lauren's station," Alex said. "Take six when it opens up. They're calling her Sarah Palin and they're half in the bag. Don't let them hassle you."

The light of battle gleamed in Annette's eyes. "Oh, I won't."

A few minutes later her cousin Bill came slicing through the crowd, his wife Sandra and Lauren trailing in his wake. Lauren was trying to get Bill to give his check—or ticket, as it they call it here—to her. Good luck with that. Bill slapped his checkbook down on the bar and wrapped a huge, callused hand around his pen. He nodded at the old guy.

Sandra and Bill, in their mid-fifties, a good twenty years older than Alex, had always seemed more like aunt and uncle.

"Well. That wasn't bad," Bill grumbled.

"Not bad?" Sandra slapped his arm. "He cleaned his plate!"

"What'd you get? No wait, let me guess." She pretended to ponder the options on her blackboard menu, as if he would actually consider anything but meat and potatoes. "Shepherd's pie."

"With lamb!" Bill snorted. "What's wrong with beef?"

If Alex weren't so busy these would be the mere opening volleys of an epic Fitzpatrick tease-fest, the dysfunctional Irish family way of saying, I love you. Or at least, I acknowledge that you exist. God forbid anyone should ever pat you on the back; that wasn't the Fitzpatrick way. Didn't matter. He'd never tell her but she knew Bill was proud to have the first Irish pub in the area bear his name.

The night wore on and the crowd started to thin. Around eleven, Barb Nichols came in and grabbed her usual seat at the corner of the bar. Barb was the owner of Book Ends, a wonderful bookstore on Main Street. Her friendly face was a welcome sight.

Alex put a coaster down in front of Barb. "Just closed up?" It seemed late for that. Barb usually came down right after she closed, or not at all. She wasn't a night-owl.

"No, I've been closed for an hour. I didn't feel like staying at home." Like Alex, Barb's home was an apartment over the shop. She pushed her tortoiseshell glasses back up her nose and tucked a strand of prematurely-white hair behind her ear.

"Glass of Syrah?"

"Perfect. It's nice and cozy in here."

"Cold out?" Barb still had her jacket on.

"Chilly. The temperature's dropping fast."

Lauren was waiting for drinks and Alex went down the bar to fill her order. When she returned, she found Barb gazing into her glass. "Is the wine that good?"

"It is!" Barb summoned up a smile but it didn't reach her eyes. She looked down into her glass again.

"Hey, is everything OK?"

Barb looked up. "Why?"

"I don't know. You seem kind of..." But her search for the right word was cut off by a bellow from the fireside tables. "Can we get our ticket here?!"

Them again. Alex was so annoyed she almost missed Barb's reaction. She froze. Like a cat does, in a split second, when it senses a danger you are oblivious to. If she hadn't been looking right at Barb, she would have missed it.

Annette was making her way over to the table with deliberate slowness but before she could arrive they all got up, throwing money on the table, pulling on their coats, shoving chairs back so hard they almost toppled over. They would pass the bar on their way out and Alex braced herself for a final barrage of complaints. But no: instead of hassling her, they shifted their collective asshole attention to Barb. As they lurched past, several of them glared at her back and Don Roberts muttered something Alex couldn't catch. Barb sat stiffly and stared straight ahead, into the bar mirror.

And as they went through the door—a beefy, beery huddle—someone called back, "Get rid of that Oprah bitch!"

Alex was shocked into momentary silence. Then, too late, she shouted, "Don't let the door hit you on the way out!" She turned to Barb. "Can you believe that?"

Barb just shrugged and looked away.

Something was definitely wrong. Alex scanned the three-quarters empty room. "Hey, I could use a break. Want to sit by the fire?" She waved Annette over to spell her behind the bar. The wait staff loved to play bartender, and she had really earned it tonight.

Annette slipped under the flap. "I heard them," she said, tilting her chin towards the door. "Pffff! Now I'm Oprah, huh? One guy kept calling me Michelle Obama."

"What? Why didn't you tell me?" Alex fumed. "I'm sorry that happened."

Annette waved a dismissive hand. "Oh, please! I can handle those crackers. I told them all black people are related, that's why we look alike." She smiled. "That shut them up."

"Atta girl." It hadn't shut them up for long, though.

Alex steered Barb over to an empty table by the fireplace. She stretched her legs out. "What a bunch of assholes."

Barb nodded. "How long were they here?"

"A while. I don't know why they came. Don's never been in here before and I'm pretty sure it was the first time for the rest of them, too. They were half-drunk when they got here. And what's up with the open racism? I thought I'd moved to the Midwest, not the Deep South!"

"Someone got drunk and let his real feelings slip out."

"But he can't be the only one." Alex took a sip of wine. "It looks like Don was finally checking out the competition. He was doing the charm thing." She rolled her eyes. "Does that work on anybody?"

Barb smiled faintly. "Oh yes. Don is the unofficial mayor of Sherman, you know. Never mind who's in office. Maybe they had a few drinks down at Don's and then came here to harass you."

"I bet that's it. Maybe they ate there and the salmonella poisoning made them crazy."

A short laugh from Barb. Then she was quiet again.

"What's going on, Barb?"

She gave Alex a direct look. "I haven't talked to anyone about this. I don't know if I want to."

"Tell me," Alex urged.

CHAPTER TWO

Barb sighed and settled back in her chair. "It's a long story. I need to go back a ways."

She could take as long as she needed. Barb was the first friend Alex had made in Sherman and she'd always lent a willing ear when Alex needed to talk.

They'd met when Alex discovered Book Ends back in March. Stumbled across it, really, on a walk down Main Street, sure it hadn't been there on her last visit to Aunt Betsy a few years back. An actual bricks and mortar bookstore in small town—though this building was wooden—was she hallucinating? Inside, it was beautiful: full of windows and light, wooden bookshelves stretching to the ceiling, deep armchairs in every corner. It smelled like good coffee. She'd been happily browsing a shelf of New and Recommended books when a woman—fiftyish, tortoiseshell glasses, clearly the owner— came over with a stack of books and they got talking. It was one of those conversations where you know immediately: this person could be a friend.

Book Ends was busy that day. Main Street was ugly, but it seemed Shermanites would support a business that sold quality stuff in a beautiful setting. Her pub could do the same. And alcohol was an easier sell than books.

Fast forward to summer, and the afternoons she'd staggered in the door of Book Ends, wilting from the intense heat and humidity, exhausted from battling the contractor who was supervising the renovation of the pub. Barb had been there for her. Like Alex, she was a businesswoman on her own. More than once she had poured Alex a glass of iced coffee and talked her off the roof.

Barb had some real nightmare stories about her renovation of Book Ends. Alex's favorite was the Floor Saga, an epic battle between Barb, who wanted to refinish the pine-plank floors they'd discovered under the goldenrod shag rug, and her contractor, who insisted that indoor-outdoor carpet was the only way to go. He and the other men who kept popping in told her how impractical bare wood floors would be. They were outraged when she stuck to her guns.

Alex had been experiencing this little-woman shit with her contractor, too. "Men still really run the show here, don't they?"

"And they want it to stay that way."

"Like when mastodons ruled the earth? Well, that didn't last forever."

Conversations like that had kept Alex sane—and laughing—last summer. But Barb wasn't laughing much tonight.

She looked up from the fire. "I don't think I've told you much about Wayne and me."

That was an understatement. Alex knew Barb was divorced, but that was all. "Your ex-husband?" And what did this have to do with what Alex had just seen?

Barb nodded. "We met at the U of Wisconsin. Wayne was in

the Ag school, going to inherit the family farm. I was an English major. Wayne's two years older than me and when he graduated he wanted us to get started with our life, right then. Lots of girls were doing the same. It seemed selfish to make him wait. I didn't have a career plan or anything at that point. So I left school after my sophomore year and we got married that June."

"You were young! What, twenty?"

"Twenty." Barb shook her head. "I should've waited to graduate first. If I'd stayed those two years at the U on my own I would have grown more, met other people. Probably I wouldn't have married him. I guess he knew that somehow."

Of course he did. Alex looked at her friend, whip-smart and funny, her beautiful shoulder-length white hair glinting in the fire. She was probably always out of his league. Grab her while she's young.

"So," Barb continued, "we came back home. Wayne was a Nebraska kid, too: his family's farm was only twenty miles from my parents' farm. Everything was fine for a while. He was so happy. All his life he'd dreamed of the day he would be farming with his Dad. Those first years we were totally wrapped up in the farm. But then things started to go wrong."

She paused, looking down at her hands. "We both started to change. Wayne was a farmer now and he wanted me to be a farm wife."

"Is there a standard farm-wife type?"

Barb chuckled. "There used to be! She canned vegetables and put a big, hot meal on the table at 7 a.m., noon and six. Wayne just about had a meltdown when I wanted to apply for a position at the town library. And the farm wife joins her husband's church, and you never miss a Sunday service. I grew up Presbyterian but Wayne was Lutheran." She paused for a beat. "Missouri Synod."

Apparently this was supposed to mean something. Not to Alex. "I grew up Catholic," she said. "Well, kind of, my family lapsed. The Shore was really Catholic then—the Irish Riviera, that's what we called it. I don't really understand the difference between all these Protestant churches." She shrugged. "All I know is, Sherman has a hell of a lot of them for such a little town."

"Well, the Presbyterian Church is pretty liberal," Barb explained, "especially on women's issues. The Lutheran Church isn't, and the Missouri Synod part of it is ultra-conservative. It's very top-down. And women have no leadership positions at all."

"Sounds like the Catholic Church to me!"

That got a laugh.

Barb's glass was empty. "Hold on a sec." Alex got up and went behind the bar. Annette was pouring a pint of Smithwick's, barely visible behind the phalanx of taps, a collection of Irish and English beers and ales that Alex had lovingly assembled. She returned with two glasses of Syrah and settled back in her chair. "You said you started changing, too?"

"I did," Barb admitted. "And I don't know if I was reacting to Wayne getting so conservative, or what. But I need to backtrack a minute here." She took a long sip.

"We didn't have children. I couldn't get pregnant. Wayne was upset about it, more than I was. Then his family—his mother especially—started asking what was wrong. But the question really was what was wrong with *me*?" Barb made a face. "It was the old story: the woman was to blame. You look surprised."

"I am. This was the twentieth century, right? Why assume that you were the one with fertility problems?"

"Well," Barb sighed. "It was the twentieth century when *I* had to get tests. And doctor said I was fine. But when it was time for Wayne...well, let's say the clock had turned back. He wouldn't get tested. Kept on and on about the big families all around us, though. His friends were producing little farmers and so should we."

"Kind of like going to church?"

"Exactly." She took another sip of wine. "I started to get restless. Bored, I guess. I felt like my mind was stagnating. I'd always kept reading, but when I wanted to talk about ideas, there was no one. I joined a couple of on-line book clubs, but it wasn't the same."

"No, it wouldn't be." Alex got up and poked at the fire, stirring up the deep, soft pile of ashes that had built up over the evening. She glanced around the room. Two of the booths were still occupied, drinking buddies ensconced in the dark wood caverns. The antique barnwood paneling throughout the pub had had been the most expensive part of the renovation.

"Finally," Barb continued, "I decided I wanted to go back to school. St. Anne's College was thirty miles from our farm; it was a commute, but not a long one. I'm sure you can imagine the fights we had about that. But I went. For some reason Wayne's father backed me up—he was a nice man—and that helped."

She lit up, remembering. "I loved it! I got back into my English major, and minored in Women's Studies."

"What did Wayne think about *that*?"

She grimaced. "He pretty much ignored it. We'd really drifted apart by then. Anyway, it took me three years to get my degree, and then I got a part-time job in the bookstore near the college. And then we started having financial trouble."

Barb looked at Alex searchingly. "Do you know much about what's been going on with family farms?"

Alex shook her head. "Just those movies about the farm crisis in the 80s. What was the one with Jessica Lang and Sam Shepherd?" There'd been several movies, she was pretty sure, but they all blurred into one plot line: evil bankers, beautiful, beleaguered farmers, injustice. "I know Aunt Betsy had some rough years, but she didn't talk about it much. Probably figured I wouldn't get it."

"Well, Wayne's family weathered the really bad years in the 80s; they owned the farm outright and hadn't borrowed much. But then in the nineties the bottom fell out of crop prices. And the government cut some subsidies for other crops. Then the big agribusinesses came in and started buying up tons of land. We managed to hold on. But it changed Wayne even more. He became harder. Didn't trust anyone." She paused.

Alex surveyed the room. It had become automatic with her now, this periscope sweep of the pub. One booth was leaving; they'd knocked a framed "Guinness Is Good For You" poster askew.

"And he became abusive."

Shit. She hadn't seen that coming.

"For a while it was just verbal. He started saying things like, I shouldn't think I was smart because I had my degree, lots of stupid people did. Or he hoped they didn't have me on the cash register at the bookstore or they'd be sure to go under soon.

Then one night as I was leaving work, a big storm hit. Some roads got washed out right away and the owner of the bookstore offered me a couch at her house in town. The power went out and Wayne refused to get a cell phone, so I couldn't reach him. I drove home early in the morning. He was waiting for me." Barb closed her eyes briefly.

"He attacked me. I'll spare you the details. Then he went out into the fields to work, just like a regular day. I packed one bag and drove to my parents. I haven't been back there since."

Alex let out a breath she didn't realize she'd been holding. "Good for you."

Barb shook her head. "I should've left him long before that. But I only stayed with my folks for a few weeks. Wayne kept calling and coming by the house at all hours. He'd lost his temper, that was all. I had to come back to him. It was sickening, really, watching him try to play sweet.

And I saw the anger in his eyes. I'd humiliated him by leaving. Everyone knew. My parents live in town and you can bet the sight of me arriving there with a suitcase was all over the county by noon."

Jesus. "That's a serious jungle telegraph."

"Oh, you bet." Barb shook her head. "He only cared about his reputation. And if we got back together everyone would just pretend it had never happened. At least to our faces."

Alex nodded. "I'm getting the picture."

"I couldn't stay in the area," Barb continued. "It wasn't safe. Madison was the only other place I knew well, and I'd loved it there, in college. My parents were really supportive. They helped me out financially until I found work in a bookstore. I ended up managing it for five years." She smiled. "Good years."

"A whole new life for you." More like another planet. And a long journey there.

"It was. Eventually though, I felt like you did. I got tired of working for other people and I'd been saving for my own place for a while."

Tired wasn't the word. Years of working in bars and restaurants (so much for that B. A. in English), watching the stupid things owners did, the way they treated employees like crap and customers like a necessary evil had driven Alex nuts. She knew she could do so much better.

"It's strange, isn't it?" she said. "There's the college here, a decent town population, and the next town is fifteen miles away. But before you came, no bookstore. And—I hate to sound like I'm bragging—" her gaze swept the room with pride, "but before I came, no decent place to get a drink and a bite."

"What's strange?" Kevin loomed above them. Alex started.

"People creeping up on other people. That's strange!" she shot back.

"Police technique!" He grinned. "Gives me the advantage of surprise." Kevin was Sandra and Bill's son: twenty-two, handsome, and cocky.

Annette was wiping down the bar, yawning. Lauren leaned wearily against the service station. More people had trickled out while they'd talked and now only a handful of customers were left.

Barb looked at her watch and started. "Twelve thirty already! I better get home. We open at ten and it'll be Saturday."

True. The busiest day of the week for both of them. But how frustrating: Barb's tale, it seemed, was only half told and Alex was none the wiser about her strange behavior, or those men's animosity. Did it have something to do with Wayne? She couldn't imagine the connection.

Barb was up and pulling on her coat. "I'll tell you the rest when we both have a few minutes. Promise. I'd like to get your take on things."

"Okay," Alex agreed. "But let's make it soon. Really."

The lights flickered on and off for last call as Barb went out the door. Alex got back behind the bar and waited for the usual flurry of final drink orders but somehow, with Kevin standing there in his uniform, nobody wanted one. Chairs scraped back, coats were donned.

"You're not going to sit in the parking lot are you? That would be really bad for business."

"Got other things to do, little girl," Kevin intoned, hands on his gun belt. "Catch ya." And he was out the door.

Her last customers waited a few minutes and then followed him out into the night.

CHAPTER THREE

She had programmed her alarm for ten on Sunday morning but instead of NPR, Alex woke at to a symphony of Jane's outraged meows. It was nine o'clock. Damn. The bed was warm and she was tired. She'd only crawled into it at 2:00.

Feeling the heavy weight of Lucy against her legs, she closed her eyes again and wrapped a pillow around her head. Time for phase two: Jane walked over the pillow a few times, then thumped from the bed to the floor and launched into a tragic, sustained wail. Cat opera. At nine fifteen, Alex surrendered. Kitchen, coffee, cat food.

Alerted by the can-opening sound, Lucy ambled in, looking pissed off and sporting a bad case of bed fur. Alex looked from Jane to Lucy. Both were named after Charlotte Bronte heroines but that was about all they had in common. And she'd gotten the names wrong. Jane, a tortie, sweet and needy and perpetually anxious, displayed none of Jane Eyre's rock-solid sense of self. Lucy, named after the self-effacing heroine of *Villette*, was a brash longhaired gray and white tabby who reigned supreme. Alex was gone a lot these days and the health codes said they couldn't follow her downstairs, but at least they had each other for company. In the pre-Jane era, Lucy, left unhappily alone, would select an object to destroy. She'd shredded a couch so badly the Salvation Army wouldn't take it.

Alex fed the girls, opened the screen door off the kitchen, and watched them scamper down the stairs and into the yard. Coffee—the great reconciler—in hand, she flopped into her armchair, yawning. They'd been packed last night with a rowdy crowd that couldn't get enough of the Harp special, and unlike her Friday customers they'd stayed till the bitter end.

The view out of her window was an endless expanse of rolling golden hills, the house of the farm they belonged to off in the distance. A combine crawled across the far fields. Aunt Betsy's farm was out that way. Bill had inherited her land this spring.

For Alex, the road to Sherman had begun on long family car trips to visit Betsy, a farmer from the only branch of the Fitzpatrick clan ever to venture west of the Poconos. Alex and her brother and sister had stared agog out the car windows at the vast cornfields, the empty roads. She was only seven on that first trip but she and Betsy had become instant buds. Aunt Betsy: short silver hair, muddy boots. She'd never married. If she'd been born later she probably would have married a woman. They'd never talked about it, of course.

When she died in March, Betsy left Alex a chunk of money in her will: a total surprise. Alex came out for the funeral, got the good news, and had an epiphany. She could open her pub here in Sherman.

Alex had spent two summers in Ireland working (illegally)

in pubs. Her photo albums of those summers held more pictures of pubs than people and she'd nursed the dream of her own pub for years. But on the East Coast it was impossible. Even in a recession, prices for commercial real estate were ridiculous and a liquor license in New Jersey ran you hundreds of thousands of dollars.

Sherman is, in a strange way, a good location. A good location is one with demand for what you offer but not much in the way of supply.

Such a place is Sherman, Nebraska, population 5,000. Sherman State College swelled its numbers to 9,000 during the school year but it had successfully—thanks to determined locals—resisted becoming a "college town." Charm was in short supply on Main Street and your options for a big night on the town were Dairy Queen, Huskers, and three grimy student bars.

Alex had been driving out to Bill and Sandra's when, about a mile outside of town, she saw a For Sale sign swinging in the wind in front of an empty building. Bob's Bar. She made an appointment to see it that afternoon. It had been a popular place, the realtor told Alex as they toured the musty rooms, but Bob had gotten into some fancy Wall Street investments that went south and he was bankrupted. Out on the driveway she looked at the huge, empty blue sky and listened to the silence, a peaceful world away from the East Coast.

Two miles away, the tall buildings of Sherman State popped incongruously out from the cornfields. It looked like Oz.

She bought Bob's in a short sale, in May.

Oz had been hopping last night, at least her corner of it. No hassles, though, and no sign of Don and company. They were probably down at Huskers, drinking tepid beer and eating microwave-scorched food. Barb hadn't stopped by, either.

Barb. On and off yesterday, she had worried about her. Barb had been so unlike herself as she sat at the bar Friday night: quiet, unsmiling, preoccupied. Then those assholes had honed in on her. Alex replayed the moment when Barb froze. Was she afraid of them? Barb wasn't the kind of person to make a scene but her passive reaction was strange.

And what was their problem? Their hostility to Alex made sense: she was taking business, and plenty of it, away from their buddy Don. But Barb? Could it have something to do with Book Ends?

Maybe Don and Co. were friends with Barb's contractor. It seemed that the Sherman Mastodon Club was bigger than she'd thought, and their extinction was long overdue. Trying to figure this out was like staring at a blank computer screen. She needed to talk to Barb again.

The phone rang. Who would call her, this early? Maybe Dad. She hopped up to answer it before the machine did.

"Hey, girl!" It was Kathy. "I drove by your place a few minutes ago and saw your shades were up. Early night?"

Alex smiled. It felt like last summer, when she'd lived in a rental house next door to Kathy during the pub's renovation. They would look over for lights or signs of life before calling.

"Not quite. We had to peel people off the walls at 1:30. I was planning to sleep in but Jane had other ideas."

"That's a cat for you."

"Yup. How'd your show go?" Kathy had been selling baskets at a huge craft fair down in Omaha.

"Fantastic! You wouldn't believe all the stuff I sold. Nick, get off the counter!" A scrambling sound. Ka-thunk. "Remember those treats you brought them last week?"

"Oops."

"I'm thinking I'll bring your girls some fresh catnip from my yard."

"Lucy will tear the place apart! No more Party Mix, I promise."

"That stuff is like cat crack!"

"Totally. So what are you up to today?"

"Cleaning. This place is a disaster, basket stuff everywhere…"
The phone clanged down. "Nick!"

Alex was still laughing when Kathy picked back up. "I'm glad you called. I feel better now."

"Why, what's up?"

"I'm worried about a friend. I'm not sure what's going on with her, but something's wrong." Alex paused. She could share the mastodon vs. Barb encounter, but clearly the story Barb had begun was confidential.

"Well, if you ever want to talk about it, we'll have a beer or something."

"Thanks. Speaking of beer, are you coming here today?"

"It'll be my reward for cleaning!"

"Good. There'll be a glass waiting for you."

Alex poured another cup of coffee and went out to sit on the broad wooden back steps. What a stroke of luck that the only rental house available on a short-term lease this summer happened to be next door to Kathy. As with Barb, their friendship developed quickly, and Kathy became Barb's co-instructor in Sherman 101: Nebraska For Dummies. Looking across the golden fields, she remembered the night she went to her first City Council meeting back in July, and Kathy's de-briefing afterwards.

Alex had gone to get the political lay of the land and hopefully meet some other business owners. The meeting had been about a proposed highway project coming through town and she had anticipated a knock-down, drag-out scene.

"But everyone was so pleasant," she told Kathy when she got back.

Kathy snorted. "Think again. Half the people there can't stand each other. Town Council is a snake pit."

"You're kidding! And you know what else? After the meeting, some people came up and introduced themselves. They knew who I was! And they were asking when I was going to open my pub, said they'd come by."

Kathy smiled. "See, you have customers, already. But listen, they knew your name before you even got here. And where you're from. And who your family is—your family out here."

"Come on! Why should they care who I am?"

"Because, honey, you've landed in Sherman, Nebraska, their universe! Little hot-shot East-Coaster pulls into town, setting up a business? You bet they're interested."

Holy crap. Alex was silenced.

"Welcome to the Midwest! Want another beer?"

They'd been out in the shed that Kathy had converted into a basket studio. Kathy was originally from Webster, a town fifteen miles away. She'd gone to college in California and had been through a number of jobs and relationships while patiently learning her craft from several master basket-weavers. When Kathy's mom got sick she decided to come back home and set up a basket business. She'd been in Sherman three years, owned a thriving business, and taught a course in weaving at the college.

"Now I need another! But what about this meeting? If it's such a snake pit, why weren't they arguing?"

"Not done. This isn't New York!"

Alex laughed. "Okay. But at least at home we know what the other person is thinking. How do you ever resolve things here?"

Kathy took a long drag of her cigarette. "Backstabbing."

"Oh, please, not that."

"It's the time-honored method. If I don't like what you're doing I won't tell you, I'll just tell other people and simmer about it. Then when the time comes, I'll get you back."

"That's Byzantine! Everybody operates that way?"

"Pretty much." Kathy wrapped a piece of wicker around

the handle of a basket and gave Alex a straight look. "Keep your eyes open. And don't be fooled by all the smiley faces."

Sundays were slow at Fitzpatrick's. The Sherman state professors—plentiful on Saturday nights—always vanished, presumably grading papers or getting ready for classes. Students were hung over and broke. Alex had learned that most of the locals would be at church in the morning and then home or out for their big noon meal, which was called dinner.

Sunday dinner was a big deal in Sherman but Alex had decided not to compete for the post-church crowd with the highway diner ten miles north. On Sundays the diner rolled out a buffet filled with dubious-looking meat, starch in its many forms, and Jell-O. Jell-O is a major food group in the Midwest. Add anything to it and it's called a salad. Including mayonnaise.

At Fitzpatrick's, Sunday refugees from sanctimony and Jell-O could take shelter. Slowly, she was building up her Sunday brunch-with-Bloody-Marys crowd. But the rest of the afternoon was always dead.

Around six, Alex was sitting at the corner of the bar, happily absorbed in a cookbook when Kathy blew in and grabbed the stool across from her. "God, I never thought I'd get here."

She raked some blond hairs off her face. Kathy was a beautiful woman but she seemed almost unaware of it. Slim and blue eyed, Kathy could make an old t-shirt and paint-spattered jeans look like designer clothes. Men noticed. But she just blew them off, mostly. Her mom accused Kathy of being too picky. Kathy's response: why *wouldn't* I be?

Alex envied Kathy's killer cheekbones. But these are not in the cards when your ancestors hail from the British Isles. Alex had short red hair and an Irish face complete with a spray of freckles across her nose and cheeks that made her look ten years younger than her thirty-five. A face destined to run a pub.

"House all spic and span?"

"I wish. I made a dent in it, but it was one thing after another today."

"What's it like outside?" A question, Alex realized, she was routinely asking these days. She used to be outside every chance she got.

"Great. There's a nice nip in the air."

Alex ducked under the bar flap. "What are you in the mood for?"

"I don't know. Not beer."

"Yeah, it's not beer weather." She scanned the shelves, her eyes coming to rest on the Jameson's bottle. "How about an Irish coffee?"

"Perfect."

"A nice fall drink. I'll join you for one." Alex grabbed two class coffee mugs.

"I love fall."

"Me too. The leaves, putting your first sweater on."

"I know. And smelling wood fires again. Can't wait to start up my stove in the studio."

They sat and sipped in companionable silence. Lauren, looking exhausted as usual, sat on her perch at the other end of the bar, a textbook spread out in front of her.

"Who's in the kitchen tonight?" Kathy waved hello down the bar to Lauren.

"John is. Quiet nights like this, I like to have him in there on his own. He's getting to be pretty good." The whisky went down with a lovely slow burn.

The door opened and two tall women came in. One had a dark brown braid down her back, the other, shoulder-length golden blond hair. They didn't look familiar. Lauren went over to their table by the fireplace and promptly came back, a puzzled look on her face.

"They asked for a wine list. Do we have that?"

They did, but Sherman was a beer town. Alex found one and wiped the dust off the lamination. "I'll take it over."

No, they hadn't been in here before. She wouldn't soon have forgotten the blonde who turned her face towards Alex, wide green eyes alight with laughter. Yow.

The blonde took the list and gave Alex a warm smile. "Are you the owner?"

Tongue-tied—a rare condition for Alex—she nodded.

"I love your place. Just what Sherman needed, an Irish pub!" She looked around appreciatively.

Alex beamed and found her voice. Just. "Thank you."

They ordered a nice cabernet—good taste—and a bit later, the lamb stew. Perched at the bar with Kathy, Alex resisted sneaking glances at the blonde by a supreme effort of will. Kathy didn't help. For some reason (not Alex's) she kept checking them out.

"I know her from somewhere," Kathy said. "I'm trying to remember who she is."

This was good news. It meant they were locals, not just passing through. "Which one?"

"The blonde."

Excellent. "Maybe at a craft show?"

"No, I'm pretty sure it's not that."

"At the college?"

"Maybe." Kathy shrugged.

They were deep into a conversation about their cats when the two women were suddenly at the bar, pulling back stools a couple down from Alex and Kathy.

"We thought we'd have an after-dinner drink up here," the brunette said.

An after-dinner drink was a pretty exotic concept in Sherman. Alex got up and poured them both a Frangelico. But now the blonde was sneaking looks over at Kathy.

Kathy gave in first. "I think we've met before."

"I think so too!" She looked relieved. "But I can't remember where!"

They introduced themselves. The women were, as Alex had guessed, sisters: the beautiful blonde was Chris Morgan and the brunette was Jess Hoffman.

"I don't think I've seen you guys in here before," Alex said, feigning uncertainty.

"It's our first time here." Chris flashed a warm smile that Alex felt in her knees. "I've been away since late August. And Jess has been breaking in new horses."

"And we have boys," Jess added. "Five and three. I haven't been out for a drink in months."

"Did you get the boys broken in, too?" Alex asked. They all laughed.

Chris, it turned out, was a freelance photographer. She'd been out of town on various assignments and was just back from a shoot for National Geographic, in Africa. Talk about a kick-ass job.

"Hey, do you teach a class at the college?" Chris asked Kathy. "I teach a class in photography there once in a while."

"That's it! I teach a class in basket weaving. Maybe we saw each other at one of those awful receptions."

"With that bad food," Chris made a face. "Where do they get it from?"

"Maybe Don caters for them!" Kathy hooted.

Alex topped up Chris's glass. "Do you like to cook?"

"I enjoy it when I have the time, but Jess here's the cook."

"No," Jess protested, "baking's my thing! Pies."

"I'm jealous. Pie crusts defeat me every time."

"You just have to make a lot of them," Chris said. "And watch how your grandma does it."

Alex laughed. "My grandmas went to Delicious Orchards

for their pies. Nobody bakes pies in New Jersey."

This led, of course, to the million dollar question. Alex told them about her Nebraska family connection, and her family back home: Dad retired, brothers in New Jersey, sister in Virginia, various nieces and nephews. Mom, gone three years now. Chris and Jess's parents had sold their farm several years back and retired to Arizona. The conversation flowed easily: family, food, travel.

Jess yawned. "Sorry," she said, looking at the Guinness clock behind the bar. "I hate to be a party pooper, but I'm beat."

They were up and pulling on their coats a minute later. Bummer.

But Chris was smiling. "Would you like to come over to my place for a drink some night? Or dinner?" She looked from Kathy to Alex. "This is assuming you have a night off," she added, to Alex.

"I don't."

"I keep telling her to give herself a break." Kathy chimed in. "Just a night!"

Alex shrugged. "New business and all. It's my baby."

"Well, maybe you could leave her with a babysitter and come out to my place for a couple hours. I'm only eight miles or so down the road, just a little ways off Highway Seven."

Alex watched them go out the door and then turned to find Kathy grinning at her. Okay, so she'd been staring a little.

"Hope she calls." Kathy's grin got bigger.

"Don't even think about it."

CHAPTER FOUR

Tuesday afternoon Alex was out running errands and and pulled, on impulse, into a parking spot in front of Book Ends. It had been a busy couple of days. She hadn't seen or talked to Barb since Friday night.

As always, the armchairs were filled with contented-looking customers perusing books with a mug of coffee in hand. Alex admired Barb's ability to remain unfazed by people lounging around and fingering her merchandise, and then maybe not buying it after all. At Fitzpatrick's, touching the merchandise meant drinking or eating it. And then paying for it.

Three kids who looked like Sherman State students posted a notice onto the community bulletin board near the front door, then sidled away. Alex had never paid much attention to this board but went over to see what was printed on the bright pink paper they'd tacked up.

She read it and did a double take. PRIDE, a campus organization for GLBT students and their friends and family, was meeting Thursday at four in the Student Center. In Sherman, Nebraska? But then, Sherman State was probably a sanctuary, of sorts, for gay students. Maybe the only local place it was safe for them to be out.

Before her move west, Alex had done some complicated calculations about her own degree of out-ness in Sherman and decided that slow and cautious was the way to go. If she pined for lesbian company, there were always gay bars—five, a Google search had revealed, in Omaha, and two in Sioux City. It would mean taking a night off and driving for at least an hour, but if she got desperate, they were there.

She thought, not for the first time this week, of Chris. Was she gay? Alex couldn't tell the other night, which was unsettling. Maybe the supreme effort not to gawp at Chris had shut down her gaydar. And could Chris tell she was?

It didn't matter, anyway. After two consecutive disaster romances, Alex was taking a break from girls. It was another point in Sherman's favor that lesbians seemed pretty thin on the ground, although on her last visit to Aunt Betsy she'd gotten the opposite impression. Every woman over thirty in Bag 'N Go had short hair and wore no makeup. Lots of flannel shirts, too. Confused, she'd emailed her friend Jen in Ann Arbor: was this a Midwest thing? A Midwest Woman thing, Jen responded. Lesbians called it—here came the laughing and winking emoticons— the False Positive. Beware.

Chris was probably straight. And if not, wouldn't it be great to have a gay friend out here?

Alex scanned the rest of the board and its announcements. Lots of action on Saturday: the high school French Club car wash, a benefit spaghetti supper for Fred Claussen, a card shower for Bill and Helen Schmitz's fiftieth anniversary.

What the hell was a card shower? She'd have to ask Kathy.

Down in the right-hand corner of the board she spotted a bright blue flyer for Equal Partners in Faith. There it was again. Back in July Alex had first noticed an identical sign, canary yellow, in the front window of Book Ends. What was this group, and was Barb in it—or just supportive? But she hesitated to ask. Even the sanest people got a little crazy when it came to religion. This time Alex took a closer look at the flyer. It invited women of "all faiths" to a meeting on Saturday at 8 p.m.

"Will you be going?" asked a voice out nowhere. Alex started. A woman had materialized on her left and was looking at the bulletin board. Who was she? And where did she want Alex to go?

"Such a sad thing," the woman continued, undeterred by Alex's lack of response. "He's only thirty seven."

She searched the bulletin board for possibilities. Must be the benefit for Fred Claussen. "Yeah, it is," she replied neutrally.

Had Alex met her? Since opening the doors of Fitzpatrick's in August, she'd been getting better at putting names to faces, but she was drawing a blank now. She sneaked a quick sideways glance. The woman was short with a petite build. Her blond hair was cut short, in a style that Kathy called Midwest Hair and which looked, depending on the hairdresser, either like a helmet or a Q-tip. Alex couldn't quite figure out her age—30s? 40s?—because her demeanor, her way of carrying herself, made her seem older than she surely was. There was something old-fashioned about her that Alex had noticed in a lot of women around here. And her cheerleader-pretty looks were fading fast.

Q-tip made finally eye contact and continued on as if she and Alex were old friends. "It looks like they'll get the harvest in all right, but all the bills...I just don't know. I sure hope a lot of people turn out for it. But then," she said, her voice rising with frustration, "everything always seems to be at the same time! I'm going to have to take the early shift serving at the supper, and then be a little late for the meeting."

Alex hoped she didn't look as confused as she was.

"Well," Q-tip said, smiling with a false brightness as she drifted off, "I hope I'll see you there."

What was that about? Maybe she'd mistaken Alex for someone else. It happened pretty regularly, people coming up and asking her if she was so-and-so's cousin or if they'd gone to high school with her. She had that kind of face.

But where was Barb? No sign of her, or of Maurice, Barb's big orange tabby, the bookstore's resident cat.

Alex poured a mug of coffee and drifted over to the magazine section. Soon she was ensconced with a holiday issue of *Food and Wine*, drooling over glossies of massive turkeys shining with butter and herbs, and pies laden with gobs of whipped cream. Food porn.

"Fantasizing?" Barb's teasing voice cut into her caloric reverie.

"Yup," Alex grinned. "But it's all work research!"

Barb plopped a stack of magazines on the coffee table and grabbed the empty armchair next to Alex. She'd pushed a pencil behind her ear and her glasses were a little smudgy. Barb looked more like herself today. Busy but happy. What a relief.

"You know," Alex said, "I'm wondering if I should do Thanksgiving dinner at the pub. Do you think anyone would come?"

Back home, there were always a few restaurants open, expensive places that served pricey holiday dinners to families where mom refused turkey duty. Maybe Don would be microwaving Swanson turkey dinners at Huskers.

"I don't know." Barb sounded a bit doubtful. "No one is

used to having anything open that day."

"I'm thinking there might be enough people on their own, or students stuck in town."

"Maybe I could come. It's a nice idea."

"You're invited then! But won't your parents want you to come home for that?"

The air suddenly went out of the conversation. "I'm sure they would but..." Barb trailed off. Her expression was troubled.

"Oh," Alex gabbled—damn, somehow she'd put her foot in it— "maybe the drive is too far for a day, huh?"

"Well, no, it's not that...but wait, won't Bill and Sandra invite you to their house?"

"Probably. But I don't want to go."

"I thought you got along with them." Barb looked puzzled.

"I do!" Alex closed the magazine on her lap. "And I want to keep it that way. My family and holiday dinners: not a good combination." A slide-show of toxic gatherings flashed across her memory screen. "Someone always ends up crying."

Barb nodded. "I hear you."

Time for a change of topic. "How's Maurice?

"He's good," Barb's smile returned. "But he still keeps getting out. Just refuses to adapt to being an indoor cat."

"The girls would go insane. I'm lucky my business isn't on Main Street, so we don't have the traffic."

"You are lucky. But honestly, he has the run of the bookstore and the apartment, people petting him all day."

On cue, here he came. "Hey, boy." Alex held her hand out for a sniff-check. No sale. He stopped tantalizingly just beyond her reach, looking at Alex a little cross-eyed. That reminded her.

"You know, I just had a strange encounter with a woman in here. I have no clue who she is."

"What did she look like?"

"Short, blond, my age or maybe a little older, Midwest hair. Kind of spacey."

"Was this just now?" Barb asked. "It sounds like Amanda Wagner. I saw her in here a few minutes ago."

Alex recounted their conversation. "The thing is, she seemed to know me, but I'm sure I've never seen her before."

"Not at the pub?"

"I can't say for sure...but I don't think so. And she really doesn't look like someone who'd even go to a bar. Too straight-laced or something."

"I know what you mean. But she could've been in for dinner with her husband," Barb speculated.

"Maybe it's like this summer, when everybody knew me, but I didn't know them."

"That could be," Barb agreed. "And I think you guessed right about the sad thing she mentioned being the benefit for Fred Claussen. It's Saturday night and Amanda's been really involved in organizing it. Her husband is one of the men helping the family to get the harvest in."

"What happened?"

"Didn't you hear?" Barb seemed surprised. "I guess I assume you hear about everything, standing behind the bar."

"I do, but not this."

"Well, Fred had been feeling under the weather but he didn't think it was anything serious. Jenny got on his case to get it checked out so he finally did. They did all kinds of tests on him, and it turns out he has lung cancer."

"Shit. How old is he?"

"Thirty seven, and they have three little kids. And he farms eight hundred acres by himself."

"Is that big?" Eight hundred acres wasn't a measurement that had much meaning for Alex. She thought in terms of single or double lots.

"Not anymore," Barb said. "It's just about the right size for one farmer. One family. Anyway, Fred's been in the hospital since then and had two surgeries. It's not looking good."

She shook her head. "And now it's time to get the harvest in. But some men have been helping out with that, and lots of women have been pitching in—cooking for them and taking the kids so Jenny can be at the hospital with him. The benefit is to help with the medical bills."

It sounded like *Witness*, Harrison Ford hiding from the bad guys among the Pennsylvania Amish. Next thing, there would be a barn-raising. Alex drew the line at wearing a bonnet.

"I'm surprised you haven't been asked for a donation, or to contribute some food. Seems most of the local businesses are involved in some way. I'm donating some books for the silent auction."

Alex was surprised, too. Seemed like she got hit up for these things ten times a week.

"Oh yeah, she said something about having to leave the benefit to go to a meeting Saturday night, as if I knew what she was talking about!"

Barb smiled wryly. "That sounds like Amanda. She probably meant Equal Partners in Faith."

At last, the opening she needed. "I've seen the signs in your window...are you a member?"

"I helped to start it!" Barb sounded proud. "It's a women's group. We talk about gender issues in our churches. Once a month or so, usually in the meeting rooms of one our churches."

This was a surprise. "But I thought you wanted to skip Mass—I mean church—when you were married to Wayne."

"Well, I did get kind of cynical when I had to be part of the Missouri Synod. But I think I mentioned that I grew up Presbyterian? When I moved to Sherman I thought I'd give it another try. It's a good congregation here."

A tall blond college-age guy came around the corner. "Barb, a customer's looking for the new Elizabeth George mystery. I can't find it." He shrugged helplessly.

"Okay, Drew, I'll be right there." She gathered her magazines and stood up. "I'd better get back to it."

Alex got up and watched Drew go around the corner of a bookshelf. "Hey, Barb?" She hesitated. "I've—well, I've been a little worried about you this week. I was hoping we could continue our conversation from Friday."

"I'm sorry I got you worried!" Barb looked guilt-stricken. "I meant to call you but we've been so busy this week."

"Well, do you think you'll be stopping by the pub soon?" Alex persisted.

"I hope so. Or you could come to my place."

They settled on Sunday at ten: Fitzpatrick's closed early on Sundays. Alex would come to Barb's apartment and bring a bottle of wine. And she wasn't going to leave until she found out what was going on.

Leaving Book Ends, Alex looked up at the windows of Barb's apartment. She often caught a glimpse of Maurice there, gazing out over the downtown rooftops, presiding over Sherman and, she imagined, finding it wanting.

This time there was no Maurice, but what she did see made her stop and stare. A pane in a window of Barb's apartment had been broken. The hole was boarded with wood. What had happened? And why hadn't Barb mentioned it?

Her short-lived sense of ease vanished.

CHAPTER FIVE

Saturday morning was bright and sunny. Inexplicably, Lucy and Jane had mercy on Alex and let her sleep in. It was 10:00 before she rolled out of bed, with a luxurious morning of coffee drinking and novel reading spread out before her. Everything seemed fresh and breezy and she whistled as she got the girls their breakfast and then went through the usual doorway negotiation: in or out?

She had no premonition of how long that day would be, how dark its ending.

❧

All week, Sherman had readied itself for Homecoming, and the onslaught of alumni and parents who would descend on Friday, nearly doubling its size for three days. Businesses had donated their front windows to student organizations, and art majors set loose with paint brushes had transformed Sherman's drab Main Street from its characteristic gray and gritty look to a mismatched rainbow of colors. Go Tigers! Sidewalks, walls, and telephone poles were festooned with paw prints.

Every food and drink business in town was getting ready for big crowds and big profits—the biggest of the year. Huge beer trucks rumbled through town and double-parked while the cops, for this week at least, looked the other way. The walk-in at Fitzpatrick's was stocked to the rafters with cases and kegs.

All through Friday afternoon and into the evening, people had poured into town: parents, friends of students, a horde of alumni, and supporters of the rival football team, Cherry State. The Cherry State fans had traveled from the western edge of Nebraska. Their loyalty was impressive: Nebraska is a wide, wide state, shaped like a business envelope with the northeast corner—where Alex lived—rounded off. North to south is no big deal but east to west, forget it. She could travel from the Jersey Shore to her sister's house in Virginia in the same amount of time it took to go from the rolling hills around Sherman to the ranchland out west.

Yesterday, cars festooned with Cherry State banners had poured into her driveway. She'd heard it was an old rivalry, but how serious was it? It couldn't be too serious on the Sherman State side. The football conversations Alex heard as she stood behind the bar were all Cornhuskers, all the time. That was kind of strange, living in a college town and rooting for another college.

The whole football insanity thing left Alex cold. She'd had enough of it growing up with a dad and brother who screamed nonstop at the TV every weekend in the fall and winter. Kathy dismissed the sport in two words: helmet-heads. Perfect.

Alex kept her helmet-head thoughts to herself Friday night, though, while she listened to a lovely sound: the constant pinging of the cash register. Fitzpatrick's was packed to bursting with a crowd of Sherman Tigers and Cherry Staters all floating happily on a sea of alcohol-induced camaraderie. Don had probably driven by and counted the cars in her parking lot. Ha.

☙

The morning sun gleamed on the cornfields, chasing away stray, troubling thoughts that had haunted Alex the past week. Thursday and Friday had been chilly, with a damp air that had settled into her bones: a depressing beginning to Homecoming weekend. As they had gotten Fitzpatrick's ready for the crowds, uneasy feelings about her conversations with Barb competed with the memory of the eerie vision by moonlight of Our Redeemer, the Missouri Synod Lutheran church.

Kathy had pointed it out to Alex as they drove by the church Wednesday night. She'd come by the pub at ten, found it dead quiet, and talked Alex into a country ride to see the almost-full moon while Annette manned the bar.

On the east side of town, Our Redeemer was a massive tan brick structure that Alex never paid any particular attention to, before.

Kathy had flicked a cigarette ash out her window and gestured her head to the left. "God's Warriors meet there. They fly a red flag when they meet."

"God's who?"

"God's Warriors. You're sure you want to know?"

"Well, now you have to tell me!"

Kathy pulled into the parking lot. "They're some kind of Christian men's group."

"Like the Promise Keepers?" Alex's heart sank. Weren't those groups a phenomenon of the 90s, long gone? Football-stadium Christianity, men crying and hugging and getting cleansed, Jesus as their quarterback. And then, as she'd once read in an article that creeped her out so badly it got stuck in memory forever, the men went home and took "Christian leadership" of their families. It was right out of *A Handmaid's Tale*.

"No, they're not Promise Keepers," Kathy said. "It's something different. And I think it's more of a local organization."

"The name is a lot more aggressive," Alex noted.

"True. But," Kathy asked, "if Promise Keepers keep promises, what do God's Warriors do?"

Alex had gazed at the church in front of them. It didn't look like the Catholic churches she knew: no thin spires, no light gothic touches. A squat bell tower anchored one end and square-shaped stained-glass windows—probably fake—went up either side. One thing she'd never noticed before was that this large lot didn't contain just the church, but several other new buildings.

"Are all these part of the church?" A glass walkway connected two new buildings. "This is huge!"

"You never noticed Fort God before? Girl, you need to get out from behind that bar!"

"Fort God!" Alex laughed. "A perfect place for warriors, huh?"

Kathy made a dismissive noise. "Yeah, I just wish they'd stay in their fucking fortress, though, and leave the rest of us alone. The last five years, that church has bought up all the land around it. They just keep expanding. Look at the size of the parking lots!"

The buildings had been dark, the only light visible coming from the big lit-up sign out front that announced service times under a Bible quote. Alex pictured the red banner of God's Warriors flying out front, the men going inside. Did they wear red fezzes? Then another image came: Klan hoods. Okay, maybe she was getting a little carried away. But the chilly feeling stayed with her.

❦

The phone rang twice when Alex was in the shower. She could hear Sandra's voice through the pounding water but the second caller was much quieter. Kathy? A few minutes later, wrapped in a towel, she played the messages.

"Hi honey." Sandra's tone was motherly. "We drove by your place last night. It looked just jammed! I think we'll be coming by tonight with my cousin Carl—do you remember him? And his wife Suzanne?" Alex didn't. "He's in the State Patrol. They went to Cherry State and they come out for Homecoming every year. After the game, we have that benefit supper first and then we'll come by. Hope we can get a seat!"

Beep.

"Hi, Alex. It's Barb and it's…eleven. Maybe you're downstairs already. I wanted to stop by last night but I was wiped out! We were so busy yesterday. Bet you were too."

There was a murmur of people in the background and Maurice meowed loudly, close by. Sounded like another busy day Book Ends. "I'll try to stop by tonight after my meeting. And if I can't, then I'll see you tomorrow night around ten, okay?" Barb paused. "It'll be good to talk. See you soon."

❦

The peace of the morning's reading and the quiet of the afternoon's food prepping evaporated in short order. At 5:00 the game ended—Sherman had lost—and at 5:10 people started coming in the door. Luckily there were lots of post-game parties so that the crowd built in fits and starts, but by 7:30 every table and barstool was taken, and people were filling in all of the available space between. Alex was glad she'd taken Barb's advice and put on a second bartender for the weekend. Annette was thrilled.

Kathy managed to beat the last of the rush. She breezed in

at 7:00, selected a prime bar stool and draped her jacket over the one next to her.

"Got a date?" Alex slid an ashtray in front of her.

"Yeah, right, with who?" Kathy cast her eyes witheringly around the room at the selection of males. It's true they weren't very tempting, even if Alex wasn't that way inclined. For one thing, the guys around Sherman tended to have really big heads.

"Be back in a few," Alex said. Jason needed a new tray of drinks and some glasses at her end of the bar were getting empty. When she made it back to Kathy she saw who the saved seat was for: Chris, defiantly clad in a faded U of Minnesota Gophers sweatshirt. They looked like old buddies. Every man in the area was eyeing them.

Kathy smiled. "I saw Chris at Bag N' Go yesterday and said she should come by." Miss Innocence.

Chris looked amazing, even in a sweatshirt. The green really brought out the color of her eyes. She pointed to Kathy's glass of cabernet. "That looks good."

Alex walked off in a daze to get Chris's wine and then was hit with another rush of drink orders. When she returned to them, Kathy was saying, "No kidding."

"No kidding what?"

"I just came from the benefit supper over at Huskers," Chris said. "It was mobbed. I was telling Kathy they didn't have half the tables and chairs they needed. People were standing around everywhere. Then they started running out of spaghetti!"

Alex didn't know it was being held at Huskers. That was probably the key to the debacle. "Where was Don during all this?"

"Oh, going around schmoozing, bragging about Sherman's community spirit."

"I can see it." Alex quickly repressed the visual of a self-congratulatory, aren't-I-handsome Don in action.

"They must have raised a ton of money, though," Kathy observed.

Alex longed to pull up a stool—the one next to Chris—and keep talking with them, but the pub was filling up, people standing behind the bar stools to order drinks and then staying there. Cold weather makes people want to huddle together and drink, and it had turned cold today. Not the damp, chilly cold of yesterday, but crisp. People came in the door wearing more layers of clothes than she'd seen in months—heavy sweatshirts, sweaters over turtlenecks, even a couple of scarves. The wind had shifted to the north this afternoon and as she was quickly learning, the wind *was* the weather in Nebraska. And it was picking up. Loud as it was in the bar, she could hear it blowing and feel the gusts as they hit the walls at regular intervals.

It was a spooky sound. To drown it out, she reached up to the CD player and popped in a collection of songs by girl groups of the 50s and 60s. "It's My Party and I'll Cry If I Want To," had just begun to play when she was blasted by an even bigger sound in her right ear.

"You should get out and see that harvest moon!" Bill bellowed as he and his crew passed the bar en route to snag a fireside table that was just opening up. Other people—people in fact closer to the table—were moving towards it too, but Bill propelled his bulk through the fray like a cement mixer going at top speed through a crowded parking lot. Within a minute of arriving, they had the best table in the house.

Alex wasn't surprised. And predictably, Bill was back at the bar in two minutes, bypassing the slower route of table service. "We need some drinks, missy!" He was in high spirits.

Next to him stood a tall, thin man in his late forties, wearing a Cherry State sweatshirt and smiling as he watched their antics. He had a long, thin face with a slightly hooked nose. Evidently Bill wasn't going to make introductions.

"I'm Bill's cousin, Alex." She put the last of their drinks on the bar.

"Carl," he returned, extending a hand to shake. "Sandra's cousin."

They made small talk for a minute, until some students with empty pints and thirsty looks caught her eye. Alex pulled pints and watched Bill and Carl wade back to their table. They disappeared behind a wall of people before she saw them reach it.

Alex had just glanced at the Guinness clock over the bar–10:00 already, the night was flying—when, over the noise of voices and music, she heard pagers going off. Neil Schaeffer, a regular, plus three guys she didn't know and a woman who looked familiar threw money on the bar and went out the door, fast. Alex made her way down the bar to Kathy and Chris and found them with their heads tilted toward the group in back of them, openly listening to the conversation.

"What's up?" she asked them. "Did you see those people take off?"

Chris, still listening to the group, held up a wait-a-minute finger. Then she leaned forward so Alex could hear her. "The guys who left are in the fire department. The woman is on the ambulance squad."

And now the wind carried the sound of sirens, faint but unmistakable. The pub had gone quiet as people cocked their heads to listen.

Déjà vu. Out in March for Aunt Betsy's funeral, Bill and Sandra had stopped dead in the middle of a conversation to listen the sound of distant sirens. Most of the places she'd lived before, sirens were so common that you only paid attention until you stopped hearing them. Bill and Sandra kept listening. Alex asked what the deal was.

"When you hear a siren here," Sandra had said, "it's usually about someone you know."

Now Chris turned to Kathy. "It's downtown, don't you think?" Kathy nodded.

Alex loved her location, a mile down the road from downtown, away from its ugliness but close enough for people to drive here in a minute. But at the moment the pub felt a bit isolated. People went out to the parking lot and came back reporting they couldn't see anything. The little hill between Fitzpatrick's and Main Street was blocking the view.

The sirens kept going and going. Whatever bad thing was happening, it wasn't small. Alex was distracted as she served drinks and her customers were, too. If they weren't talking about it they still seemed to have half their attention fixed on that eerie sound. She kept hearing snatches of conversation as she poured beer and mixed drinks.

"Is it over by the college?"

"Doesn't sound like it—the trucks are closer than that."

She brought drinks down to a group at the end of the bar. They'd gone quiet. A big man in a canvas jacket and seed cap, looking like he'd just come in from the cold, held forth in their midst. "I couldn't get through," he told them. "Had to go back out of town and take the county road over here."

"Main Street? Oh dear." An elderly woman shook her head.

"Where?" several voices asked at once. "What block?"

The man held his hands up, fending off the barrage of questions. "The police have Main blocked off at Fourth. They're turning everyone south."

Kevin. He must be there.

Now the man's friends were calling out, all at once, "Which building? What did you see?"

"Fire. Going straight up, high." His eyes were wide. "It looked bad. I don't know what building. Maybe a couple blocks down from where they stopped us."

"North side? South side?"

"South, I think."

"I hope it's not in the middle of the block," a man in the group put in. "They can control it better if it's on a corner."

Alex's mind raced. What part of Main Street were they talking about? She'd never really registered the numbered streets that crossed Main and she wouldn't know north from south without a compass in her hand. Which block was Book Ends on?

For many of her customers, though, talking about it was not enough: they had to go see for themselves. She glanced over to Bill's table. They were gone. About a third of her customers paid up in a hurry and left.

Alex went back over to Kathy and Chris. She gestured at the departing people. "What are they doing?"

They both looked at her blankly. Then Chris explained. "Everyone wants to see what's going on. It's always like this with fires."

"Half the town will be there," Kathy affirmed.

"Are you kidding? They're going to drive over to see it?"

"Of course!" Kathy turned to Chris. "Should we go?"

Chris was up, car keys in hand.

Alex protested as they pulled their jackets on but they ignored her. "We'll be back soon," Chris reassured her. "Along with the rest of the crowd who left."

Kathy held up her cell phone. "If we don't come right back we'll call you."

"Be careful!" Alex called after them, ineffectually.

She hoped the pub would be filled up again soon, with customers laughing at themselves for running down to a fire that turned out to be nothing.

Her gut told her different.

❦

Alex was grateful to her customers who stayed put: mostly students and Cherry State people. All of the Sherman residents, it seemed, were at the fire. Had they gone running over there as concerned citizens? Or voyeurs? The sirens had stopped blowing but the crowd who stayed at Fitzpatrick's was past noticing. The pace of their partying was increasing with the night and she and Annette were scrambling to keep glasses filled.

It was a good distraction. But only a surface one. When the phone rang at the other end of the bar Alex went racing down to grab it and almost knocked Annette over on the way. She put a finger in her other ear to shut out the bar noise.

"Alex? Are you there?" Kathy's voice was tense. She was half-shouting over the sound of wind and people and police sirens.

"Yes!" Alex yelled back. "Can you speak up? What's going on?"

There was a pause. She heard Kathy take a deep breath. "I have bad news. It's Book Ends."

Oh no. No. "Are you sure?"

"I'm sure. We're about a block down but we can see it."

"Where's Barb?!"

Another pause. "They don't know. We were hoping you'd say she was there—Kevin asked us to call you. Hold on." Alex could hear Kathy talking to someone. "Kevin said the firemen got into part of the first floor but they couldn't find Barb. They can't get up to the second floor."

"Her apartment is on the second floor." Alex sat down hard on an empty barstool.

"Could she be somewhere else tonight?"

"No. I...I don't know." Alex couldn't think clearly.

"Listen. She might be okay. She could be anywhere."

"Oh my God, I hope so. How bad is the fire?"

"It's bad. Fire's coming out of all the windows. They've been hosing down the buildings around it, trying to keep it from spreading. There are fire trucks here from Westfield and

Byron, too." The connection suddenly cut out.

"Kathy? Are you there?" More silence. Cell phone reception was lousy around Sherman, but it had never mattered so much as at this moment.

"Alex!?" Kathy's voice came back. "I'm losing you. You wouldn't believe how crazy it is down here."

"Come back here, then," Alex urged.

"We'll be back soon. Check your cell, I'm sending you a picture." A gust of wind hit the wall of the pub and more static came down the line. "Call me right away," Kathy shouted, "if Barb shows up at the pub! We'll see you soon."

Numb with disbelief, Alex looked down the bar and saw a handful of concerned faces.

"Are you okay?" It was Tina Davis, a pub regular.

"The fire," Alex said. "It's at the bookstore and they can't find Barb Nichols."

"Oh no!" Tina exclaimed, then turned to the man next to her to share the news. Within minutes Book Ends was on everyone's lips.

It was unbearable. Alex wanted to race down to the fire, do something. Could she? She surveyed the loud, hard-drinking crowd. Most of her staff was college kids and she would be leaving Annette alone behind the bar. Not possible.

She grabbed her cell phone from beside the register, ignored for hours now in the rush of the night. Two new picture messages from Kathy. Loading. She opened them: no text, just pictures. The first showed orange and red flames shooting up in the air over a sea of flashing lights and dark heads. The second was a head-and-shoulders shot of Chris in profile, one eye squinting as she aimed her camera lens at the fire.

She scrolled back to the first picture and squinted. Behind the flames she could see the outline of the building. It was Book Ends. This was really happening.

But Kathy wanted her to call if Barb turned up at the pub.

That gave Alex hope. No one knew where Barb was. She could be anywhere.

Barb's phone message this morning: what had she said? Think! She couldn't. Quiet—she needed a quiet place. "I'll be back in a minute" she called down to Annette, then slipped under the bar flap and walked into the kitchen.

Robin turned from the grill, looking confused. "Jason'll bring your orders out—" she began, but Alex only waved a hand and continued out the back door and into the parking lot. She leaned against a pickup truck and looked up at the stars. Breathe. Focus.

The phone message. It was what, eleven o'clock? Barb had called from Book Ends; they'd been busy last night and sounded busy again. But...that's right! Barb had said she was coming over here tonight after her meeting, if she could.

Alex had heard the first sirens at ten. What time was Barb's meeting? She visualized the bright blue flyer at the bottom of the community bulletin board at Book Ends. Eight o'clock, wasn't it? Surely a group of church women would adjourn by ten. Then why hadn't she come by here? But maybe she had another place to go, first. That must be it: Barb had gone somewhere after the meeting, and then was coming to Fitzpatrick's. She could walk in any time.

For the next hour, the front door of the pub was the center of Alex's universe. People started coming back from the fire and every new arrival brought in a blast of cold north wind that she could feel all the way to the bar. She held her breath each time it opened. But it was never Barb.

And Maurice, she thought with a sudden stab. Where was he?

The muscles in Alex's neck and shoulders were nearly frozen with tension by 11:30. Why hadn't Kathy called her back? But the connection had been really bad before. Maybe all the police and fire radios were interfering with the signal.

Then Alex looked at the door again and her stomach tightened with dread as she realized another reason they might not have called her: bad news. She'd give Kathy ten more minutes, then call. At 11:37, Kathy and Chris walked in the door, looking eagerly left and right as they came towards the bar. She knew what that meant.

The three of them looked at each other expectantly. "Barb's not here?" Chris asked.

"No, no. I would have called you."

"The signal went down a while ago," Kathy explained. "We didn't know if you'd been trying to call,"

"She's not...they haven't found her? I mean," Alex corrected herself, "seen her?"

They shook their heads gloomily. Kathy ran her hand back through her hair. "No, she didn't show up and it's still really chaotic down there."

They both looked worn out, strain etched around their eyes, soot dusting their jackets, hair, and faces, which were red with cold. Their clothes smelled like smoke.

Two bar stools opened up near where they stood. "Grab those," Alex directed them. "I'm getting you something warm to drink. Chris, do you like Irish coffee? Good."

They sipped gratefully at the big, steaming mugs Alex put down in front of them. Kathy wrapped her hands around hers, soaking up the warmth.

"What's happening down there? Did they get it put out?" Alex knew she was gabbling but couldn't stop. "Kathy, did you see Maurice at all?"

Kathy shook her head, frowning. "No. I was looking around for him."

"It's almost out," Chris said. "They managed to save the buildings next to it, but they're damaged."

"The water damage will be as bad as the fire," Kathy put in.

"The wind." Chris's eyes widened. "That north wind made

it so much worse. I think they could have got it under control but every gust that came along just stoked the flames again."

Kathy lit a cigarette. "I bet your pictures are going to be amazing. I'd really like to see those."

"Kathy sent me a picture of you in action."

"Sorry." Chris looked embarrassed. "I know Barb is your friend. It's just engrained habit." She patted the camera bag which Alex only now noticed, hanging on the back of her barstool. "Something like tonight—a fire, a big storm—I'm shooting on auto pilot."

"Do you know Barb?" Alex asked.

No. I've been in her store a couple times, but I never met her." Chris paused. "I shot a lot of pictures down there. Tomorrow I'll upload them, see what I got. Good thing I had the digital Nikon. I would have run out of film on my older camera."

"Weren't you too far away to get good pictures?"

"I snuck up pretty close. I thought I'd be noticed less if it was just me, so Kathy stayed back. I thought." She gave Kathy a wry smile.

"Of course I didn't stay back! I did get up closer, just not right where Chris was."

"They let you take pictures, right there?" Alex was surprised.

"Well," Chris said, "I'm used to being places I'm not supposed to be with my camera. The best thing is just to be quiet and stay out of their way. When I first got past the barricade a cop moved me off, but I waited a couple minutes and then went back. I think they were too busy to bother with me. Lots of times firemen and police just assume you're from a newspaper, and I don't tell them any different."

"What did you see?"

Chris blew out a breath and focused on the back of the bar, as if seeing it all again. "There were fire trucks from all over, police, firemen everywhere. They had the hoses on the second floor of the bookshop when I got up closer. Flames were coming out of all the windows up there."

The second floor. Barb's apartment.

"A Westfield fire truck had a cherry-picker and they were hosing it from above, too," Chris continued. "The flames would go back some and then a huge gust of wind would come along and then," she made a whooshing sound, "they'd flare right up again."

"Goddamned wind," Kathy agreed. "Why did it have to be blowing like that tonight? It just went on and on like that. That's why we were down there so long."

Chris nodded. "Along with half the world. I swear the the whole town was there, and I saw some out-of-county plates too. Bet people from Westfield and Byron followed the fire trucks over."

"Yup," Kathy agreed. "Better than TV."

Fucking voyeurs. "And then," Alex said, "think all the people in town for Homecoming. When my customers started heading over to see it, it looked like the out-of-towners mostly stayed, but some didn't. But that's just the people at my pub. There are all those parties going on in town, and the student bars on Main Street, and then there's Huskers."

"And Huskers is only a few blocks down from there. An easy walk."

Hopefully a few people in the crowd had paused in their enjoyment long enough to think of Barb. "Was anybody trying to get inside?"

"No," Chris said. "There was just no way, at least when we saw it. They'd tried to get in earlier. Did Kathy tell you?"

"Yeah. What time was that, do you know?"

Chris and Kathy shook their heads.

"Because I'm thinking that maybe Barb wasn't there when it started." Alex told them her hopeful theory. "I've been watching that door like a hawk."

Kathy half-turned to look at the door. "You've been doing this for how long?"

"Since you called."

"Well, I really hope you're right." Kathy paused. "I don't want to be pessimistic…"

"What?" Chris pressed.

"Well, where could she be? Barb said she might come over here after her meeting, right? But she didn't. The only thing I can think of is maybe she went out of town after that. Did she say she might do that?"

"No."

"Because if she was anywhere in Sherman, how could Barb not know about the fire? She would have been down there."

They got quiet again. But their somber mood was out of tune with the rest of the pub. It was midnight, and it got louder and more raucous with every minute and every new arrival back from the fire. A world away from last night, when Alex had been caught up in the Homecoming energy of the rowdy crowd. Tonight the same people were strangers, unsympathetic—menacing, almost.

Right after she had, with relief, announced last call, Bill appeared at the bar with Carl. They carried the cold wind in with them, and their coats and faces had a heavier layer of soot than she'd seen on anyone tonight.

"Last call," she said to Bill, "What can I get you guys?"

Bill unbuttoned his coat with stiff fingers. "Whisky! Two doubles." Of course, no one would be carrying gloves on them the second week in October. No one had been dressed to stand out in that cold wind.

They took the bar stools next to Chris and Kathy. Bill nodded at Kathy and Chris. "Damn!" he patted the pockets of his jacket. "Left my cigarettes out in the truck."

"Here, take one of mine." Kathy slid her pack over to him.

"Thanks, appreciate it. This should do the trick." He

wrapped a big, calloused hand around his glass and threw back half its considerable contents—closer to a triple than a double—in one go.

Carl took a more modest drink but signaled his satisfaction with a slow smile.

"What's going on?" Alex asked Bill.

"They got it out. Finally." He frowned. "It's a real mess down there."

"What about Barb—the owner?" Alex wasn't sure how well Bill knew her.

"Don't know. They couldn't get up to the second floor."

"I heard that. But what about now?"

Carl spoke for the first time. "Too dangerous now. No one knows if the structure will stand, so they can't send anyone in till they see what's what, in the morning. Sun'll be up when, Bill?" He looked at his watch.

"Yeah, you're right." Bill threw the remainder of his whisky back. "We should turn in. Not too many hours before you need to be back there."

"At the bookstore?" Kathy asked. She hardly knew Bill and didn't know Carl at all, but that wasn't going to stop her when her curiosity was aroused.

Carl was standing, zipping up his jacket. "I'm gonna go with the Fire Chief on the first walk-through."

Bill relieved their puzzlement. "Carl's an Investigator in the State Patrol and he knows the Chief here. And the State Fire Marshall."

Small world.

"Bill was saying the owner was your friend?" Carl looked at Alex with a sympathy that boded the worst for Barb. "Did she smoke?"

"No. Why?"

"Just wondering," he said, and without further explanation he and Bill headed out.

It was only later that Alex realized he'd talked about Barb in the past tense.

CHAPTER SIX

Barb was dead. Alex knew it as she climbed the stairs wearily to her apartment, knew it as she went numbly through the routine of taking out her contacts and re-freshing Lucy and Jane's dry food and water bowls.

In her dreams, she knew it too. Her exhausting night at the pub didn't reap the reward of the deep, obliterating sleep she craved. Instead, she woke almost every hour with a jolt, from nightmares filled with fire and smoke, sirens and flashing lights. In one dream her apartment was filled with smoke and she searched frantically for Lucy and Jane, unable to find them as flames spread across the walls of her living room. The worst one woke her bolt upright at five: Barb behind a windowpane, flames all around her, reaching out her arms for help.

She dozed in fits and starts after that, never fully asleep, afraid to slip back to a place where she could have those dreams again. Then she finally crashed and woke with a start at 10:30.

Did they know yet? They must; the firemen were going back in at first light. She fed the girls and drank coffee, gazing across the quiet fields. They brought her no peace today. Would someone call her? She wanted to know but dreaded the call.

From downstairs sounds and voices drifted up: Jason and Lauren had arrived and were finishing the cleanup from last night. Jane and Lucy wanted out, so she opened the door to the back steps for them, then headed down the inside ones to get to work.

The smell of stale beer hit her like a wall. Jason and Lauren were opening the windows. The north wind, the enemy at the fire last night, seemed like an ally today as the cold, fresh air blew through. It was so quiet now, chairs turned upside down on top of tables and sunlight streaming in. The ice machine hummed in the silence. Hard to believe how many people had been in here last night for a party Alex hadn't felt a part of.

Bickering mildly, Jason and Lauren set to work with mops and table rags. "What a mess," she complained. "People are slobs." She had scraped her brown hair back into a ponytail. Sarah Palin cleans the pub.

"Quit your bitching," Jason grunted. "Let's just get it done."

Alex turned her attention to the bar. She'd done most of the cleaning last night, washing glasses and wiping down the bar while Kathy and Chris lingered to talk over their Irish coffees after the crowd had gone. Time to check the stock. Hard liquor was fine but the beer supply was low. The kitchen stores were pretty depleted, too, and she needed something for brunch. With a sigh of relief she discovered a trove of still-fresh eggs and enough smoked salmon and cream cheese to improvise some omelets. Dill she had in the garden. If only all life's problems could be solved so easily.

The phone started ringing as she was climbing the stairs

back into her apartment.

It was Sandra, sounding subdued. "Has anyone called you yet?" Clearly, she hoped that someone had.

Alex's stomach churned. "No."

"Well," Sandra took a deep breath. "It's bad news, honey. They found Barb's body this morning. She was up in her apartment."

"Oh God." Tears welled up. She hadn't really been ready for this, after all. "Who told you?"

"Bill. He went down there with Carl hours ago."

"What did he say?"

"He said the structure was okay and they were able to go in." Sandra paused.

"It's okay. I want to hear."

"Well, they found her right away. She was near the stairs that went down to the bookstore. What was left of them."

She didn't want any more details. The pictures she was starting to get were too vivid already.

But Sandra added one more. "Bill said they found a fire extinguisher near her. Looks like she tried to use it."

Worse and worse. Although Barb fighting back was better than the passive, helpless victim of her 5 a.m. nightmare. "Do they know what started it?"

"No, they can't tell that yet."

"Thanks for calling. I'm opening soon," she told Sandra. "I'm glad I didn't hear this from someone sitting at the bar."

In the shower, the warm water rushing over her, Alex cried a little, the news just beginning to sink in. It was true. Barb was dead. No, it couldn't be. She closed her eyes and saw Barb behind the counter at Book Ends, laughing at a customer's joke, her tortoiseshell glasses slipping down her nose. She couldn't be gone, she and her bookstore, just like that.

Visine took care of her red eyes and she tried to pull herself together. Good thing it was Sunday. She gratefully anticipated the quiet interval that would give her space to think.

At noon, Fitzpatrick's was hit with its biggest Sunday crowd ever. For two hours Alex, Lauren, and Jason worked flat out. In the weeds. In the weeds means you have fifteen things to do. Simultaneously. Today, Alex didn't mind: she'd take crazy busy over soaking sadness. Most of her customers were patient about delays. They were probably too exhausted and hung over from Homecoming weekend to complain.

It was her personal philosophy that everyone should work in a restaurant—at least for one night. That one night would go a long way in the understanding department. And anyone who hadn't worked on the floor of a restaurant had no business owning one. Like Don. She was sure he'd never waited tables. One night early in the summer she'd been at Huskers, drinking a tepid beer, when they'd been hit with a rush. Don was sitting at a corner table with a group of male friends, rudely calling for a waitress to come and take care of them. He should have gotten off his ass and helped out. But he sat there like a lord, sneering at his staff while loudly complaining to his friends about their incompetence.

For most of those two frantic hours, Alex didn't have time to be sad. But there were moments. The fire was, of course, the talk of the town, and as she poured drinks or ran out to cover tables she couldn't avoid hearing snatches of conversation:

"Yeah, they found her this morning."

"Did you know her?"

"Such a shame."

"Lucky it was only that building."

On a normal day, Alex lingered at a table if she found the conversation interesting. Today she hurried away.

The crowd had come in a big herd and they left the same way. Jason and Lauren clocked out a little after three and the pub felt suddenly empty. And lonely. Into the emptiness, Barb came rushing back with renewed force. Had she stayed inside to fight the fire, hoping to save her store, rather than escaping immediately? Or had she just been trapped upstairs and tried to make an exit route with the extinguisher? Please let it have been quick for her in the end.

These were things they might never know. But Alex had to know one thing: how the fire had started. All last night, through the rush of events, and this morning while Alex waited for the phone to ring, she hadn't been able to stop thinking, *how*?

Carl had asked if Barb smoked. That wasn't the answer: Barb had quit long ago and hated cigarettes with the zeal of the reformed. And of course Book Ends was No Smoking. Alex scrolled through her scanty knowledge of fires as she headed into the kitchen. Restaurant fires were really common. Commercial kitchens were deadly places with open-flame gas stoves, and all that oil and butter handled by people working under pressure in a small space. Fitzpatrick's had plenty of fire extinguishers—more than the fire codes required.

At the Jersey Shore, unprofitable restaurants were particularly fire-prone, especially if they had red-and-white checkered tablecloths and were owned by "family." No Mafia in Sherman though, and Alex was pretty sure Barb wasn't in witness protection.

The the walk-in refrigerator was almost empty. Her suppliers were coming tomorrow, but she had to scrape something together for tonight in the unlikely event anyone showed up.

She was pulling out of the driveway before she realized that her route to the store would take her through downtown and right past Book Ends. The dread of last night swept back. Maybe she should take a detour.

No, she had to face this. Odds were, Alex was the only living soul in Sherman who hadn't seen it yet.

It was a beautiful fall day, the fields golden with stubble. Alex drove slowly towards town. The air was crisp and she'd put down the top of the Cabrio down to breathe it in, but as she got closer, the crispness abruptly went away, replaced by a heavy, bitter smell. Smoke. It hung in the sky over downtown, barely moved by the light breeze that had succeeded last night's north wind. A thin, dark column of it spiraled lazily in the air two blocks down.

This was going to be bad. Traffic had slowed to ten mph as Alex joined the end of a line of cars crawling past the store, people rubbernecking, unable to get their fill of disaster. Cars were parked all the way up and down Main Street. Two yellow Sherman fire trucks and some police cars filled the block, still barricaded, between Fourth and Fifth. She followed the line of cars detouring down to Hogan Street, and then back on Main lucked into a parking spot vacated by a young family in a pickup truck.

Nothing could have prepared Alex for the sight of Book Ends. What was left of it. Against a perfect blue sky stood a hollowed, blackened shell. The front was gone and the building gaped open obscenely, like a burned-out dollhouse. The charred remains of bookshelves, stranded in lakes of water, still smoldered. Burned books were everywhere: in piles inside the store, on the sidewalk, on the street. Bits of sooty paper swirled in the air and stuck to everything in sight, including the dry cleaner's next door, whose left side was heavily scarred with fire.

And where was Maurice? Had they found him yet?

It was only when Alex got right up to the barricade at the corner of Fifth and Main that she saw the yellow tape that had been put up around the perimeter of the building.

Crime Scene.

"Alex? Hey, Alex! Are you okay?" It was Kevin, standing at the barricade, looking concerned. That jolted her out of her trance. Kevin's normal expression was totally self-absorbed.

"Crime scene?" she asked blankly. "Why are they calling it

a crime scene?"

He looked over his shoulder at the remains of the building. "I don't know." Her face must have registered disbelief; he held up his hands. "Honest. The State Fire Marshall guys are doing the forensic stuff, and they haven't said anything to us." He emphasized the last word resentfully.

Carl stood next to a police car, talking on a cell phone.

"Kevin!" A Sherman cop called him over.

Alex walked numbly back to her car, trying to concentrate on the immediate stuff she had to do: drive, shop, cook, open the pub. But she couldn't focus. All she could see was that yellow crime scene tape. And what it said.

That the fire at Book Ends was arson.

CHAPTER SEVEN

Fitzpatrick's was empty that night. Alex had half-expected some die-hards to show up, wanting to pro-long the weekend for just a little longer. But the party was over. Homecoming was done and the fire was yesterday's news. Sherman would be zipped up tight tonight, the streets quiet, blue lights from TV screens reflecting out into the yards.

Alex was glad. She was a mess. She'd gone through Bag N Go on auto pilot, seeing nothing but the ruin of Book Ends, barely aware of what she was putting in the shopping cart. In her apartment, the answering machine was blinking: short messages from Kathy and Chris. They'd heard about Barb, it was terrible, how was she doing? She reached for the erase button but stopped short. There was one message she didn't want to erase. She hit the back arrow.

"Hi Alex, it's Barb and it's...eleven." Alex put her hands in her face and the tears –tears she'd been holding back all day— came now. Barb's voice carried on as if she were still down the road at a busy Book Ends. She be coming by tonight, if she could. Through the tears, images of Barb came one after the other: Barb laughing as she told her renovation stories; Barb at the pub, on her favorite corner bar stool, sipping wine; Barb at the register at Book Ends, petting Maurice as he sprawled on the counter. All the years of friendship Alex had looked forward to—gone.

She had to lie down for a bit after that. The girls immediately appeared once she was in a prone position and Lucy's loud purr provided a little comfort.

But even a short bout of crying gave Alex a headache and she had a whopper starting now. She popped three Tylenol, washed her face, and stumbled downstairs, leaving the outraged girls staring at her in disbelief from the bed. Leaving again?

❧

At eight o'clock, Alex sat at the empty bar, remembering the strange atmosphere the night before. At the first sirens, there had been that all that focus and sense of unease. Later, everyone had been talking about the fire, sharing whatever news came in. Now the whole town would be doing that again. Only now the question would be, what crime had happened there? Arson. Unbelievable. Who would want to kill Barb? Or was it the bookstore, not Barb, which was the target? But again, *why*?

"You open?" Bill's voice boomed across the empty room as he walked up to the bar with Carl.

"Doesn't look like it, but we are." At the other end of the bar, Jackie slid off her bar stool and John disappeared into the kitchen. What was Bill doing here? He never came on Sunday nights. And there was Carl. How long had he been down at Book Ends?

"Have a seat!" Alex gestured at the empty bar stools and ducked under the bar hatch.

Carl eyed the empty pub. "A little different from last night, huh?"

Bill and Carl certainly looked different. Gone was the soot and exhaustion of last night. They looked rested and relaxed, almost sleepy.

"That's okay. After Friday and Saturday, I could use a rest." She saw Bill begin to form a retort and cut him off. "Hey, I'm not complaining. I'm just tired. You guys looking for some dinner?"

"Supper," Bill corrected her. "No, we ate. Sandra and Suzanne really went to town tonight."

Carl nodded agreement. He had a nice, gentle smile

"Came out to stretch our legs," Bill said. "Get some fresh air."

Alex snorted. "By driving over to the pub?"

"Well," Carl chuckled, "we did have the windows down."

"Got anything to help us wash down supper?" Bill surveyed the bottles lined up in front of the bar-back mirror.

"I have a new French cordial I'm trying; it's made with apples and it's nice and light..." Alex trailed off in the face of Bill's sarcastic expression. "Okay, Bailey's it is."

Carl said, "I'll try the French stuff."

She was starting to like this guy. He had better taste than Bill, for starters. And he didn't seem like a cop. No I-need-to-be-in-authority vibe from Carl.

Alex wanted to ask Carl about the fire. But she'd just met him and besides, she knew from TV cop dramas and murder mysteries that police weren't supposed to share info with civilians.

She didn't have to ask. As she put his snifter down in front of him, Carl looked at Alex searchingly. "I'm sorry about Barbara Nichols," he said. "It's hard to lose a friend."

He caught her off-guard. Her throat tightened and the tears she'd just gotten under control threatened to come right back. She nodded and willed them back down.

Even Bill's craggy face had softened. "It's rough," Bill said. "A bad way to go."

There was a silence. Alex poured herself a Grand Marnier and lifted the bar flap. She pulled up a stool on the corner facing them and looked at Carl. "I saw you down at the store today. Are you part of the investigation?

"No, but Tom Norris—he's the Assistant State Fire Marshall—we go way back. Went to Cherry State together, and we've coordinated on some cases." He sipped his cordial. "This is good. Sure you don't want to try some, Bill?"

Bill raised an eyebrow at Carl. "No thanks, it's a little fruity for me." Zing. Bill knew Alex was gay. Didn't he realize that was a homophobic remark?

She was about to zing back that real men didn't worry about the masculinity quotient of their cordials when Carl cut in. "I was wondering if you could tell me a few things about the bookstore."

"Sure. But I didn't see the fire. I couldn't get away from here."

"No, it's not about the fire. Just some background you might have. It could save Tom some time." Carl's tone was soothing. He must do this a lot, interviewing people, making them feel comfortable. John and Jackie resumed their seats at the other end of the bar. That wasn't allowed when customers were there; they must have sensed her absorption in the conversation. She'd let it slide, tonight.

"But this is a criminal investigation, right? I saw the Crime Scene tape down there."

"Oh, there's always an investigation when there's a fire. Home, business, whatever. As for arson, we don't know yet. But the procedure is, when someone dies in a fire it has to be treated as a crime scene until we know the cause. Once that's known, the crime scene tape might come down." He paused. "Or stay up."

Alex slumped with relief. "When I saw that tape, I assumed

the worst."

"It's just a precaution. It preserves evidence."

There was a little pause. Carl had been leaning comfortably against the back of the barstool, drink in hand, looking like he had all the time in the world. Now he sat up straighter, his gray eyes suddenly losing their sleepy look.

"You were good friends with Barb?" he began.

"Yes." Alex took a soothing sip of Grand Marnier.

"How long did you know her?"

"I met her last March. But I became friends with her in June, when I moved here."

"When did she open the bookstore?"

"About three years ago."

"So it was an established business. Sandra says it was a nice place."

"Really nice." She looked at the bar mirror and saw Book Ends again, the floor-to-ceiling book shelves, armchairs in the corners. "You never went there?"

"No, I'm not a big reader." he admitted. "But Suzanne is and she loved it. She was planning on going there to stock up on books for the fall."

"You don't have a bookstore in your town?"

"Just the little one at the college. But the next nearest one is probably an hour away."

Like Sherman was, before Book Ends. And now would be again. What a bleak thought. "Barb's place filled a big gap in the area. She had customers who drove here from several counties."

"Do you know what her hours were?"

"Open seven days, wasn't she, Alex?" Bill put in. "Seemed like she was open all the time."

"Well, not exactly, but almost. She was closed on Monday. Let me think...she was open ten to eight, Tuesday through Thursday, but she closed earlier on Sundays—at five—and she stayed open till ten on Friday and Saturday."

"Ten o'clock?" Carl looked surprised. "That's pretty late for a Main Street business."

"That's right," Bill said. "Sometimes she'd be the only thing open on that stretch of Main."

Main Street could be spooky at night, the street empty of cars and people, the shop fronts darkened. The college bars were clustered together down at one end of Main Street, but Book Ends, in the middle, was surrounded by nine to five businesses, pockets of darkness. Light from Barb's big plate glass window would spill out onto the street, onto the cars and bikes parked in front. The smell of coffee wafting out was irresistible.

"She was," Alex confirmed, "except the college bars, at that hour. Book Ends is—was—" she stumbled on the past tense, "a nice alternative, if you didn't want to be drinking or watching a second-run movie at the theater."

"Did college students go there?" Carl asked.

"Yeah. Whenever I went in, students were there. And a lot of her staff was students. I don't know how much they bought. Sometimes I think they just came there to hang out. But Barb seemed to like having them around. Oh," Alex remembered, "and she was thinking about stocking some books for college classes next semester, see if she could get some of that business. The college bookstore is owned by one of the big chains and their prices are ridiculous. The kids who work for me complain about it. They try to buy their books online, but that's no good for last-minute purchases, and a lot of them seem get the book the day before they need it for class." She paused. "Or the day after."

"So Barb was going to set up as competition with this chain?"

"No, not for textbooks. But she thought she had room for the ones assigned for English classes. Novels and anthologies, some poetry."

"Competing with the big chain, huh?" Bill grunted. "Wonder how they would have liked that?" A small independent farmer, Bill was no fan of corporations.

"Not much, I'm sure." Alex wouldn't shed a tear for corporate America, either. "But I don't think they could do anything about it. You know, I'm not sure she was doing it, though; I hadn't talked to her about it in...I don't know, the past few weeks."

"Did you talk to Barb on Saturday?" Carl asked.

She told him about the answering machine message. How Barb had been really busy on Friday and too tired after to stop by after. "I kept looking for her to stop by last night—praying for it, once I heard about the fire."

"Thought you were an atheist!" Bill mocked. He and Sandra kept up the faith of the Fitzpatrick ancestors. Not a conversation she was about to have.

Carl steered them back to the topic. "Was the store open for its regular hours yesterday?"

"I'm not sure. Oh, but I did ask Barb about it one time." It was last month; Alex had swung by Book Ends one afternoon. She'd been asking around about what to expect during Homecoming weekend, and was wondering how it had gone for Barb the past few years.

"She told me the Friday was always great; she did a lot of business, and Saturday morning, too. Sounds like it was the same this year." A busy Friday, and Saturday morning too, when Barb had left her message. "But then Barb said the rest of Saturday was a real bust. People were all tied up with the parade, and the game, and the parties."

Alex smiled. "She was so funny, talking about how the parade passed right by her window but no one came in. All these people walking by! So this year she was going to put out some signs on the sidewalk, try some gimmicky thing to get people in."

"Like what?" Bill scoffed. "A poetry reading?"

Carl chuckled. "Come on Bill, you know you can't resist a poetry reading."

"Try me."

"I have to say," Carl admitted, "I didn't even notice Book Ends when we were at the parade."

Bill shook his head. "We were blocks down from it. But hell, nobody's thinking about books on Homecoming Saturday. I want to look at the bands and floats...and cheerleaders," Bill leered. "And then go watch us pop those Cherries!"

"Not this year." Carl leaned back in his chair, looking smug.

"Not most years, from what I hear...isn't that right, Bill? Like some more, Carl?" His snifter was empty.

"Just a little bit, thanks. So, was Barb cutting her hours this Saturday?"

"I'm pretty sure she wasn't going to be open past six or seven...oh wait, there was a benefit Saturday night, for a local farmer with cancer, and I think she was going to that. We talked about it when I stopped by there on Tuesday." What had Barb said? "That's right, she was donating books for the silent auction. And then she had her meeting. That was at eight, I think."

"Yeah, we went to that benefit, too. Sure was a lot going on that night," Carl remarked. "Now this meeting—what was it? A book club?"

"No, this was a group called Equal Partners in Faith."

"So what do they do?"

"I don't know exactly." Alex shrugged. "It's a women's group, and Barb said they talked about gender issues in their churches."

"Gender issues!" Bill hooted. "Bunch of femi-nazis, I bet, griping about their husbands."

She refused to be goaded. "I got the sense it was a little more interesting than that," she told Carl. "But that's all Barb told me about it. Sorry."

"You wouldn't know where they met?" Carl didn't look hopeful.

"Barb said they met at the meeting rooms of their churches—the women were from different ones."

Carl made a note. "You were saying that you and Barb had talked about Homecoming, and what to expect. Did you two talk about your businesses a lot?"

"All the time," Alex affirmed.

"So if she was having problems at Book Ends, you would have heard about it?"

"Problems at Book Ends?" This threw her for a loop.

"We don't know if there were any, but it's something the Sherman P.D. will need to find out. Would Barb have talked to you about it?"

"I think so, yes. I mean, I told her about everything going on here—new stuff I was trying, problems with staff. But," Alex amended, "it was all everyday stuff. We never got into the details of our finances or anything."

"You must have had a sense of how she was doing, though?"

"Yeah. Like I said earlier, she was doing well. Barb drew in people from town and the college, and all over." Alex had envied all the out-of-county plates in front of Book Ends, proof of a far-flung customer base that made the difference between just getting by, and success. Barb told Alex that she too would soon have a loyal following willing to drive a bit to spend some time at Fitzpatrick's. She'd been right. Actually, Barb had helped that along, recommending the pub to her customers who were looking for somewhere to grab a bite before a long drive home. Those people would be reading about the fire in the Sunday papers. How sad.

"You mentioned staff," Carl continued. "Did Barb have any trouble with her staff—lately, or that you heard of in the past?"

The disgruntled ex-employee-as-arsonist theory. Alex

couldn't help him there. "No. Barb had a good crew: college students and some people from town. It was a nice place for them to work, a lot nicer than the fast food places, where most of the jobs in Sherman are. Barb was a laid-back boss. In fact, she had a big backlog of applications from people who wanted to work there."

Carl nodded, folding his arms across his chest. "Sounds like things were going well there. Do you know if she was she having any..." he paused. "Any personal problems lately?"

"Personal problems?" Alex parroted his question back. "Why, have you heard about something?"

She was stalling. It had been just over a week ago that Barb had sat where Bill and Carl sat now, worrying Alex by her quietness and preoccupation.

"No," Carl said. "Eric, the police, they haven't heard anything. But investigations turn up stuff you wouldn't expect. If it wasn't an accident, Barb's personal life becomes a factor." He looked intently at Alex. "Any problems that you knew of?"

Up to this moment she'd been completely open with Carl. But now she hesitated, pretending to search her memory while she decided what to do. On the one hand, she had little to offer him: Barb's partly-told story, some formless misgivings. On the other hand, nice as he was, Carl *was* the police. Did she want the very personal story of Barb's marriage and divorce to become part of the police record? Stuff got turned up in investigations, Carl said. Including stuff that didn't need to be. Barb was such a private person.

"No," Alex lied. "She seemed fine."

"Okay. Thanks. This is helpful. I'll pass it onto to Tom." He looked at her a bit doubtfully, though. He'd caught the hesitation.

Hiding her emotions wasn't Alex's strong suit. And she wasn't great at lying, either. "Will I need to talk to the Sherman police?"

"No. They're talking to some folks, but I doubt they'll come to you. If you think of anything else, though, will you give me a call?"

"You know the number," Bill said.

"I'll be here tomorrow, maybe Tuesday. But after that," Carl added, handing Alex a shiny white card with a blue police shield, "if you think of something, here's my cell and office number."

Not a soul had come into Fitzpatrick's the whole time they were talking. Bill and Carl walked out the door. It was high time she and her staff did the same. Jackie ran around turning chairs over the tables at top speed, delirious at the prospect of release, while John shut down the kitchen with equal speed.

Her bed, the cats, and a warm tot of Jameson's beckoned, but wasn't she supposed to be doing something, going somewhere still tonight? Alex checked her Blackberry calendar: 10pm, Barb's. Bring wine.

At 10:00, she dragged herself upstairs with a heavy heart.

CHAPTER EIGHT

It felt like forever since she'd talked to Kathy, though it had only been since Saturday night. Monday morning, Alex dialed her number as she sipped her first cup of coffee. Kathy got up with the dawn—or before. No worries about waking her. When they lived next door last summer, Alex would look out her kitchen window, eyes barely open, and see Kathy cheerily trekking to or from her basket studio with an armful of willow, her cats Nick or Eliot in tow. In the winter, Kathy said she often got up at four, made coffee, and wove baskets by candlelight. Alex had an open invitation to join her. "Coffe'll be on! We can watch the sun rise."

Not likely. Years of bar and restaurant work had forced Alex to become a night-owl. It had been a hard fight against a biorhythm that naturally gravitated towards mornings.

Kathy's machine picked up after three rings. Rats. No weaving this morning. Or probably—Alex looked at her wall clock: nine—weaving begun hours ago and now errands well underway. She left a message, hoping it wasn't the beginning of a long round of phone tag. Phone tag had become the norm with her long-distance friendships. She and her friend Erin had had a four-month round once.

Alex had slept hard and felt more like herself this morning. The exhaustion, the fogged sense of unreality she'd been living in since Saturday night was gone. Last night, curled up in bed with the girls, she'd dreaded another bout of nightmares and anticipated that the yellow crime scene tape would flutter through her dreams. It hadn't. Not that she could remember, anyway.

But once awake, the crime scene tape came back, framing the image of the burned-out bookstore. It flickered through her mind as she dressed, and as she stocked the bar refrigerator and helped Robin prep for lunch. The soundtrack to the image was Carl's questions.

He'd asked a lot about the business, how it was doing, opening hours. Probably the most important thing she'd told him was that Barb hadn't planned to be open that night. Businesswise, it made sense not to sit waiting for customers who had football and partying on their minds. But it might have been the worst decision Barb ever made. The first sirens had sounded at ten; the fire started some time before that. On a normal Saturday, Book Ends would have open and busy, the fire quickly detected, the store vacated and the fire trucks on their way.

But then Carl had veered into more disturbing territory: unhappy employees, personal problems. The possibility that the fire wasn't an accident. They clearly didn't know much about the causes of the fire, but Carl had been serious about those questions. He'd been doing his job a long time. Maybe he had a feeling. It was all very unsettling.

Lunch was slow. Not as dead as last night, but slow enough that the overhead was more than what the sparse lunch checks were adding up to. At 1:30 the bar phone rang, breaking into the quiet and Alex's gloomy thoughts.

"Hey girl!" It was Kathy. "I thought I was gonna leave a message that you're it."

"No, we're actually live."

"It's been a crazy couple of days over here," Kathy reported. "Mom wasn't doing well yesterday. We had to take her to the hospital."

"Oh no! Is she okay?"

"She's better now. Dad and I just took her home a while ago."

Her mom's health was one of the reasons Kathy had come home after all those years away and her Dad, who was in his late seventies, really relied on her. It was the only topic she was reserved about. Alex didn't press her for details.

Kathy switched topics. "So how have you been? I heard about Barb on the local news yesterday afternoon, at the hospital. I figured you already knew by then."

"Yeah, Sandra called me in the morning. She'd heard it from Carl; he was down there with the fire investigators. Then he and Bill came to the pub last night. Carl asked me a bunch of questions." She heard a truck rumble into the parking lot and looked out the window. "Hey girl, I gotta go. The Guiness guy's here. Are you coming by today?"

"I've got a ton of things to do. Can you come over here, tonight? It's Monday—you always say Mondays are slow."

"That's what I thought about brunch yesterday, and we got swamped!"

"Well, why don't you see how it goes and if it's quiet, come over around nine? I bet you can get someone to cover the bar for a while. And you can go back to close."

"I'll try," Alex half-promised.

Kathy went in for the kill. "I'll see if I can get Chris to come, too."

Hmmm. "I'll see if Annette can come in. Anyway, I wanted to talk to you about the fire, and I can fill you in on last night."

"Really? I want hear all about that! See you tonight, okay? I'll make some snacks."

"Don't make anything that can't keep! I might not—" But Alex was talking to a dial tone.

❧

Kathy was right. Alex got Annette on the first try. She had no plans for the night and jumped on the opportunity for extra cash.

A couple of peaceful hours stretched ahead. Her armchair under the windows had never seemed so luxurious as she settled into it with a cup of tea and a Miss Marple mystery she'd been reading in fits and starts for weeks. Since opening the pub, reading had become a lost pleasure. She used to gobble up a little novel like this in two days, max.

Of course, the moment she got comfortably ensconced, Lucy and Jane emerged from wherever they'd been sleeping, clamoring for attention and treats. Then they went out. But there was a catch. They wanted her to come out too, and hang with them on the back steps. Lucy gazed imperiously up at her through the screen door.

"Sorry, sweetie. I need to sit down and relax for a while. In a chair." Lucy blinked huge green eyes, reached up to a full stretch on the screen door and tore her claws all the way down, leaving two perfectly parallel tears.

"Bad cat!" she called to Lucy's back as she moseyed deliberately down the stairs, tail flicking. She'd made her point.

Alex returned to her chair and became quickly immersed in the world of St. Mary Mead. A knock on her screen door wrenched her out of it.

For people who grew up in Sherman, drop-by visitors were just a part of life. In Jersey, and everywhere else Alex had lived, arriving at someone's door without prior warning guaranteed a startled and frosty "welcome." Your home was your castle and if the building codes allowed it, people would have moats and drawbridges. They had to make do with fences. In the summer, Alex told Kathy how struck she was by the almost total absence of yard fences in Sherman.

Kathy had laughed. "Fences? Then we couldn't see what everyone else was up to!" Then she'd told Alex about drop-bys. "You're supposed to put up a pot of coffee in the after-noon and always keep some cookies or pie on hand."

Not likely.

"Alex, are you home?" a familiar voice called out.

It was Sandra, standing at the screen door with Suzanne. She was holding a big orange cat. Not Lucy: wrong color, and Alex was the only person in the world allowed to pick Lucy up. He looked vaguely familiar.

"They just found him," Sandra explained as they came into the kitchen. Maurice, his paws draped over Sandra's shoulder, gazed imperturbably at Alex.

"Oh my god, Maurice!" Tears pricked her eyes. "Where were you?" She stroked his broad head.

"So this *is* Barb's cat? We figured you would know."

"Carl called us," Suzanne explained. "He was down at the bookstore, and he said this cat just showed up. He wouldn't go away."

"I thought..." Alex trailed off. She thought he'd died with Barb, up in the apartment.

"That's what I thought, too," Sandra said. "I guess he got out somehow."

Clearly Maurice had had a rough couple of days since then. He was thinner, and his normally sleek and burnished fur looked dull. Alex scratched his cheek. "Poor guy. He must be starving."

He was. Alex put down a plate of Whiskas and he was on it like a shot. A few minutes later he followed them into the living room, flopped on the rug, and began a leisurely clean-ing of his face and paws.

Sandra voiced the question they'd all been thinking. "What are we going to do with him?"

Maurice sprawled on the rug, looking totally at home in Alex's living room. Could she keep him? He was a great cat, big and sweet, and he already knew her so the adjustment for him wouldn't be that hard. And he was Barb's cat.

As if on cue, the girls made their presence known at the screen door. Jane began a series of piercing howls and Lucy clawed the doorframe. Reality check. She couldn't adopt an adult cat and then leave the three cats to get to know each other while she ran the pub. "I can't," she sighed. "My two would go nuts and I'm hardly ever here."

Sandra squatted down to pet him. "How about if I take Maurice out to our place for now? He'll have to be outside with the other cats, of course. Was he an indoor cat?"

"He was supposed to be, once they moved in over the shop; Barb worried about the traffic on Main Street. But he'd been an outdoor cat before and he wasn't having it. She said he snuck out all the time."

"There's the shelter in Sioux City," Sandra said. "But I think he'd be happier with us out on the farm, at least for now."

Suzanne had an idea. "You know what? Maybe you can run an ad in the Sherman paper, for someone to adopt him."

"Great idea," Alex said. "We can include a picture. Maybe a Book Ends customer will want to adopt him. Everybody knew him down there." He would go from room to room, tail up, greeting everyone, commanding attention. "And he likes people."

After they left, Alex reheated her coffee in the microwave and picked up Miss Marple, but she couldn't concentrate. Where had Maurice been since Saturday night? Probably he'd been near the bookstore the whole time, checking it out when no one was around. Looking for Barb.

She should have remembered his habit of slipping out the

door with customers. He was very nonchalant about it, and often Barb wouldn't even know he'd gone out until he reappeared, scratching on the front door to get in. Alex had seen this happen a couple times. Barb would throw her hands up in frustration, then laugh at his ingenuity.

Chris called on the pub phone when Alex was setting up with Sarah and Kristen. "The message I left yesterday...I heard about Barb on the radio and wasn't sure if you had."

Seems the story had been covered everywhere. Nothing like a grisly death to spice up a slow news day. But Alex thanked her for calling.

"Of course." Of course. She liked the sound of that.

Chris hadn't talked to Kathy yet and had been planning on coming by the pub to say hi tonight. Alex told her about Kathy's invite.

"Sounds good," Chris said easily. "Something to look forward to, today."

"For me too." Maybe too much. Time to slow down. And put the gaydar on tonight. Of course, she could just cut to the chase and ask Chris some leading questions about her love life. But she didn't want to be that bold.

Maybe Kathy would do it for her.

CHAPTER NINE

"**C**ome on in, girl!" Kathy called.

Alex stood at the screen door, looking into Kathy's lighted kitchen. It was a flashback to last summer, and all the nights she'd stopped by for a beer, or for a cup of coffee in the morning before heading over to the pub renovation. Kathy was always at work on a basket—or two or three—and they would perch in the middle of her current projects, talking as she wove.

Her house was a beautiful two-story Victorian. The owners before her had really let it slide, so the price was right when she came along. Kathy had scraped and painted and, with a carpenter friend, restored the original gingerbread trim that made her fall in love with it.

Nick and Eliot came running in to greet her, tails up, eyes wide. Both cats were long haired: Nicky a stripy silver tabby and Eliot, a big regal black and white. Kathy was pulling cheese puffs out of the oven. The kitchen smelled amazing.

The dining room table was filled with yet more temptations: guacamole and chips, quesadillas and salsa. Chocolates in a bowl. Eliot jumped onto his customary chair and settled himself in for a social evening as Alex opened the bottle of Pinot Noir she'd brought. The room was softly lit with candles.

"Hey, did you get a hold of Chris?" she called into the kitchen, attempting a casual tone.

Nice try. Kathy arrived with cheese puffs on a plate and mischievous twinkle in her eye. "She should be here soon."

Alex pretended she was too preoccupied with her first bite of guacamole to see it. "This is fabulous. If you don't get a chip in here soon, I'm gonna polish it off myself."

Kathy reached for a chip. "Not to worry. Friends don't let friends eat alone."

Alex laughed. Two days worth of tension began to ease out of her shoulders. "Did I ever tell you about my friend Erin? In Florida?"

"I don't think so."

"Erin was renting a house, and her next door neighbor had an avocado tree. And it was so big it would drop avocados into Erin's yard. Her neighbor said, hey, take whatever falls into your yard. Can you imagine—avocados falling into your yard?"

"A guacamole tree!"

"Right? But Erin won't touch them: too fattening. She calls them Nature's Little Twinkies!"

Kathy laughed. "Perfect! If it tastes great, you know it's loaded with fat. Even if it grows on a tree."

"Hello?" Chris's voice called from the back door. And then there she was, in a butter-colored suede jacket and faded jeans, her cheeks rosy from the cool night air, a bottle of red wine in her hand. Alex had just put another loaded chip in her mouth and her cheeks were full of guacamole. Smooth.

"I didn't know you lived here!" Chris exclaimed. "Isn't this the Baker house?" She put the wine and a loaf of fresh-baked bread on the table.

Kathy anticipated Alex's confusion. Nebraska 101 time. "The Bakers are the people who owned it before me. So that's what people still call the house. And will, for ten more years, probably."

"You did a lot of work, huh?" Chris was clearly impressed. "The house hasn't looked this good since I was a kid."

Kathy beamed. "A labor love." She summarized the restoration for Chris. Alex listened. She was eager to talk about Book Ends but reluctant to break up the lighthearted mood.

Kathy beat her to it. "Have either of you heard anything else about the fire?"

Chris shook her head. "Just what's been on the news. Which isn't much."

"I have—kind of," Alex turned to Chris. "Bill and Carl came by last night; I was just starting to tell Kathy about it when I had a beer delivery. Oh but wait—guess what? Maurice showed up!" She re-capped Sandra and Suzanne's visit. "Now we need to run an ad, see if we can find him a good home."

Kathy pondered for a minute. "Hold up on that ad. I might have room for a third cat. The boys might be okay with that."

Alex sighed. "I wish I could take him. The girls would have a nervous breakdown."

Chris was looking into the candle. "Smoke likes other cats," she mused. "And Charlie—my dog—just ignores them." She smiled. "Maybe I'll go by your cousins' place and meet Maurice. I should be near there tomorrow."

Alex melted. Kindness: nothing was more important. Or more attractive. Chris was kind.

They grazed for a few minutes, talking only about the food. Then Alex resumed her story. "It was weird last night. Like, it seemed all casual but underneath it really wasn't." She paused. "Carl asked about the store hours. He wanted to know if Book Ends was doing well. I told him it was."

"They always want to know that." Kathy re-lit a candle that

had flickered out. "That's the first thing, with a business fire."

"Isn't that strange, though?" Chris asked. "That they have to rule out the victim, first—as arsonist?"

Kathy shook out the match. "But could the cops really be thinking that? Because when people set their businesses on fire, when do you ever hear of them dying? They're always long gone."

Barb setting fire to her beloved store: impossible. More bizarre than any science fiction she had ever stocked. "Hopefully they'll get off that tack soon," Alex said. "I wonder if they'll have access to her bank records."

"But, wait," Chris pointed out. "They don't even know if it was arson."

Kathy lit a cigarette. "Sounds like they think it's a possibility, though."

"Definitely." Alex leaned forward. "Carl asked if Barb had any unhappy employees. Or any personal problems. Freaked me out."

There was a silence as they digested this.

"Did she?" asked Chris.

Alex hesitated. Chris noticed it.

Kathy, busy refilling the chip bowl, didn't. "Chris, do you remember when the Dairy Queen burned down a few years ago?"

"I heard about it. I was traveling."

"Dairy Queen burned down?" Alex was confused. "But we have one."

"Oh, "Chris explained. "They rebuilt it, fast. That place is a real moneymaker."

Kathy rolled her eyes. "God forbid we should have a Midwest town without a Dairy Queen. Anyway, that was a bad fire—like Book Ends. The building was gutted. But I don't remember an investigation. They figured out pretty fast it was a grease fire and that was that."

"But what time of day was this?" Alex asked. "I mean, if

they were still open it would have been a no-brainer to figure it out, right?"

Kathy took a long drag on her cigarette, thinking. "No, it wasn't during the day. I'm pretty sure it was at night and they were closed. Because there was no one there, no danger of anyone getting hurt. I remember that part."

"So what was the cause?"

"Oh, I think a kid didn't turn one of the fryers off, something like that."

Alex's gaze swept over the many lit candles in the dining room. She tapped the top of a hurricane lamp, a red candle glowing within. "I love these. But I wouldn't have them on my pub tables."

Chris nodded. "Probably a good idea. Especially when it gets really packed, like it was Saturday."

"Yeah," Kathy added, "and people are drinking up a storm."

"No candles or fryers at Book Ends," Alex said. "And no smoking. So what *started* it?"

Chris gestured to Kathy's big oak bookcases, lit candles perched on the edges of the shelves. "There was plenty of fuel. When I heard it was Book Ends, my first thought was, all those books. But how did it start? Jess and I were talking about it yesterday and I wondered if Barb had started serving food since last time I'd been in there. Sandwiches and cookies and stuff. I read some bookstores make more profit on that, than on books."

"I bet," Alex agreed. "But Barb wasn't into the designer coffee and scones thing. People can go up to the big chain bookstore in Sioux City if they want to pay three dollars for a cup of coffee. Barb's was free. It was all part of that cozy feeling in the store." Sadness swept back.

"Those chains are so sterile," Chris grumbled. "Exactly the same, wherever you go. So boring."

Alex nodded. "Like McDonald's. When Barb was renovating the store, everyone told her she could never compete with that chain. The chain was struggling anyway, with the online competition. But she thought there were enough people who still loved bookstores. And she gambled that they were burned out on the chains and wanted somewhere a little warmer, smaller, with a real bookseller as opposed to some minimum-wage drone. Turned out she was right."

"Where did she make the coffee?" Chris asked. "Did she have a kitchen?"

"No, just a little area in the back with a counter for the coffeemaker and a sink. A Bunsen with three pots. I noticed it because it's the standard restaurant kind."

"Huh." Chris pushed her chair back and stretched her long legs out. "I can't see a big fire like that starting from a coffee maker."

Kathy shook her head. "No way."

Alex saw another possibility. "What about Barb's apartment? It could have started up there."

"I hadn't thought much about that," Chris admitted. "Just all those books in the store."

"You know, maybe you're right," Kathy said. "Maybe she just left an iron on. Or it started in her kitchen, somehow."

"What was her place like up there?" Chris asked.

Alex thought for a minute. She'd been to Barb's apartment three of four times this summer, before the pub opened. "Small, but homey. Four rooms: living room, kitchen, bedroom and bathroom. There were bookshelves in the living room, maybe in the bedroom too. Her bedroom was small and the kitchen was *tiny*. But Barb said she didn't care; she didn't use it much."

"I know lots of single people who don't cook," Chris said. "I do, but then I'm on the road so much, I really get into doing homey things when I *am* home."

"Right," Kathy agreed, "so then it's kind of a treat. When you're doing it day in, day out, though, it can really be a drag, just cooking for yourself."

Alex had been there. "I know, where's the motivation?" She had plenty of motivation these days, of course. For her customers, anyway.

Kathy shrugged. "I go through periods where I'm living on microwave popcorn, or whatever. My friend Jill, she just can't be bothered. She just stands at the counter and eats ice cream out of the container or soup off the pot on the stove."

Chris raised her eyebrows. "I thought only single men were that bad."

Uh-oh. Was this the voice of experience? Alex had resolutely switched on her gaydar when Chris arrived, but either there was nothing to read, or her old system had broken down from attrition these past few months. But Alex wasn't getting a straight-girl vibe from her, either. She pictured those guys who swept the beach with metal detectors on summer mornings, searching for coins and watches. No loose change for her today.

"Well," Alex steered them away from the dining habits of straight men, "Barb told me she used to cook three square meals a day for her husband. So I bet not cooking was really liberating for her, after her divorce."

"She was divorced?" Chris asked.

"Yeah, a while ago. Anyway, after I opened the pub, she was a regular for late dinners after she closed up." A bowl of soup, a basket of bread, and a glass of red wine: that had been Barb's ticket.

"Well, then," Kathy looked from Alex to Chris, "doesn't sound like it was a kitchen fire."

"What about an electrical fire?" Chris asked. "Those are really common, too. Especially in older buildings. How old was it?"

Kathy knew. "Old. It was one of the original buildings on Main Street. Turn of the century. Beautiful. And solid, like they used to make them. Too bad it was wooden instead of brick, like most of the other ones."

"That's true. But did Barb have it re-wired?" Alex thought

back to the renovation stories, but couldn't remember anything about wiring.

"Who was her contractor?" Chris asked.

Alex came up blank again. "I don't know if she ever mentioned a name. Some jerk."

Chris shook her head. "I could tell you stories about when my log cabin was being assembled. I just about killed the crew—and some of them were guys I'd grown up with! The worst guy," she rolled her eyes, "was an old boyfriend." Old boyfriend. Crunch. The words rang in Alex's ears as Kathy and Chris traded stories about their maddening experiences with workmen. She heard their voices faintly in the background as she processed the information. Old boyfriend. Damn. No doubt there was a current one, somewhere.

"So," Chris was saying, when Alex tuned back in, "I stood there with steam coming out of my ears. But he could have cared less."

"Yeah," Kathy commiserated, "I've been down that road."

"These guys talk down to you, too? " Chris asked. "But you're so handy!"

"Right, but they never expect that. So I let them start the condescending shit, then I pull the rug out from under them." She cracked a wicked smile. "It's fun. But you know, it shouldn't be hard to find out who Barb's contractor was."

"Well," Alex said, "I hope we find him, and find out she had really old wiring, and that's what it was. Or they discover she left an iron on. I really want this to have been an accident."

Kathy nodded. "Me too. Sad as that would be, it's better than the alternative."

"The alternative being arson" Alex looked from Kathy to Chris. "But arson to get Book Ends or to get Barb? Was Barb murdered?"

Murder. The word hung in the air.

The wind was picking up outside. High above them, the branches of Kathy's elm tree creaked.

Chris cupped her hand around the flickering flame of the big green candle in front of her, looking at it thoughtfully while she spoke. "I have to say...I have a bad feeling about this. Have had, since Saturday."

"Me too," Kathy put in quickly. She pulled the band off her ponytail and readjusted it. "The atmosphere at that fire felt really different. Off."

"I agree."

"Different from what?" Alex asked.

"Other fires," Kathy and Chris said in unison.

"Wow. How many fires have you guys been to?"

"Listen, city girl," Kathy said. "When you lived back East and you heard a siren, what did you do?"

"Wished it would stop."

"Well, when I hear one I listen for what it is. Is it fire? Ambulance? Then I listen for where it's going."

"I know. Sandra told me about that, and I saw everyone doing it Saturday night. I get that. But why go running to see it?" She'd asked that question on Saturday night and never gotten an answer. "Come on, isn't that just voyeurism?"

"It's just..." Chris groped for an explanation. "It's just what everyone does." She shrugged. "Small town thing, I guess."

"I think people just want to know what's going on. It's contagious. Come on," Kathy teased, "if everyone on your block was running over to see a fire, wouldn't you be tempted to go, too?"

"Well, maybe. But it wasn't on my block!"

Kathy continued. "Dad told me people used to run right over if they saw a fire or accident. To help out. Way back in the old days people brought buckets! In Mom and Dad's day it was blankets and medical kits, or coffee and sandwiches. Now people pick it up on the police scanner or the TV, and just drive by. Or stand around, getting in the way."

"That's true," Chris said. "But maybe they still have that impulse, wanting to help. Even when they know they can't." Chris assumed kindness in others. Bad assumption.

Kathy turned to Chris. "But it wasn't like that on Saturday." Chris nodded.

"The men I was standing near, they didn't want to help." She paused. "They were enjoying it."

"I know," Chris said, looking somber. "I heard a comment that I wish I hadn't."

Kathy frowned. "Me too. What did you hear?"

"Some guy said, 'Nice night for a fire,' and some other guys laughed."

"Mine was worse," Kathy replied. "I heard somebody say, 'About time.' "

Alex was horrified. "Are you shitting me?"

"Wish I was," Kathy said. Chris shook her head no.

Did you see who it *was*?"

"No," Chris looked at the wall, her eyes narrowing as if conjuring the scene. "It was in back of me, and I turned around to see but there were so many people. Men, mostly. No way to see who it was." She shook her head. "Sorry. I figured it was just some asshole, probably drunk. And I wanted to think maybe I'd heard wrong. That's why I didn't mention it to you, Kathy. But now..." she trailed off.

"Well, I know who said 'about time.'" Kathy mashed the last of her cigarette into the ashtray. "It was that little creep who owns the video store. Whatshisname, Ken Miller."

"Over on Sixth?" Chris asked. "I haven't been in there in a while."

"He bought it last winter," Kathy said.

"I know who you mean," Alex fumed. "That little troll! I went in there a couple times in the summer. I couldn't believe how rude he was." She imitated his lemon-sucking expression. Kathy laughed.

"That's the way he is with everybody," Kathy said. "I heard a lot of people have stopped going there."

Chris was bemused. "You'd think with Netflix so popular he'd have the sense to at at least be polite. What does he look like? Maybe I've seen him around."

"He's about four foot ten, for starters," Alex said, seeing him again as he stood behind a dusty glass counter filled with equally dusty candy and used videos and DVDs.

"Oh no," Chris snorted. "A little man." The three of them looked at each other in silent understanding. They were all tall.

"And he's a real looker," Kathy added, deadpan. "Just picture Austin Powers...on a bad hair day."

"`About time,'" Alex repeated Ken Miller's words. "About time for Book Ends to burn down?"

"Or for Barb to die?" Kathy asked.

"Or both?" Chris turned to Alex. "Did Barb have a problem with him?"

"Not that she ever said. We did talk once about how unfriendly he is, and she said she never went in there, either. But then, she's—was," Alex corrected with a twinge, "too busy to rent movies anyway Do you think he might have a problem with women?" The short-man syndrome. "Women generally, not just tall ones?"

"I bet he does," Kathy sipped her wine. "A little loser like that, you just know he's been rejected a million times."

"And Barb was one of the few women in Sherman who owned her own business. A much more successful one than his crappy little place," Alex noted with a shiver. She fit that profile too.

"Where were you when you heard this?" Chris asked Kathy.

Kathy blew out a breath. "I was maybe half a block from Book Ends? You were a little ahead of me, then. Where did you hear those guys laughing? "

"Same place, at the barricade closest to the fire."

"Who would wish that on Barb?" Alex burst out. "This is horrible!" The grief and sadness were burned away. She was angry.

There was a silence.

Alex wished she'd been there. Then she remembered Kathy's picture texts, and Chris's camera bag hanging on the back of her bar stool. "Have you downloaded those pictures yet?"

"I will tomorrow."

"How about those cell phone pictures you took?" Alex asked Kathy.

"I need to send those to my computer," Kathy said. "And the video."

"You took video, too? I didn't know that!"

"Hey, don't expect much," Kathy held up her hands. "I just got this phone and I don't really know what I'm doing with the video part, yet. I had it on for maybe a couple minutes."

"What kind of phone?" Chris asked.

"IPhone. The latest."

"Good quality pictures, then. Can you send it all to me? I can print some stills from it."

"Can we look at them together?" Alex asked.

They'd just begun comparing schedules when Nick, who'd been sitting peacefully by Kathy's feet, jumped up onto the table, snagged a piece of Muenster cheese, and took off into the kitchen with it.

"Nick!" Kathy yelled after him. But he was long gone.

"Slick move!" Alex laughed. "I wonder how long he's been thinking about doing that?"

Chris was smiling. "Maybe he got tired of waiting for us to leave the table. I could imagine Soot doing that. Charlie only raids the food when I'm not home."

Not home. "You know," Alex said, "with the fire, I keep wondering: was Barb there when it started?"

Kathy was still scouting around for Nick. "I've been thinking about that too."

"What time was that meeting she was going to?" Chris asked.

"Eight. At one of the churches. I don't know which."

"Okay. Let's say the meeting lasted an hour," Kathy theorized. "And Barb goes back to Book Ends at nine. The sirens went off, when? Ten o'clock?"

"Yes," Chris said. "So she could have been up in her apartment when it started. Maybe even asleep."

"But wait, at ten?" Alex protested. "She was planning to come over to the pub."

Kathy yawned. The curse of the early riser. "Who knows? Maybe she was just exhausted from the day and was lying down for a bit, and then nodded off. Happens to me all the time."

"Or maybe she came back," Alex said, "and found the fire had started and tried to do something, and then got trapped."

"Would you go into a burning building?" Chris asked, doubtfully.

"She might have only seen a little smoke. I might do the same, with the pub."

Nick sauntered by them, licking his chops, unrepentant. Kathy, watching him, suddenly looked up. "I just thought of another reason. Maurice."

Of course. Barb had thought Maurice was trapped inside. "I would have done it, too," Alex said. "Especially if I thought the fire had just started."

Chris and Kathy nodded agreement. They all got quiet for a minute.

"Well," Kathy broke the silence, "when are we all free again?"

Not till Wednesday night, it seemed. "Want to come over

to my place?" Chris asked. "Sevenish."

Alex shook her head. "Sorry, it'll be happy hour at the pub."

Kathy chimed in. "Happy hour will just be ending! Can't you get someone to cover for you? Annette's been doing a great job, you said. Or Lauren?"

Chris's house. Tempting. She'd love to see it. "Well...I'll see if one of them can bartend for a couple hours. Wednesdays aren't that busy after happy hour. But I'd better wait till 7:30 to make sure." She paused. "There's something I'd like to run by you guys—about Barb. But we can talk then." She needed to get back to the pub.

She drove home under a black starlit sky, her mind full of soft green eyes and deep mellow laughter. And might have beens.

CHAPTER TEN

Tuesday morning her clock radio woke Alex out of a sound sleep. Reluctantly, she opened her eyes into the brightness—sunlight blazing through the shades—and found she couldn't move. The girls had her pinned in.

The weather reporter on the radio sounded chipper, but didn't they always? It had dropped to forty last night, and there was a hard frost advisory for tonight. He repeated it: a hard frost advisory—as if a big storm were coming. So the ground was going to freeze. So what? One strong cup of coffee later she picked up the phone. Sandra would have been up for hours by now. And maybe she wouldn't laugh at the question.

No such luck. "Go into your living room," Sandra directed between cackles, "and look out your window."

Alex did as instructed. "I'm looking."

"What do you see?"

Fields. Slowly, a light dawned. "Oh. Because it'll hurt the crops."

"A hard freeze—a black freeze, some people call it— will kill whatever's left in the ground. Like tomatoes. Better get out to your garden today!"

"I will, thanks. Maybe after I take a smarten-up pill."

"Oh honey that's all right, you're not a farm girl! I'm sure I'd be confused about a lot of things back East."

"You're sweet." Alex started to say goodbye, when a falling-asleep thought of last night returned. "Oh wait. Is Bill out in the fields today? I need to get a phone number from him."

"Can I help?"

"Maybe. Remember this summer Bill wanted me to use this contractor he really likes, but that guy was busy?"

"I remember. So you got stuck with Ray...who wasn't busy. They say that's not a good sign."

"It wasn't! But who was the guy Bill wanted me to hire?"

"Robbie Pierce." She sounded definite. "Do you need more work done?"

"No, I just want to talk to him about a couple ideas I have, maybe for next summer," Alex said. And get some information out of him.

Sandra gave Alex his cell number.

❧

The sun was warm on her back that afternoon as Alex picked the last of the tomatoes and basil, thyme and hot peppers, tossing it all into two baskets Kathy had given her. The baskets were big. And beautiful: one a natural-colored brown, short and wide, the other tall and deep, a green Jeremiah basket. She'd told Kathy they were too nice to drag around outside. But Kathy's philosophy was that baskets were functional, working things, made to be used. These were designed for harvesting. The wide slats in the bottom let the dirt fall through and the produce could be washed right in the basket.

The baskets had a solid feel, and it was good to be using

them; good to be outside wearing old work boots, playing farmer. Looked like the girls thought so, too. After the outside stairs, the garden was their favorite place. Today was typical. Lucy took up position near Alex, carefully supervising her work, while Jane rolled luxuriously in the warm dirt.

Alex's hands were in the dirt, but her head was elsewhere. Arson at Book Ends, Barb as a murder victim; her own half-formed fears: so improbable, so melodramatic before last night. But there was nothing fanciful about those malicious comments and the laughter that Kathy and Chris overheard. Carl's line of questioning Sunday night had been disturbing. But her unsettled feelings about the fire pre-dated that. It wasn't just panic she'd felt Saturday night, but a deep sense of unease. Because the week before she'd died, Barb had been uneasy, too.

Alex pulled up the dried-out remains of another tomato plant. Barb wasn't herself Friday night. She admitted something was bothering her, but she wasn't sure if it really was "anything." Barb wasn't a worrier: she rolled with the punches, never wasting energy or anxiety on things she couldn't help. If Barb was worried, it was serious. Somehow, though, she'd mistrusted her instincts, second-guessed herself. Like Alex often did. Big mistake.

She'd promised to tell Alex the rest of her story on Sunday. *It'll be good to* talk. Talk about what?

On Sunday her bookstore was a shell. Was there a connection?

❦

Her cell phone rang as Alex was hosing the dirt off her garden tools. It was Robbie Pierce, returning her voicemail.

A youngish, friendly voice came down the line, apparently from a moving car with the windows rolled down. "Robbie here. I got your message and I'm coming up on your pub. You need some work done?"

"Not just now, but—"Alex began, when Robbie cut in.

"I'm pulling into your lot. Hold on."

Alex met him in the driveway, dripping garden clippers in hand. He hopped out of a dirty white pickup truck, a tall guy in his thirties with already-sparse ginger hair. His eyes swept over the pub. Assessing it with a contractor's eye, probably seeing things he would have done differently.

"Nice place," he greeted her. "Would have loved the job here but I was booked up all summer. You thinking of making some additions?"

"And I would have loved to have you do it. Bill says you're the best. And the easiest to work with."

Robbie grinned. "Well, there's some guys with big egos in this job. You had Ray, right?" He gave her a knowing look.

Alex smiled. "But I won't have him again. Actually, I don't have any work to do right now, though I'll definitely call you when I do—well in advance this time." She would have felt less guilty about wasting his time if this had been a phone conversation. "I do have something in mind for next summer, if my budget allows it. A thatched roof. I wondered if you knew any thatchers."

Robbie blew out his breath. "A thatched roof! You really want that authentic look, huh? Well, it'd sure make the place stand out!"

"I just love them," Alex admitted. "Though Bill told me it's totally impractical with the winds here."

"Oh, I don't know," Robbie mused. "Thatching's been around a lot longer than roof shingles. I'll put some feelers out and let you know. There's an outfit in Ohio, I think." He began heading back to his truck.

Alex walked alongside him. "Did you see the fire, Saturday?"

"Yeah, caught the end of it." He shook his head. "Terrible thing. And the owner killed, too."

"Barb Nichols—the owner—we were friends. She had a lot of work done on the building, three-four years ago, when she bought it. Were you her contractor?" Surely not. She was looking for Mr. Mastodon of the Floor Saga, not this pleasant, chatty man.

Robbie didn't hesitate. "Nope, didn't get that job—too bad, beautiful building, and I love restoration work. Gerry Arens did a good job, though."

After Barb forced him to. "I was lucky," Alex said. "The previous owner had started a big renovation here before he went bankrupt; the plumbing and electric is all new."

"Oh I know, I put it in!" Robbie chuckled. "And *I* was lucky. He paid me before he went broke."

This was news to Alex: good news. The best contractor in the area—and a nice one, to boot—had done the trickiest, most expensive work on Fitzpatrick's. He was climbing into his truck now. Time for the most important question.

"Do you know if Gerry Arens did new plumbing and electric for Book Ends?"

Robbie turned the ignition key and then paused, elbow on the window ledge and one hand on the wheel. He didn't seem suspicious. In his world, this must be a staple of conversation: who got what job, what it entailed.

"Plumbing—no, pretty sure not. Not important for a store like that and I don't think the system in there was that old. Electric—that was all new. I remember Gerry was bitching because his usual guy was sick and he had to hire someone else."

Robbie waved and drove down the drive, then turned right towards town. An all-new electrical system. The walls of Book Ends hadn't been full of frayed wires and connections, dangerous things held together with old tape. The wiring was only a few years old and, as at Fitzpatrick's, the store would have undergone a thorough inspection before opening to the public.

So the most benign explanation—electrical fire—had just

become much less likely. The autumn sun that had seeped into her bones had begun to make Alex drowsy. Now she was awake again. And suddenly cold.

⌒

She barely had time to get cleaned up and back downstairs to open up for happy hour. But she needn't have rushed: the first hour was dead. The second wasn't. At six-thirty they got hit with rush that lasted on into dinner.

Around nine, Alex was unloading a third set of glasses from the small dishwasher behind the bar. She looked up to find that Bill and Carl and Sandra and Suzanne had suddenly materialized at the bar, perched on their stools like pigeons on a phone wire. She started.

Bill guffawed. "Lost in the stars! How bout some drinks, missy?" Bill slapped his huge hand on the bar.

She looked around. "I don't see any Missy."

They'd been driving around, Sandra said. It was such a beautiful night, clear and starlit, they didn't want to stay in.

The last time Alex had driven around without a destination had been high school. But here, people did it all their lives. It's the reason, Kathy told her, that you can't get anywhere quickly: because half the people on the road with you aren't actually going anywhere.

"It really is beautiful out," Suzanne said. "But cold!" She cast a longing glance over at the fireplace.

"I bet it is. Why don't you guys take that table over there?" Alex gestured towards the empty fireside four-top. "Just tell me what you want—I'll send your drinks over."

Suzanne gave her a grateful look, and after a few minutes and some token resistance from the men—men always preferred barstools, for some reason—they settled in, drinks in hand and talking comfortably.

She was glad somebody was. The sight of Carl had snapped

out of her post-rush slump. He would know more than almost anyone about what they'd learned at the fire site today and she was itching to talk to him. But she could hardly pull up a chair and start firing questions at him.

Would Carl put his official hat on now and just keep her hanging? Or show her some mercy?

He took the mercy route. Just when Alex had decided she was SOL, he came up to the bar. "We're gonna have one more round." He took a worn brown wallet out of his back pocket.

"I can send Lauren over."

"That's okay, I wanted to get up and stretch my legs."

This sounded like an excuse. She started mixing their drinks, but took her time. Carl looked to his left, at the couple sitting a few stools down. They were college students, deep into a conversation. Oblivious. "Sue and I are heading home tomorrow," he announced.

She put two vodka tonics on the bar. "Are they done getting evidence or whatever at the book store?"

He seemed about to say something, then stopped. Damn.

"Hey! What's the hold-up?" Bill's voice boomed across the floor, startling her, so concentrated had she been on Carl's reply.

Alex gave Bill an exasperated face and framed a lie. "I'm brewing fresh decaf for Sandra's Irish Coffee!" (A half-full pot sat in the kitchen). "Or Sandra, would you be okay with regular?"

"No, honey," Sandra said, holding up her hands, "if I had a cup of regular…"

"Don't even think about it!" Bill warned. The three of them launched into an animated discussion. Alex heard "caffeine" several times. Middle age must suck.

"When Sandra called to tell me, she said you were down there."

The hesitation again. Then he spoke. "I went over the scene today with Tom and now they have to look at what they found there. That might take a little time." He was being awfully vague.

She prodded. "What kinds of things?"

Carl put on his official hat. "I can't be specific, since it's an ongoing investigation—and I'm not even officially part of it. They have things that'll be tested at the lab in Lincoln, and lots of pictures to analyze."

Her disappointment must have shown. Carl's expression softened a bit. "I wanted to tell you they're still not sure about the cause. They should know soon, though."

But there was another thing on Alex's mind. "I don't want to seem morbid but..." She hesitated. "Can you tell me what's happening with Barb?" Barb's body.

"Oh." He cleared his throat. "They took her to Omaha for an autopsy. When the cause of the fire is undetermined that's the procedure."

Horror on horror. What might they have already done to Barb? She wished she hadn't watched so many crime shows. Then another thought struck her. "But wait, if she died in a fire, isn't the cause of death obvious?"

"It seems obvious. But in these circumstances, we don't know if it was the fire that killed her."

"Whoa." The idea hit Alex like a brick. "She could have been dead before the fire?"

"Right."

"Is there any reason to think that's what happened?"

"Not as of yet."

Slowly, Alex spooned whipped cream onto Sandra's coffee. "It wasn't an electrical fire, was it?"

Now it was Carl's turn to be startled. "Why would you say that?"

Alex assumed a bland expression. "Oh, just asked around. I found out who her contractor was and that the wiring was all new when she renovated a few years ago."

"That doesn't mean it couldn't be an electrical fire. New wiring has problems too, sometimes. But you're right," he conceded. "It doesn't look like it."

Their eyes met and locked for a moment. Carl sighed. "You're not gonna play detective, are you?"

She laughed as if dismissing the notion. "I just asked a couple questions!"

"It's not a good idea. This isn't a TV show."

"That's for sure. When a TV show ends, you turn off the set and forget about it." She paused. "I really want to know what happened. I have a bad feeling about it—and it's getting worse."

He nodded. "You may be right. We'll know soon."

Bill suddenly loomed up beside Carl. "What are you two so deep into discussing?" he asked suspiciously, snagging two of the drinks. "We're parched!"

"Nebraska football." Carl deadpanned. "Alex wants my take on the defensive line this year."

"Yeah, right!" Bill threw over his shoulder as he headed back to the table.

Carl grabbed the other two drinks. "You have my card. Give me a call. Maybe I can keep you up to date."

"Thanks." He was doing more he needed to, maybe even more than he was supposed to.

He leaned in towards Alex. "Just don't go nosing around on your own, okay?"

She held up two fingers. "Scout's honor."

Alex had never been a scout.

CHAPTER ELEVEN

They say soup is good for the soul, and Alex was a believer. Wednesday afternoon found her chopping and stirring, putting together a big pot of Manhattan clam chowder. It was a soup from her childhood, and evoked a favorite memory: the day after a Nor'easter, she and Mom collecting the clams that had washed up onto Manasquan beach and lay everywhere, live but stranded. They'd forgotten to bring something to carry the clams and ended up using Alex's red sweater, the one she'd worn for her third-grade picture just weeks before. In her sixties, Mom still chided herself about ruining that sweater. She'd died three years ago, of cancer.

Basking in the homey smell on a chilly October day was therapy. Alex needed it. Needed not to think about the grim, hollowed shell of her friend's bookstore just down the road. Or that she may have been...murdered.

Her conversation with Carl had left her unsettled and restless, and she woke up too many times to count. But her wakeful thoughts hadn't brought any closer to understanding recent events.

She stirred dill into the pot. Better to take a break—however brief—from obsessing, and concentrate on the good things. The smell of the chowder, thickening and intensifying as it simmered. The sun coming through the window of the pub kitchen. Her pub, a dream at last come true. New friends, family down the road, and upstairs two cats to love and spoil.

Such peaceful moments are only interludes, alas. The sound of the front door opening and heavy boots crossing the floor broke the spell. That must be John, who was scheduled to come in at four and help Alex finish prepping. Ashley would be following in half an hour to set up.

"Smells good in here!" John pushed through the swinging kitchen doors, cheery as ever.

Alex liked John. He'd grown up on a farm outside of Sherman and had told her, one afternoon as they were prepping together, that as a kid he'd always wanted to be a farmer. Too bad for him that he had three older brothers, and that only one of them could inherit the farm. Not too long ago, according to Sandra, a family farm could sustain several generations of one family. No more. These days a farm could barely support one family. And so the kids leave.

But he was empty handed. "John, didn't you pick up the bread?" The weekend had almost wiped out the huge supply she'd ordered from a craft bakery in Sioux City and Alex had just about eked through lunch today. John was supposed to make an emergency run to Bag 'N Go on his way in.

"Shit!!" He grabbed his jacket. "I'll go right now. Sorry."

"Hold up," Alex pulled her apron off. "I want to get out for a bit. You need to prep the fish and chips. Don't worry, I'm glad to have an excuse for a drive." She just hoped Bag N Go would have some edible bread.

It had warmed up since she'd been outside earlier, and Alex

put down the top of the Cabrio for her drive into town. She drove past the big NRA billboard. Assholes.

Her East Coast friends had teased her mercilessly about the gun-happy locale she was relocating to. Would she mount a gun rack by the door? Under the teasing though, Alex had heard their worry about where she was moving, a terra incognita most of them couldn't find on a map without a minute of intense searching.

Had Sherman ever been a wild-west town? Alex lived in fly-over country now, but she was as ignorant about its history as were her friends ensconced—presumably forever—on the East Coast.

She knew from the sign at the edge of town that it was founded in 1889; young, by East Coast standards. Sherman's population ebbed and flowed with the school year. At the Jersey Shore, Memorial Day signaled the onslaught of the summer tourists—they called them Bennies—and all the money (and aggravation) they brought. Just the opposite here: graduation day in May meant an exodus of students that left the streets quiet, the residents delighted, and business owners facing some lean months.

Main Street and the business district in Sherman was a hodge-podge of styles from different eras: mostly nineteen-thirties and sixties, she guessed. Away from Main Street, the town got prettier. In the older neighborhoods, Craftsman cottages sat next to Victorian houses covered with gingerbread trim. Alex drooled over one cottage in particular, white with green shutters and a big flower garden all along the front, red roses climbing up a lattice and purple clematis trailing down the side of the house. Someday. She didn't intend to live over the shop forever.

All the old, beautiful trees in town were in these neighborhoods and on the Sherman State campus. Student-rental houses dotted these streets: big, rambling wrecks, dumpsters out in front overflowing with beer bottles. The Sherman State campus, small and pretty, all red bricks and big trees, dominated the northern end of town.

An old railway station, now converted to a cell phone store, anchored the southern end of downtown. Alex always noticed that building when she drove by because she had a memory associated with it. When she was a kid, out on one of their Nebraska visits, they'd driven by the old station, deserted then, and Aunt Betsy told them how once the train had run through here. Sherman, she said, was where it was because of those train tracks. And that still amazed Alex: that a town was founded not because of a river or ocean, but because of train tracks running west.

≈

The bread racks were luckily near the door of Bag N Go and she got in and out quickly, before the strange smell of the store—as if you'd spent some quality time in a dumpster—permeated her clothes. The loaves she picked, purporting to be fresh-baked, were a step up from Wonder Bread, but just. They'd need to be rescued somehow. Garlic bread?

On the way through town she'd put on the blinders, refusing to look at Book Ends. She wanted to savor her brief peaceful mood. But that was over now, anyway: Bag N Go had cast its usual pall on her spirits. She drove slowly past this time, then pulled into a spot half a block down from Book Ends and walked up as close as she could.

She would never feel that first shock again. But it was appalling, the black hole that stood where the center of Barb's life, her pride and joy, had stood only last week.

It was still roped off with that terrible yellow tape. Crime Scene. In the dim interior, Alex could see two people, police or forensics. They'd been at this for days; would so much time and money have been spent if there weren't serious suspicions?

A flush of anger went surging through Alex like adrenaline. What sicko had done this to her friend?

Getting back behind the wheel, Alex glanced across the street and saw the lit-up plate glass window of the town newspaper. *The Sherman Telegraph* was published once a week and circulated to all the towns around. Had there been a new edition since the fire?

Alex walked across the street. A bell on the door jangled and a girl sitting behind a desk looked up. She sat behind a counter piled high with newspapers. The workings of the paper were hidden behind a door to her left.

Alex read the *Telegraph* sporadically. In the summer, the front page was splashed with color pictures of 4-H contest winners at the county fair; in the fall, group pictures of service club members or winning high school teams went above the fold. You could get through the *Telegraph* in about eight minutes.

It was an intensely local paper. Sherman was the center of the universe and the rest of the world basically didn't exist. A mirror image of that old *New Yorker* poster, it put Sherman in the foreground, the coasts and big cities dimly seen at the vanishing point. And if a newspaper could be said to have a theme, the theme of the *Telegraph* was community. It was full of ads for open-invitation, come-all events. Even to weddings. The first time Alex saw a wedding dance advertised in the *Telegraph* last summer, she scurried over to Kathy's house for an explanation.

"Oh yeah," she'd said casually, "everybody's invited to those."

"Everybody who? Everybody in town?" This couldn't be right. "People don't send out formal invitations here?"

"Sure. If they're having an expensive reception with a sit-down dinner, and an open bar and all that. But if it's in the town auditorium or the armory it's called a wedding dance, and the whole town's invited—to the reception part. There's dancing and a cake and all that, but the food is just sandwiches and salads on a buffet. And there's always kegs of beer. Tons of people show up. Wedding dances are a blast; we'll have to go to one, you'll see."

Alex was astounded. "The whole town is invited?"

"Well, not in Sherman!" Kathy clarified. "That'd be a bit crowded. But in some of these really small towns, like Byron, everyone's there: babies, 100-year-old great-grandmothers, escaped convicts passing through."

Today, it would be different. Today, there would be real news. The girl hopped up from her chair and came up to the counter. "Like to buy a paper?

Alex took a *Telegraph* off the pile and snapped it open. And there it was: a large-font headline: "*BOOKSTORE BLAZE KILLS OWNER*," over a half-page color picture of the burnt-out front of Book Ends. Below the fold was a grainy black and white picture of Barb. It didn't even look like her.

"Um, that's fifty cents?"

"Sorry." Alex fumbled for change, her eyes riveted to the opening paragraphs, which described the fire on Saturday night in vivid—if not lurid—detail. Then halfway down the second column, she read:

The cause of the Book Ends fire is still undetermined, according to Fire Chief Eric Frisch. "But," said Frisch, "we have identified the point of origin. It was on the first floor of the building, in the bookstore." To determine the point of origin, fire investigators trace the path of the fire backward, to the area with the greatest damage.

Pending the release of autopsy results from the Medical Examiner's Office, the cause of Nichols' death is also still undetermined. Smoke inhalation, which causes disorientation, is the most common cause of death in fires.

Frisch noted that the fire could have been much worse if the Westfield and Byron fire departments hadn't responded so quickly.

"It could have spread right down Main,'" Frisch said.

The article concluded by noting Book Ends' popularity in Sherman and surrounding communities. It directed readers to the obituary for the victim on page three.

"Would you like to sign up for our home delivery service?"

Alex dragged herself back to the surface. "Uh..." She certainly didn't, but how to diplomatically tell this eager young woman that the *Telegraph* sucked?

"A subscription will save you money," she pressed. "Do you live in Sherman?"

Here was a born saleswoman. Alex smiled. "Just up the road," she pointed. "I own Fitzpatrick's."

"Oh, then you can advertise with us!"

She knew when she was defeated. "Are you a reporter?"

"No. Well, not yet! I'm a Journalism major at the college. This is my internship. My first one," she amended.

"Do you take plastic?"

The intern ran her debit card and Alex turned to page three. The awful picture of Barb from the front page was repeated here. In the company of the other obituary pictures on the page she looked like a teenager, but then it didn't look much like her anyway. Boy, would Barb be pissed. She told Alex she'd always been camera-shy and this was like a final insult.

The obituary was as stark as her picture: birth, hometown, education, when she came to Sherman and opened Book Ends. Barb was survived by her parents, two sisters, and a brother. And an ex-husband, but of course he wasn't mentioned. The funeral would be this Saturday: 10 a.m. at St. Andrew's Presbyterian Church in Cooper.

Alex folded the paper up signed the debit card slip. The intern was looking out the plate-glass window at the ruins of Book Ends. "They're sure spending a lot of time over there," she observed. "I bet it wasn't an accident."

It was the bluntest assessment Alex had heard yet. She followed the girl's gaze. "Too bad you're not a reporter yet. You could talk to the forensics guys."

The girl groaned. "Tell me about it. And I'd do a better job than—" She cut herself off.

"I bet you hear a lot about it, though. Being in the middle of it and all." Unlike Carl, now back in Cherry. And journalists loved to talk.

"Sure do."

"Well, the owner was my friend."

"Oh. Sorry."

"So if ever you want to come by Fitzpatrick's and give me the latest, the beer is on the house."

The intern beamed. "You got it! Oh I'm Tiffany." She extended a hand, practicing professionalism.

"Alex." They shook hands. "Come by any time."

❧

Alex got back just ahead of her first happy-hour customers. Fitzpatrick's was the first bar in Sherman to offer a happy hour that featured fun cocktails, not just beer, and it had become popular with the after-work crowd, especially from the college. What she lost in mark-up, she more than made up for in volume. And food.

At seven fifteen the bar had cleared out and she pulled the *Telegraph* out from behind the register and read the story again. Then she turned to the obituary and the funeral details.

She had to go to the funeral. But hopefully not alone, to a strange town and a congregation filled with faces she didn't know. She called Kathy.

"Hey, girl! Did it quiet down over there yet? Do you want me to come pick you up?"

"So far, so good. Lauren's ready to cover for me. What time?"

"Soon!"

"Okay. Have you seen the *Telegraph* yet?"

"Yeah. Pretty depressing." Water was running on Kathy's end; a sink full of reeds, probably. "And that picture of her is awful. Tell you what, when my time comes my family better find a better picture of me than that!"

"I know. I was wondering about the funeral. Are you going?"

"I was gonna ask you the same thing. Want to go together?"

"Definitely. Where's Cooper, though?" Hopefully not hours and hours west of them. You never knew, in Nebraska.

"Cooper? That's over by Ewing."

"And Ewing is..?"

"Oh," Kathy caught on. "It's maybe an hour and half away. We'll take Twenty-Five over."

"Okay." Alex paused. "I'm dreading this."

"I know. I'll see you soon—half an hour."

They say two heads are better than one, and three are better yet. Alex hoped their collective heads could start to make some sense of this.

Clarity might go a long way towards a good night's sleep.

CHAPTER TWELVE

As they drove away, Alex cast a last, anxious glance back at the lit windows of Fitzpatrick's. Please let it stay quiet.

"Don't worry," Kathy said. "It'll be fine. And they'll call you if there's a problem, right?"

"They better!"

Alex had volunteered to drive, but Kathy had a better vehicle for the ride: her old Ford truck. Chris's place was out of town, down a county road. County means not paved. There were miles and miles of these roads, a whole network of dirt roads with a little gravel on top.

She had some vague memories of these from her childhood visits, but nothing as sharp and real as the first time she attempted to drive on one last summer and slid from side to side in white-knuckle terror, waiting for the inevitable moment when her car would topple into one of the steep ditches on either side. Her car felt like a boat, unmoored, with no sense of tires hitting pavement.

Alex brought this up as they rolled down one of these, a hilly ribbon that wound through places you never saw from the highway. "You know, I've been wondering," she said, suppressing panic as she listened to the truck's back wheels slide around behind them. "Why aren't all these county roads paved?"

"Why would they be?" They were having a cultural moment.

"Because," Alex ventured, "that's what roads are...dirt that's gotten paved?"

"Why does it have to have blacktop to be a road? It goes somewhere, right? So it's a road."

"That's true," Alex conceded. "But why not throw some blacktop on it, and make it a really good road? Like, with traction."

"Farm vehicles don't need pavement for traction."

Point taken. Something weighing ten tons wasn't going to be stopped by a little loose gravel. And Kathy, who'd grown up driving on county roads would find them as natural as Alex had found little balls of tar on the beach when she was a kid. She'd thought the off-casts from oil tankers were part of the ecosystem. A native Nebraskan just drives on down the county roads, going with the floating sensation, as Kathy was effortlessly doing now. But it would never feel right to Alex. "How about if *I* need traction?"

"Then drive the highways, city girl!" Kathy crowed.

"Oh, I will!" But 'highway' in Nebraska was an exalted designation for a two-lane road. And the signs were pretty minimalist. If you knew where you were going, fine. If you didn't you were an urban sissy, the kind who relied on maps or GPS rather than navigating by an iron-sure internal compass. Directions in Nebraska were along the lines of, go three miles north and then go west at the Jenkins' place. In New Jersey, it was the Parkway exit, the number of stop lights, and the jug handle to watch for after the Dunkin Donuts on the corner.

"Do you mind?" Kathy shook a cigarette out of her pack. She knew Alex didn't, as long as she hung the cigarette out the window and blew the smoke that way

Kathy looked at the fields as they drove amid them, like everyone here did, farmer or not—especially everyone over fifty in a pickup truck. And like Bill and Sandra, she didn't remark on anything but just quietly registered the progress of the harvest. Or what she could see of it through the dust of the combine that was rumbling through the field to their left. Please don't let that thing jump onto the road with us. It was her second request to a greater power in the past ten minutes.

She added a third: please let me not make a fool of myself tonight.

❧

Chris's log-cabin house, surrounded by trees, sat at the end of a long driveway lined with young trees. It was the prettiest place Alex had seen since she moved to Sherman.

"This is Chris's house?" Kathy exclaimed. "I've driven by it lots of times but I never knew who owned it. I love this property!"

The house and the land around it really stood out in an area dominated by weather-beaten farms. Oddly, the barns in the country around Sherman often looked better maintained than the farm houses. What was that about? Kathy had said that's how you know it's a German farm. The Swedish farms are always pretty. Kathy's ancestors, of course, were Swedish.

Chris was sitting on an Adirondack chair on the porch. She looked even more beautiful tonight, if that was possible. Stop looking, then.

Inside, Chris had a fire going and a nice bottle of cabernet sauvignon breathing. The house was filled with mission-style furniture and comfortable chairs, accented by rugs and bowls and pictures from Chris's world travels. She even had endearing pets: Soot, a shy little black cat and Charlie, an exuberant sheep dog. She was perfect. Please let her be straight.

They sat in armchairs in front of the fire. "Have you seen this?" Chris tapped the *Sherman Telegraph* that lay on the coffee table. Next to it was a laptop and a manila envelope. The pictures.

They nodded.

"The picture of the fire is pretty good," Chris observed, gesturing to the *Telegraph*.

"But where'd they get that one of Barb?" Alex complained.

"Looks like a driver's license photo," Chris said.

"That would explain it!"

They talked for a few minutes about their weeks so far. Kathy and Chris were both getting ready for shows. Kathy had a booth at a big craft fair in Sioux City and Chris was taking part in a photography exhibit in Lincoln. They'd been going flat out and seemed happy for an excuse to take a break.

But the *Telegraph* lay in front of them, and the picture of Barb's burnt-out store was hard to ignore.

Kathy picked it up and scanned the front page. "Cause undetermined."

"At least we know it started down in the store," Chris noted. "So we were right, it wasn't the coffee maker or something up in the apartment."

"Score one for us."

"Carl was at the pub last night," Alex said.

Chris put her wine glass down. "Any news?"

"Nothing concrete. He did say they took a lot of pictures and were sending lab samples down to Lincoln." Alex paused and took a sip of wine. "I told him I had a bad feeling about the fire. He said I might be right.

And here's the other thing. I asked him what was happening with Barb." She grimaced. "I felt really ghoulish about asking. But get this: he told me they were doing an autopsy because they couldn't assume she died in the fire! She may have died before."

Silence.

"Shit," Kathy finally said.

Chris blew out her breath. "I hadn't thought of that."

"Me neither. Though I've seen it in cop shows and read it in mysteries. Someone is murdered and the murderer sets a fire to make that look like the cause of death. Gets rid of the evidence that way."

Kathy took a long sip of wine. "Well that's pretty grim. And honestly it seems kind of far-fetched. Don't you think?"

"I know; it seems crazy to me too. But do you remember on Monday I said I wanted to run something by you two?"

They nodded.

Alex sighed. "The thing is, I was worried about Barb *before* the fire."

"You were?" Chris leaned forward, her eyes intense.

"Hey," Kathy asked, an idea dawning on her face, "is this who you were talking about last week? When you said you were worried about someone but couldn't tell me about it?"

"Yes."

Chris and Kathy were good listeners. They settled back in their chairs and took in all the things that had, the week before the fire, set off alarm bells for Alex. How unlike herself Barb had been when she'd come in that Friday night. The hostility of Don and his asshole crew and her strange, passive reaction to them. Barb's uncharacteristic worry, and her incomplete story. The boarded-up window in her apartment. "What do you guys think?" she asked.

Chris looked into the fire. "It's disturbing. That's what I think."

"Absolutely," Kathy agreed. "It's a lot, when you add it up." She leaned forward and dragged a chip through Chris's spicy black bean dip. "Do you think those creeps at the pub were any part of her story?"

"Well, that's it. I didn't get the whole story. It's so frustrating!"

Kathy blew out a breath. "That's too bad. But let's look at what she did tell you. She's worried about something, but to explain it she has to go back a ways, right?

"Right. Mostly about her about her marriage and how she broke away from being a farm wife. And how she ended up here."

"But that wasn't the whole story," Chris observed.

"No. And it may have been a lot longer. You know, until that night Barb was always reluctant to talk about herself. The past, anyway."

"Then," Chris said, "someone from her past was coming back to haunt her?"

Kathy didn't hesitate. "Well, my vote goes to the abusive ex-husband!"

"Wayne." Alex said. She tried to picture him. If he looked like the farmers around here, of German or Scandinavian stock, he'd be big and fair. But was he the same stock? "I just realized I don't know his last name. Barb may have changed hers back, after they divorced."

"This might tell us." Chris grabbed the *Telegraph* and turned to an inside page. "Yup," she confirmed. "Nichols is her parents' name too. She did change it back."

"Where is he?" Kathy asked. "Does he still have the farm?"

"It sounded like it," Alex said. "But I don't know."

"Was there a fight over the divorce settlement?" Chris asked.

Alex shrugged. "Barb didn't say anything about that."

Kathy and Chris exchanged glances. "The thing is," Kathy said, "the farm was probably their major asset and if Barb got half their assets, he might not have been able to keep it."

That would be a big deal. Alex shared what Barb had said: that when Wayne started farming with his Dad it was the happiest day of his life. If she'd taken that away from him—and that's how he, no doubt, would view it—Wayne would be carrying a very big grudge.

They got quiet for a minute. The silence was broken by Charlie, barking like crazy outside. The sudden explosion of noise made Alex realize how absolutely silent it had been.

"Someone coming?"

Chris cocked her head toward the window. "Just a car going by."

"I guess you're never going to be surprised by anybody coming up to your door, huh?"

Kathy shook her head. "Not with farm dogs! They'll either greet you or bark like hell, but they're never going to ignore someone on the property."

The car must have been out of sight and sound now, because Charlie stopped barking. And now silence returned—a silence where not even the chirp of a cricket could be heard. It was like outer space.

"Don't you ever get scared, living out here?" Alex wondered.

Chris and Kathy's eyes met: city girl. "No, it doesn't bother me," Chris said. "But I grew up on a farm. So the quiet seems normal. Comforting, I guess."

"Me too," Kathy agreed. "Actually, I think towns are the scary places. All those people on top of each other."

This was probably how Aunt Betsy had felt. She'd lived out alone on that farm for years, refusing to move into town in her old age and sell the house, though by then Bill was farming the land. Were you really safer out here, away from everyone? In terms of statistics—how many people were hacked up in apartments vs. farmhouses, for example—Kathy was probably right. But if someone wanted to get you out here, in the dark and quiet, you were on your own. Shades of *In Cold Blood*. Was this why all farms had dogs?

"So," Kathy asked, "had Wayne been in contact with her?"

"She didn't say so. Really, the way she talked about her marriage, it was like it was another lifetime."

"He *was* violent," Chris put in, "even if it was only that one time."

"And let's not forget the stalking after she left him."

Alex shook her head. "What a Neanderthal,"

"Oh, I don't know if he's such a relic," Chris countered. "They wouldn't admit it, but I bet plenty of guys would like to go back to the old ways. Women at home and all that."

"Did you ever think," Alex asked, looking from Kathy to Chris, "that maybe *we're* the freaks around here?!"

Chris lifted her glass. "To us freaks."

Alex lifted hers. "And to more like us. But you know, Barb was one of us. And I want to know what happened to her."

Chris nibbled thoughtfully on a tortilla chip. "Well, let's think about what we do know. She had a violent ex-husband. But we don't know if there was any recent trouble with him."

"Then there were those nasty comments you and Kathy heard at the fire." Alex frowned.

"And that thing at the pub, with Don Roberts and his friends," Kathy added.

Wait a minute. "Was Don Roberts at the fire?"

"Did you see him, Kathy?" Chris asked. "I didn't."

"No, I don't remember seeing him. But it was so chaotic down there."

Chris slid the manila envelope toward her and opened the laptop. "Let's see what we got. I haven't had a chance to look closely at these yet." She clicked a few keys and turned the screen to Alex and Chris. "Kathy, here's your video."

Chaos, indeed. Kathy's cell phone video had picked up the sounds all and sights all too well: people yelling, sirens, lights flashing. The wind blowing—a roaring sound. For a moment, Alex was there.

This was when they'd first gotten there and the burning

store was a couple blocks down, a huge red background to the police cars and fire trucks parked nose to tail like they were on a used car lot. Kathy had been on the move and the video—about two minutes long—went up and down, left and right. Alex felt car-sick. Then abruptly, it stopped.

"It looks way worse on your screen!" Kathy looked chagrined. "Oh well, I told you it wasn't gonna be anything great."

"Why'd you stop filming?" Alex asked.

"I felt stupid. I hate how everyone is always holding up their goddamned cell phones to take pictures and video, and there I was, doing the same."

"I didn't have time to enhance any stills from that, sorry. But I printed these." She pulled a stack of photos from the envelope.

Chris's pictures took them closer to the fire, up to the last barricades on Main Street, where police stood, motioning people to stay back. There was Kevin in his uniform, talking with a fireman.

"Is this when you guys talked to Kevin?" Alex asked.

"No," Chris said. "That was a little later." When he'd asked them to call and see if Barb was at the pub. When they'd still held out some hope.

The next sequence was the worst. Chris had stood across the street from a Book Ends consumed in fire. You could hardly see the store beneath the sheets of yellow and orange. But the apartment hadn't disappeared yet: there were the window frames. Oh, Barb. But if the *Telegraph* article was right she was probably dead by then, from the smoke.

The pictures alternated now between the building and the people trying to save it. Firefighters directed huge jets of water onto the flames. Two stood in a cherry picker above the store, backlit by the flames, the arc of their hoses intersecting with those from below. There was the Sherman ambulance and next to it, the volunteer first aid squad, waiting. Alex recognized the woman whose beeper going off in the pub had been the first warning of trouble that night. And there was Carl, standing next to a Sherman fire truck, talking with a short, beefy crew-cutted man she didn't recognize. Maybe that was the Fire Chief.

Chris picked up a handful of pictures and riffled through them. "Now these might be helpful. From where I was standing," she pointed to the pile they'd just looked at, "I turned around and got shots of the crowd at the barricades." She fanned them out.

"Good," Alex leaned forward for a closer look. "Let's see who just couldn't stay away."

In her first pictures, Chris had captured the man vs. nature drama of a fire out of control. Here she had captured the human drama. It wasn't pretty. Alex was startled to see some of her regular customers right up in front. More surprising were their expressions, caught with clarity by Chris's lens. Several looked neutral and a couple, worried. But there was no mistaking what Alex saw in the rest. Eagerness. Excitement. Like kids at Disney.

"God." Kathy was disgusted. "This is worse than I remembered."

"Well, at least a couple of them look like they gave a shit." Alex pointed to their faces. "But the rest..."

"The rest they could have charged admission to," Kathy spat out. "And they would have paid!" That was saying a lot. Nebraska natives were famously tight-fisted.

"But wait," Alex was puzzled. "If people always race over to watch fires, they must see them as entertainment, right? So is this any different?"

"That's true," Chris conceded. "But I don't think people are always so open about enjoying it."

"Especially when someone might be in there!" That's what blew her away.

"Yeah, but nobody knew if she was or not," Kathy pointed

out. "And there was no rescue going on, and no one had spotted her at the windows. So I'm sure a lot of people assumed she wasn't there. Hey look," she said, peering closer to the picture nearest her. "There he is. Don."

They leaned in. Kathy was right. There was no mistaking Don. He stood in the middle of a crowd of men, wearing a Huskers sweatshirt—the football team, not the bar—radiating ego, even from a distance.

Then Alex looked closer. He was laughing. So was the man next to him, who wore a seed cap and a shiny baseball jacket, his arms crossed over his chest. The seed cap shadowed his face, but Alex recognized him. It was Paul Nielson, of the farm supply store.

On Don and Paul's left two men stood talking as they watched the blazing building in front of them. They looked familiar. "Who are these guys?"

Chris took the picture. "I can tell you who he is." She frowned, pointing to the man on the right. "Dick Wagner. He has a farm a couple down from my folks' old place. The other guy I don't know."

"But look behind them, you guys." Kathy stabbed her finger at the enlargement. "It's that little creep, Ken Miller!"

Sure enough, there he was, craning his neck to get the best possible view of the fire. The fire glinted off his big black frame glasses as he gazed his rapturous fill. He looked demented.

Alex put the picture down before her stomach started heaving and picked up the next enlargement. And there was Chuck Bauer. Things clicked into place. "Damn," she said, leaning back in her chair.

"What is it, girl?" Kathy shook a cigarette out of her pack.

"These men in the pictures?" She flicked a glance at them. "They were the ones hassling Barb that night!

"All of them?" Chris fanned the enlargements out over the table.

Alex leaned forward, her eyes raking over the freak show of satisfied faces. "Okay, Don. He came in a little after the others did that night. Paul Nielson." She pointed at his fat, laughing face. Kathy and Chris nodded. They recognized him.

"Chuck Bauer." She slid that one towards Kathy and Chris. "You know who he is, right?"

"Mr. Fresh Produce?!" Kathy made a face.

"If I have to buy one more head of wilted lettuce at Bag N Go..." Chris began.

"Or one more mushy cucumber..." Kathy added.

"Now there's a place that I could watch burning down and not shed a tear!" Alex said. "Though I don't know if I'd actually stand there laughing,"

Kathy snorted. "I might want to clap a little. You know, I did hear a while back that Chuck wanted to get a farmer's market going."

"Yeah," Alex mused. "I bet produce manager at that gross store wasn't Chuck's dream career. Well, good luck to him on the farmer's market. I'd love to see that."

Kathy pointed to a picture. "Who's Dick Wagner, Chris? You said he was a neighbor?"

Chris nodded. "Mean guy. If he ever found kids cutting through his land, or sitting by his creek, forget it." She laughed grimly. "One time he chased Jess and me across a stubble field. We were scared shitless."

"I bet!" A pitchfork-waving madman. Holy shit. "What did your parents say?"

"Stay off his property." Chris grimaced. "We did."

He didn't look dangerous. Just a big late-middle aged guy. But you could never tell. "I think he was in here that night, too." Alex said.

"And Ken Miller," Kathy sneered as she picked up another enlargement. "Looks like the best time he's had in years. I bet he stayed till the bitter end."

"I wonder if they all did," Alex said.

Kathy shrugged. "Probably. Don's dive is close by. I bet they were there and walked over when they heard the sirens."

"They seem to spend a lot of time together," Chris mused. "Some of them, anyway."

Kathy scanned the pictures in front of her again. "This guy," she pointed to the man next to Dick Wagner, "I've seen him around." He was thinner than Wagner and slightly shorter, and wore a dark sweatshirt and a light-colored baseball cap.

Not a farmer, then. Alex had soon learned that they only wear freebie caps from the seed or ag equipment companies. All the time. She thought that farmers sweated in these caps all day and then put them right back on at night, after their shower. But then Kathy set her straight: there are work caps and town caps. When they pick you up in the surrey they have the town cap on.

Kathy pointed to another face. "And this one too." A short dumpy guy stood to the right of Don and Paul, smiling as he watched Book Ends burn. The little John Lennon glasses weren't the best fashion choice for his pale moon face.

Chris leaned in and looked at Moon Face. "I know him from somewhere, too." She narrowed her eyes and looked closer. "I can't place him, though."

They all sat, thinking their own thoughts for a minute. Chris refilled their glasses. "So what do you think?" Alex asked. "Should we be looking into this?"

Chris took a sip of wine. "Seems to me like we already are." She cocked her head to one side and looked at Alex. "Did you tell Carl that you were worried about Barb the week before the fire?"

"No."

"How come?"

"It's kind of hard to explain. I mean..." she shrugged. "Part of it was, it just seemed far-fetched to link that to the fire. And come on, when do cops ever really want to hear theories from a non-professional?"

"Well, what do you think now?" Chris asked. "Do you want to tell Carl? Or the Sherman police?"

Alex looked from Chris to Kathy. "My gut feeling is still no. But maybe I should."

Kathy leaned back in her chair. "I know what you mean. Still, it might help them to know Barb was worried about something."

"True," Alex said. Then something that had been niggling at the back of her mind all day came suddenly to the front. She picked up the *Telegraph*. "Wait a minute, this thing about where the fire started..." She skimmed through the middle paragraphs of the article on the fire. "The point of origin. The Fire Chief said it was downstairs, in the store. But how would they know what *part* of the store it was—what section—unless they knew Book Ends well? I can't see how that would be in the blueprints."

"Where are you going with this?" Kathy wanted to know.

"I'm not keen on going to the cops. But this makes it easier, this point of origin thing. See, I can go and ask if they know what part of the store it started in, and if not, offer to give them info on the store layout. They may blow me off on that, too, of course. But at least it's something concrete to approach them with."

Chris was nodding approval. "Good plan. Who will you talk to?"

"Well, I do have a cop in the family. Should I start with Kevin?"

Kathy pushed a few strands of hair behind her ear. "If it was me, I'd just go down to the station. If they're interested, fine. If not, whatever." Kathy was a cut-to-the-chase girl.. And she was right.

"I'll go down tomorrow."

"Chris, can I hang onto these pictures?" Kathy asked. "Maybe I can figure out who these two guys are, if I look at them more."

'No problem. I'll make another copy and see if I recognize him." She pointed to Moon Face.

The fire was down to red coals. "So what do we do now?" Alex asked. If they were going to be detectives they needed a plan.

"I want to find out more about Wayne," Chris said.

Alex leaned forward. "And you know who else?"

"Don and his friends?" Kathy asked.

"Exactly." Alex agreed. "For one thing, I'd like to know why they always travel in a pack."

"And what their problem was with Barb," Chris put in.

"Well, girls," Kathy said, "I think it's time for us to have a night out on the town." She cracked a wicked grin. "At Husker's."

CHAPTER THIRTEEN

The Sherman police station didn't inspire confidence. Alex dragged her reluctant feet up the path to the door Thursday morning, taking in the architectural details, such as they were. It was an ugly little building. Perfectly square, with tiny windows, it looked like a small prison. The sand colored brick didn't do a lot for her either. It reminded her of that monolith up the street, Fort God.

The huge lawn in front was way out of proportion to the building, as was the parking lot out back where five police cars gleamed in the sun. Sherman was short on many things. Law enforcement wasn't one of them. Near the door, two tiny new trees were putting up a valiant effort to survive.

Alex pulled open the heavy front door and quickly found herself belly up to the reception counter. No space wasted here. A middle-aged woman with a serious perm and granny glasses was on the phone. She cast a cranky glance at Alex.

"*Where?*" She practically shouted at the caller, apparently a deaf person or a young child.

A long pause ensued. "He's in your yard? What is your address, sir?" A brief pause. "Fourth and Jefferson, right. We'll send a car over." She banged the phone down and looked up at Alex. "Can I help you?"

She'd been idly looking at the Norman Rockwell calendar on the wall, expecting a little more delay as the dispatcher followed up on that call. But she wasn't reaching for the earphone set on her desk. Hopefully nothing too serious was going on at Fourth and Jefferson.

"Yes." Alex looked at her closed face and suppressed the instinct to flee. "I need to talk to someone about the Book Ends fire."

"This is regarding?"

"The fire." Hello. "I'd like to talk to someone on that investigation."

"And this is about?" The woman tapped her pencil impatiently on the desk blotter. Alex was getting the picture now. This was one of life's natural gatekeepers, the self-appointed human call screener for the Sherman P.D.

One last stab. "I have some information the investigators might like to know." And that's all you're getting, bitch. The showdown theme from *The Good, The Bad and the Ugly* had begun to play in her head when the glass door behind the dispatcher swung open and a bulky blond cop in his thirties came through from the back, unbuttoning a light windbreaker. He looked familiar. Alex was sure he'd been in the pub more than once.

"Any messages, Dee?"

"None." Not that Dee chose to share, anyway.

His eyes swept over Alex briefly and back to Dee. Dee gave a little exasperated sigh. "She's here about the bookstore fire. Won't say what it's about, though."

The path to sanity lay in ignoring her. Alex repeated her

request to the blond cop.

He looked a little puzzled but at least he wasn't hostile. "Come on back." He held open the wooden gate in the reception desk. Dee watched Alex pass with narrowed eyes.

The smell of stale coffee permeated the station—basically one big room with several desks and chairs and file cabinets crammed into it, plus one separate office with Chief of Police stenciled on the glass pane in the door. What was up on the second floor? Jail cells?

The desk he took Alex to was in the corner, cluttered with papers. He dragged another chair over and peeled his jacket off. "I'm Officer Karsten."

"Alex Fitzpatrick. I own Fitzpatrick's—the pub."

"Yep." This he already knew. "Nice place. So," he picked up a pencil. "You have some information on the fire?"

"No," she clarified, "not on the fire itself, but a couple things before it. But actually, I wanted to ask you something first."

He looked surprised.

"I read in the paper that they'd found the point of origin."

"Right."

"Do you know where exactly in the store? What section? Because I knew Book Ends well and I was thinking I could help you pin it down more."

"We can't be specific about that," he said, frowning and crossing his arms over his chest. "But don't worry, that's all being looked into."

So much for being helpful. And that was supposed to be the easy part.

"About this information you have?"

This was starting to seem futile. But Alex thought of Barb, took a deep breath, and began. This was way different from sharing ideas with Kathy and Chris though, a glass of wine in hand. She was talking to a stranger in a uniform, in a room with institutional green walls. In the face of his blank look she jettisoned their theories about the hostility of Don and his friends, and the possible role of Barb's past.

Officer Karsten didn't seem too interested about Barb acting differently that Friday. He made a note about the broken window. "I'll pass this along," he said.

A minute later, back in her Cabrio, feeling the burning gorgon stare of Dee still singeing her back, Alex resisted the urge to give herself a dope slap. Why did she never listen to her instincts? When they were teenagers, her best friend Nan was the only one of them smart enough to refuse to rise to the challenge of dares. "What do you have to lose?" they would goad her. "My pride," was Nan's standard response. Indeed.

This hadn't been a dare, though. Her friends' advice to talk to the cops had been sensible, and she hardly gone in spouting wild theories. If the cops didn't want to take her seriously, that was their tough luck. But it better not be Barb's tough luck, too.

❧

It was the usual busy Thursday lunch at the pub. Alex liked Thursdays. On Thursday her customers' internal clocks clicked into weekend mode and they all relaxed their work ethic and their death grip on their wallets. She didn't even have to run a special.

Being busy was always the best medicine. By the time she sat at the bar tallying up a stack of lunch receipts, she had put her waste-of-time police visit in perspective. She summoned her Inner Jersey Girl, and channeled a classic Jersey response. Fuck 'em.

She filled out a deposit slip and put a stack of cash and credit card receipts in her bank bag. Three o'clock and the place was deserted, the hum of the bar fridge and ice machine the only noises. That, and her fingers tapping on the bar. Think.

But Alex thought best when she was moving. She grabbed a new bar towel and started polishing up some smudgy-looking bottles on the speed rail.

Was she really at a total dead end with the police? It seemed so, at least with cops she didn't know. But she did know two: Kevin and Carl. She blasted a bottle of Bacardi with Windex. Kevin might know about the investigation. And he was family; he couldn't just blow her off, like Officer Karsten basically had.

But he wouldn't help her just because they were second cousins, or whatever they were. Kevin was cocky and self-absorbed and ambitious. Last month Alex had seen an "It's All About Me" T-shirt on the internet and nearly bought it for him. If she could convince Kevin that helping her out was to his advantage, she had a chance. And what could he do for Alex?

Get her into the Book Ends. That would be the fastest way for her to learn where the fire had started. For her part, she could tell him what section of the bookstore it was in. It might be significant. If he wanted, Kevin could bring that info to the cops. Him, they'd listen to.

Her cell phone wasn't in her usual spot next to the register. Shit. She dashed up the inside stairway to her apartment, startling Lucy, who'd been sound asleep in a spot of sun on her armchair.

"Sorry, sweetie." She absently petted Lucy's head as she scrolled down the screen, not sure if she had put Kevin's number in, this summer. There it was. She highlighted his number and hit Send as she headed back downstairs.

❧

Alex's day was definitely getting better as it went along. Her conversation with Kevin had been short and sweet. And it had gone her way.

Kathy called just as they were opening for happy hour.

"How'd it go this morning, with The Man?" They were having a 70s moment.

"The Heat wasn't too cooperative." Alex filled her in.

"Huh. Well, it was worth a shot."

"I guess. And he did make a note about the broken window."

"That's something at least! You know," Kathy said, "I meant to ask you last night. Do you have any ideas about that window?"

Alex sat down on her favorite corner barstool. "No ideas. Just a bad feeling."

"And you said it was boarded up, so you couldn't tell what had happened."

"Right. I thought about it some last week, until we got hit with the Homecoming insanity and then everything else just went out of my head. What about storm damage?"

Kathy thought for a minute. "I doubt it. We haven't anything big since that hailstorm back in August—remember?"

"Remember? It took a year off my life!" She wasn't likely to forget the huge thunderstorm that had swept through Sherman a week before she opened Fitzpatrick's, or the sound of hail, like shovels of stones being dumped on her roof. Luckily it had been smaller than it sounded.

"And," Kathy continued, "that was a while ago. If she lost the pane then, she would have replaced it by now."

"For sure." Barb was meticulous about her building.

Kathy paused, and Alex heard the creak of her screen door opening. She could picture her standing on the porch, looking around for the boys.

"So," Alex said, "the other option is, someone broke it— threw a rock or something at it. And the window was pretty high up. I mean, it's not a logical place for some random vandalism. Or a baseball to come flying through."

"That would require kids outside playing baseball!" Kathy

scoffed. "When do you ever see that anymore?"

"True." Alex walked over to the front door and unlocked it, scanning the empty parking lot and the highway beyond. "I wonder if Barb ever reported it."

"If it was me, and I knew it wasn't from storm, I might have called the cops. Or my insurance company."

"It was a small window, though. I wouldn't have called insurance for that. No point— it was probably way below her deductible. But I could ask Kevin to see if Barb called the police." She told Kathy about her evening plans. "After the thing this morning at the station, I went to Plan B. Sincere and honest didn't work. So I'm moving onto manipulation and family pressure."

"Attagirl!" Kathy's laughter rang down the line. "Let me know how it turns out."

Alex heard the creak of Kathy's screen door again and then the phone clunked down. "Eliot! Drop that bird, goddamnit!" A silent minute later, Alex was about to hit the End button when Kathy came back on. "I've got a situation here," she said breathlessly.

Alex was laughing as she watched her first customers arrive. "People are here, I gotta go. Good luck with that bird— and Eliot!"

"Be careful tonight!" Kathy warned. "That building's still dangerous."

"I will," Alex promised. "And I'll wear dark clothes."

CHAPTER FOURTEEN

Alex loved fall, but she hated to see the days getting shorter. In a couple of weeks daylight savings time would end and it would be dark twelve hours a day. Rural darkness. Granted, the sky was beautiful: blackest velvet with a million stars of incredible brightness. But they weren't casting much light down on Sherman.

Main Street at 7:30 felt more like midnight. The dim street-lights outlined shadowy buildings. Only last week Book Ends had cast a glow of light and comfort on this block. Now it was a dark, eerie ruin.

The sight of a police cruiser gliding up behind Alex's car and killing the lights would normally make her heart skip a beat, but tonight it was a reassuring sight. She glanced at the dashboard clock. Kevin was right on time. His quiet approach signaled that he didn't want to be noticed much more than she did. Maybe she should have worn black burglar-clothes after all.

She'd left Annette pulling pints a few minutes ago. Annette was a natural bartender, quick on her feet with an easy, bantering style. If rednecks didn't like being served by a black woman they could suck it. And go to Huskers.

But when she clambered out of her car, Alex saw that Kevin wasn't alone. Did he have a partner on patrol with him tonight?

No. The guy wasn't wearing a uniform. Through the gloom Alex could see he was tall and beefier than Kevin, with a dark beard. They stood by the cruiser talking quietly and then he turned towards Alex. She knew him. It was Neil Schaeffer, one of her regulars. And a volunteer fireman, as she'd learned last Friday. He'd gone tearing out of the pub to respond to the fire at Book Ends.

Neil nodded and smiled at Alex. Not a big talker, Neil, but a nice guy.

Kevin rested both hands on his belt, looking official. As usual, his belt looked like it weighed a million pounds, an armory of stuff hanging off it. Gun. Baton. Flashlight. Alex felt a twinge of sympathetic back pain.

"Hi Neil."

Neil cleared his throat. "I'm on the fire squad," he said, gesturing with his head at the shell of Book Ends. "Went back in there after the Fire Marshall guys were done. I know the danger areas."

Good thing to know. "Are we going inside?"

"Maybe." Kevin said as he started across the street. "If we do, he's gonna keep us out of trouble." He flashed a grin at Neil. "Maybe you could give Neil a couple beers on the house?"

"Absolutely." He could have a keg if he kept them from getting crushed under some beam.

The yellow Crime Scene tape bordering the store glistened in the darkness. They stood on the sidewalk that fronted Book Ends, up against the tape. It smelled like the inside of a fireplace, only twenty times stronger. And darker. This was the closest Alex had been since the fire. Maybe this wasn't such a smart idea.

Neil had brought along a great big flashlight, like Kevin's, and he snapped it on. Kevin did the same. They shone their beams into the first floor, this way and that. One beam hit a floor-to-ceiling bookshelf, now a charred wreck, covered with melted black piles. Next to it, where another bookshelf had once stood, nothing. It all looked so unrecognizable that Alex was disoriented, the layout of the store washed from her mind.

But she couldn't afford to stay spaced out. She took a deep, smoky breath. Focus. She peered into the charred mess, trying to recreate what had been where when she'd visited last week.

They shone their flashlights into the front room. "This," she told them "is where Barb had the best sellers: the thrillers, the hot nonfiction books." It was a smart strategy. That room was usually hopping with activity as customers perused the latest titles, and passers-by on Main Street were lured in. It was the same with restaurants and bars. An empty one will scare people away, but busy ones just get busier. Not fair, but there you have it.

The community bulletin board had been in that front room, too. Last week, she had stood there reading and laughing at the announcements. It was where she'd talked to that strange Amanda woman.

"Kevin, can your shine you light over there?" Alex pointed to the right wall of the front room. That had been a favorite spot of hers; she'd often stood there browsing through the mystery section, letting Barb's hand-printed recommendations guide her to new authors.

All gone now. Kevin and Neil's beams played over a blackened wall, then down the floor. What was left of the shelves was a small pile of burned wood that looked like big chunks of coal. Their lights didn't reach beyond, to the second room, which had been defined by partial walls.

"Can we go in?"

Kevin and Neil looked at each other. Neil nodded.

"Two conditions," Kevin said with heavy emphasis. "One. We follow Neil. We only go where he says it's safe. Got it?"

Yes, Dad, Alex nearly said. But she nodded obediently.

"Two. You don't tell anyone about this. *Anyone.*"

Alex lied and vowed silence. They ducked under the Crime Scene tape. Debris lay everywhere underfoot. They got into Indian file, Neil leading the way.

A bit of the wall into the second room remained. "That was all fiction," Alex said, pointing to the wall on the right. Yards and yards of it. It was the same story as the front room: the charred pieces of books and shelves everywhere, destroyed by fire and water.

A large object in the middle of the room attracted her attention. Kevin and Neil shone their lights on it and she saw that it was the remains of the big round oak table for the coffeepot, mugs, and creamers. "This was a high traffic area," she told them.

"Yeah, I remember." Neil prodded the table with his boot. "I came in here a few times." He moved forward, pointing his flashlight towards the back of the store. "This is where it started."

"Holy shit," Alex murmured, slowly taking in the scope of the destruction as their flashlights traced paths across the empty spaces. They were now in what had been the third and last room of Book Ends. It was totally unrecognizable. The walls were gone and nothing, not even a partial bookshelf or burned book was left.

This is where Alex had sat last week, ensconced in a cozy armchair, flipping through food magazines. Where she and Barb talked about Thanksgiving dinner at the pub.

Neil's voice broke into her reverie. "The point of origin, that's where the most damage is."

"So what was in here?" Kevin asked Alex.

Alex surfaced. "Magazines. Newspapers."

"That makes sense," Neil said. "Stuff like that burns really fast, even faster than books."

"And all the shelves in the store were wood," she told them.

"Seen enough?" Kevin suddenly shone the strong beam of his flashlight right into Alex's face, blinding her.

"Hey!" she grabbed ineffectually for the flashlight as his adolescent laughter sounded through the hollow space.

"Well, now I bet she can't see anything," Neil observed.

"Idiot," Alex muttered in Kevin's general direction. Then, her vision recovering, she looked up. Straight up, into a sky full of stars.

Neil turned his light to where she was looking. "That's how it got started on the second floor," he said. "From this room."

"Jesus." Alex stared up in horror. It had gone from here up into Barb's apartment. And she'd been there.

❧

The air on Main Street had never felt fresher than it did a few minutes later as they stood by their cars. Alex gulped down big mouthfuls of it, trying to wash out the dirty ashtray taste. Her clothes, her hair—everything, she was sure—reeked of smoke. "Thanks, guys."

Neil made a dismissive, 'no problem' kind of noise.

"Come on over for those beers whenever you want, Neil." She looked at Kevin. "You too, I guess."

"Better get back to it," he said, slipping behind the wheel of his patrol car. Could Kevin just go off the radar while on duty?

He tapped the radio thing on his shoulder and spoke into it. "Car two to base." He inclined his head and assumed a serious expression. "Fire site is secure." Then he grinned at Alex and Neil.

She really should stop underestimating him, Alex thought, as she drove back out to Fitzpatrick's through the black night.

So much for slipping right back behind the bar. Alex stood in the shower scrubbing the smoke smell out of her hair, Jane perched on the rim of the tub, eyeing her reproachfully.

Lucy, as usual, took the other route, acknowledging Alex's hurried, acrid-smelling entrance with imperial disdain. But curiosity had gotten the better of her. As Alex changed into fresh jeans and a shirt, she spied a pair of enormous green eyes peering out from behind the pile of smoky clothes she'd bundled together and thrown on the bedroom floor.

"Caught you!" She scooped Lucy up in her arms.

Two servings of treats later, Alex was back down the stairs. In the hour she'd been gone, things had gotten a lot busier and Annette flashed her a look of relief as she joined her behind the bar.

The pub stayed busy till a little after ten and then, as often happened on Thursday nights, they were suddenly empty. Downtown it would be another story: the bars that catered to them would be packed exclusively with drunken Sherman State students, lured by the ads for Bladder Buster specials. Twenty-five cent beers, pounding music, and hook ups.

The quiet gave Alex a chance to check on supplies for the weekend. She emerged from the walk-in to find Chris sitting on a barstool with a glass of wine in front of her.

Quietly absorbed in the Weather Channel, she didn't see Alex. For the first time, Alex gazed her fill at Chris, taking in her long tapering legs, the elegant way she held her wine glass, the way the simple oatmeal sweater brought out the gold of her skin and hair. Black boots peeked out from under faded jeans.

She pulled up a barstool and joined her. "Any good weather stories?"

Chris turned and smiled. "People in Florida might not call it good."

On the map which filled the TV screen, a menacing green blob was headed straight for Fort Lauderdale. Erin would be running around buying masking tape and vodka.

She looked sidelong at Chris. They'd never, she realized with a small jolt, been alone together until now. Or sat this close. Not that it mattered now. But her heart beat a little faster, all the same.

"What does the bartender recommend?" Chris asked, with a teasing smile.

Ouch. Alex could think of a few things, like giving up boyfriends. She rummaged in the cooler and pulled out a bottle of white wine, its green glass beaded with water drops. "Try this Fumé Blanc. It's out of this world." Really it was a summer wine, but it was warm and toasty in the bar. The fireplace, burning brightly, was helping.

Chris took a sip of wine. "Very good. And guess what?" She turned her wide green eyes on Alex. "I have a new cat in my house today."

"Maurice!" Alex clapped her hands.

"I stopped by your cousins' today and met him. He's a real sweetie."

"That's absolutely the best news I've heard all week. Thank you for doing that."

A couple of women came in—college students—and settled themselves noisily at the other end of the bar. This obviously wasn't their first stop of the night. What were they doing here, far from the college action? Maybe just taking a breather. "Annette," Alex waved her over. "Get them started and then you can go. The party's over here, for tonight."

"So did you go to the police today?" Chris asked

"Yup," Alex frowned and told the story again. As she finished it, her cell phone rang.

"Hey girl! How'd it go at Book Ends?" It was Kathy, talking through heavy static.

That's the last thing Alex heard clearly. After a minute or so of playing "I can't hear you" tennis Kathy shouted, "Be there in five!" Then the line went dead.

Chris, like Kathy, wasn't all that surprised at the outcome of the cop story. But she did enjoy the description of Dispatcher Dee, who of course she knew from way back.

Alex had a Frangelico waiting for Kathy when she blew in a few minutes later, a long tan raincoat flapping elegantly behind her and a manila envelope under her arm. "What a drive!" she called out.

Alex and Chris looked at her blankly.

"Haven't you seen the fog out there?"

One of the students called over to Kathy. "Still heavy?"

"Go take a look!" Kathy said. But they didn't budge from their stools. Alex walked over to the door, Chris following. Total whiteness. The parking lot, the highway beyond, the lights of Sherman had all disappeared.

Alex turned back to Kathy. "How did you manage to make it here? I can't believe you're not in a ditch!"

Kathy laughed. "I just beat it here—it only rolled in on me the last quarter-mile or so. And there was no one else out there with me. I think." She peeled off her coat and sat down next to Chris, plopping the envelope on the bar and reaching for her glass in one fluid motion. "These are the pictures you loaned me last night." She took a sip of Frangelico.

"I looked at mine again today but no luck," Chris said.

Kathy slid out two pictures. "Well, I had some." She tapped her finger on Moon Face. "Him," she said. "It finally clicked today, who he is. He's at the college."

Chris leaned in and narrowed her eyes. "You're right. "Isn't he a professor?"

"You got it. I went on the Sherman State website today, and there he was. Dr. Vanderberge. Math department."

"I think I've heard that name somewhere," Alex said.

Kathy reached back into her raincoat and pulled out a piece of paper. "It sounded familiar to me, too. "So I surfed around some more on the website. You guys ever read *The Tiger*?"

They nodded. *The Tiger* was the Sherman State College newspaper and sometimes Alex's staff brought in a copy. For a student paper with a fierce name, it was pretty tame. The rumor was that the administration censored it—so much for the First Amendment—but sometimes the Editorial page was entertaining.

It was the editorial page that Kathy had printed off. Alex and Chris leaned in to read it, their shoulders almost touching. The date was a few weeks back and the letter was titled, "Reclaim America!"

Purporting to be an editorial, it was essentially an ad for a new campus group of students and faculty who wanted to "Take back America" and return it to the place "we all once knew and loved." From the Heartland, they would send their angry message to Washington: cut spending and government, respect traditional values, reject "foreigners" running for office.

"Foreigners from Hawaii, I guess," Alex frowned. "I hope he doesn't force his students to listen to that crap in class." She took a closer look at the enlargement. "I wonder if he hangs out with Don's crew." He sure seemed to fit the profile: racist, angry. From the picture it was hard to tell. He wasn't talking with any of them, but he had the same rapt, pleased expression.

"Same demographic," Chris pointed out. "White, male, middle-aged."

"And the America 'we once knew' was white, right?" Kathy added. "Or at least white people were in charge."

"White men," Alex noted.

Kathy picked up the second picture. "As soon as I figured out that Moon Face is from campus, I knew that's where I'd seen this other guy, too." It was the man in the ball cap and dark sweatshirt, thinner than the group around him. He was younger too, maybe thirty.

"Wait a sec," Chris said, taking the picture from her. "I do know him! He works in the Administration building. I had to deal with him about a student auditing my photography class one time. Something was wrong with her paperwork. He didn't want her sitting in until it was straightened out—kept sending me emails about it."

Alex looked at the picture. Another Don groupie? He had more of a neutral expression than the other men, but he definitely didn't look worried or concerned.

Kathy slid a cigarette out of her pack. "I want to hear about your adventure!"

Chris looked puzzled.

"I went into Book Ends tonight with Kevin." Alex tried to remember every detail as she recounted their walk-through. Kathy and Chris listened quietly, taking it all in.

"You're a braver woman than me," Kathy said when Alex had finished.

"It was awful. Like something out of a movie."

Chris sipped her wine. "Did you find anything out?"

Alex thought. Her night had been such a rush: the dark, eerie tour of Book Ends and then zooming back here to two busy hours behind the bar. There'd been no time to process anything. But the impact had been mostly emotional. "Seeing how bad it was, that was the main thing. It's much worse than what you see driving by." She shook her head as the images came back. "At least now we know where it started."

"What do you make of that?" Kathy asked.

Alex shrugged. "No idea, really. Except now the speed of the fire makes more sense. But *how* it started in the magazine section? You got me."

"Well," Chris looked at them intently, "if I were going to

set a fire in Book Ends, that's where I'd do it."

Kathy tapped her nails on the bar. "Me too. Lots of paper. But also, think of the layout. Magazines were in the back. Wasn't Barb usually up front? That's where I always saw her."

"That's right." Alex grabbed a bar napkin and pen and sketched the three rooms of the bookstore.

"So." Chris picked up the pen and drew an X where Alex had drawn the counter in the front room. "Barb is here. Maybe she's at the register, busy with some last customers." Then, at the other end of the floor plan, in the corner of the magazine area, Chris made another X. "I'm the arsonist, and I'm back here." She put the pen down.

Kathy nodded. "Easy enough, if no one was back there. No way could Barb have seen."

"But," Alex objected, "didn't the fire start when the store was closed? How could someone have started it when the store was still open—and Barb was there?"

"Maybe it took a while to get going," Chris said. "I saw something about that on one of those true crime shows. There are all kinds of delaying devices for starting fires."

"If someone knew what he was doing." Kathy shrugged.

"I could ask Neil when he comes in next. I owe him a couple of beers for tonight." But she knew someone more expert than Neil. "Or I could call Carl."

"Have you heard from him?" Kathy asked.

"Not since they left."

Chris pulled her jacket off the stool next to her. "I tried to do a little research myself, today," she said, extracting a thick piece of paper from her pocket. "But I didn't get very far."

She unfolded the tattered paper on the bar in front of them. It was a faded map of Nebraska, the creases so heavy that some had become rips. She traced her finger from Sherman to somewhere southwest of them. "See, here's Cooper, Barb's hometown." They leaned forward. Cooper was in small print, with a big red circle drawn around it.

"Alex, you said that Barb's hometown was about was twenty miles from their farm—she and Wayne's farm."

"Right."

"We need to know where he is. Or was. So I calculated twenty miles in all directions from Cooper. Their farm has to be somewhere in here."

Alex looked at the area within the circle, an expanse of emptiness only broken by four towns. "It's not exactly a metropolitan area, is it?"

Kathy winked at Chris. "Well, it's not New Jersey!"

"I'll say!" Alex retorted. "I mean, how can you have towns like twenty miles apart? That's not normal. When one town ends, another should start."

They burst out laughing. "Let's take her out to the west of the state sometime," Kathy said to Chris. "Then she'll see sparse."

"The Cooper area is like a suburb compared with western Nebraska," Chris added.

Alex's eye traveled west across the map, to counties that were surely bigger than her whole home state. They had about two towns each. "No thanks."

With her finger, Chris traced the circle she'd drawn around Cooper. "This is as far as I got, though. We need his last name."

"Well, look," Alex said. "There are only these four little towns. Why don't we check the phone books for those towns and see how many men with Wayne as a first name are listed? These are pretty small towns, I'm assuming."

"Probably two to three pages in the phone book for each," Kathy estimated.

"How about if I take Valley and Grant?" Chris proposed.

"I'll look up Petersburg. You do Eustace, okay?" Kathy pointed to a town northwest of Cooper.

"Got it." Alex wrote the name on a bar napkin to get the

spelling right. "Let the Wayne hunt begin."

I hate to bring up a sad topic," Kathy said, "but about Saturday, Alex? I was thinking we should be on the road around eight."

"For the funeral?" Chris looked alert.

"Mmm-hmm. It's not far." Kathy glanced at the map. "About an hour and a half over to Cooper, I figure."

Alex would never get used to the concept of distances in Nebraska. An hour and a half drive in Jersey is a trek. It usually meant you were going to another state. And of course it would involve traffic, something people here never had to factor into drive time.

"Can I come too?" Chris asked.

"Of course!" Damn, they should have thought to ask her. "Sorry, I just—"

Chris waved off her apology. "Don't worry about it. I didn't know Barb, but I'd like to go. And I can drive us. How 'bout if we meet at your place?" she asked Kathy.

Later, climbing wearily into bed, Alex realized this would be their first road trip. She hoped the future would hold more pleasant ventures. Cooper. What did it look like? She tried to picture it as sleep crept up. They'd be paying a visit to Barb's past, in a way, and the past was where Barb's unfinished story began. A vision of a sandstone church, much like Fort God, floated before her eyes as she felt the heavy, comforting weight of Lucy settle against her legs. Then she was asleep.

CHAPTER FIFTEEN

"**We're stranded, huh?**" Alex said to Jane the next morning as they looked together out the living room window into a wall of fog. She'd watched her friends disappear into the white void last night but never imagined she'd wake to find the pub still surrounded. Jane regarded her anxiously.

Fog, fog, go away. Her regular Friday customers would never venture out onto the highway in this. They'd be stuck in town for lunch at Dairy Queen or Huskers. And she'd be empty.

But that first glorious cup of coffee worked its usual magic. Why not just pretend it was a snow day and enjoy it? For now, anyway. She climbed back into bed and propped the pillows up to a reading position. Miss Marple was covered with dust and cat fur, neglected all week. Jane settled in at her side.

Colonel Protheroe was dead, shot in his study. Alex sank back into the world of St. Mary Mead, following Miss Marple as she discovered, chapter by chapter, that everyone in the village hated the colonel and had a motive to shoot him. Plenty of suspects. And a village which Miss Marple knew as well as she knew human nature. But as a detective, Miss Marple had another big advantage over Alex. She knew Colonel Protheroe had been murdered.

Alex put the book down and looked out her bedroom window, into the fog. She was in a fog herself: sadness, anger, that nagging sense of unease. Why? People died. They died in accidents all the time. Why couldn't she let it go, accept that bad things happened to good people—more often than to bad people?

Alex believed in reason, in logic. That had been the closest to a faith system she'd ever known. Her parents were recovering Catholics—fully recovered—Dad a biochemist. Her family had, however, retained the Irish-Catholic code of suppressing emotion. Anger was okay. But try to share any other feelings and you were labeled an emotional cripple. Intuition was for New Age freaks. You trusted your brain, not your gut.

And yet her gut was there, with its persistent if often ignored messages. In the quiet, the fog pressing up against her windows, she tried to listen. She breathed deep, tried to empty her mind of all the clutter. But then, more strongly than she'd felt it yet, unease swept over her with the intensity of panic. Her stomach churned; her pulse raced.

This was no accident. Barb was murdered.

The cell phone rang. She started. No ring tone, just the generic ringing sound for people not in her phone book. Normally she'd let a call like that go to voice mail. Not today.

"Alex, it's Carl."

"Carl! I was going to call you—today if I had the time."

"I can call you back if you're busy."

"No, I'm socked in with fog right now. We're looking at a slow day if this doesn't clear."

"Oh, it'll lift soon, I bet." He cleared his throat. "I said I'd keep you up to date if I heard anything. Eric Frisch called this morning." The Fire Chief. "They heard from the coroner's office last night. The cause of death was smoke inhalation."

So it had been the smoke that killed Barb. Not something—not someone—before the fire.

"Alex? You there?"

"Sorry. Just thinking."

"I thought you'd be relieved it wasn't something else," Carl sounded puzzled.

"Well, yeah, that's good. But have they figured out how the fire started yet?"

"No. They've ruled out electrical causes, though."

"Then it still could be arson," she pressed.

"Could be."

"Carl, I gotta tell you, I'm sure this wasn't an accident."

"Have you found something out?" His voice was sharp.

Alex ignored the stern tone. "Yes. I think I have. Not that the police were interested." Shit. What she'd tried to share with the Sherman P.D. yesterday, she'd withheld from Carl on Sunday night. Oh well. Might as well just spill it all to him, now—minus the tour by night of Book Ends. She didn't want to get Kevin in trouble. Carl might even listen.

He did. When she'd finished, there was a brief silence. "I can see why you're worried," he said, finally. "But you know, Officer Karsten couldn't have done much with what you gave him. It's too vague."

"I guess," Alex conceded. "But what about the cause? Don't they usually figure that out sooner?"

"Sometimes. Depends on a lot of factors." Alex could hear people in the background, the crackle of a radio. "Eric said they're still waiting on some lab results."

"What are they testing?"

"One thing they're looking for is evidence of accelerants. Gasoline, things like that."

The back room of Book Ends: a shadowy figure, a lawn-mower-sized gas can in one hand and match in the other. She could see it. "Do you know what the Sherman P.D. are looking into?"

"Couldn't get anything out of Kevin?" he teased.

"Not much!" And Tiffany, the intern at *The Telegraph*, hadn't shown up with any scoops, yet either. Oh well. Carl's info was right from the horse's mouth.

"Eric said the police are trying to trace Barb's movements that day and evening. And they're looking into her financial situation. Nothing suspicious there, so far."

A clamorous scratching sound erupted at the back door. Damn. Alex had forgotten Lucy was out there and scrambled to let her in. Her thick grey fur beaded with moisture, Lucy tromped in and paused to give a great shake, ensuring that a shower of drops covered the floor, cabinets, and every surface in her vicinity.

"The broken window." Carl said. "Do the police know about that?"

"That's the one thing Karsten wrote down."

"I'll give Kevin a call, see if they've got a record on it."

"Carl, if someone set the fire at Book Ends, could it have taken a while to get going? Kathy and Chris saw something on TV about delaying devices."

"It could have happened that way." He sighed. "I hope not. Those devices can get burned up, so there's no almost trace left. And someone who uses one of those…he's no amateur."

"Or she."

Suddenly, out her living room window, a tree appeared. Then, dimly, the road.

A sedan cruised slowly by. If that car could make it out here, so could others. "Hey, the fog's breaking up. I'd better get a move on. Thanks for calling."

"Tell you what, I'll ask Kevin to let you know about that

window. And I'll call you when I hear anything—anything I can share," he qualified.

"Great." She was pulling jeans and a shirt out of her closet, her mind on the prep for lunch.

"And you'll let me know anything you find out?" Carl asked.

"I will."

"Alex," he paused. "I don't know what all's going on out there. But please be careful." He wasn't kidding around. His words and tone chilled Alex more than any fog could, and she carried them with her as she hurried downstairs, turning on the lights.

~

The pub was slammed at lunch. Freed of the blanket of fog, people drove out with a single-minded determination to have fun, as if they had been trapped in Sherman for months.

Her conversation with Carl was never far from Alex's mind, though. In the kitchen with Robin during the rush, behind the bar pulling draft beers, chatting with people at the bar, part of her was always mulling it over.

Carl was worried—a little scared, maybe, about what was going on around here. That made two of them. She poured drinks and looked around at her customers, laughing and talking as they sucked down beers and lunch. Barb's killer could be here right now.

By 2:30 the mob had departed, most of them heading back to clock in a few more reluctant, somewhat buzzed hours at work before Friday officially began. At 3:00 she was alone in a clean and empty pub. The sun shone through the windows. The fog seemed like a distant dream.

But it would be cool again tonight. Better set the fireplace up. Alex snagged a pile of newspapers from behind the bar and wadded them under the grate. Paper would get it going fast. Just like at Book Ends.

Alex replayed their walk through the ruined interior of Book Ends. Arson. But how? And the big question: *why*? Her conversations with Chris and Kathy, Carl and Kevin, with Robbie the contractor and Tiffany swirled around in her head like a drink with too many ingredients. Two weeks ago all she had on her mind was Fitzpatrick's. It was all starting to blur together.

Maybe she should make a list.

Some people love lists. They have "to do" lists, they have shopping lists, they have lists of resolutions. They buy country kitchen-themed list pads at stationery shops, stick them on their fridge, and zestfully draw lines through the completed items.

Alex lost lists. Now that she owned a business she typically had about ten lists in progress, but she always picked up the pen with a heavy heart and the knowledge that half the lists she made would go missing right when she needed them.

Today, though, there was no way around a list. The various threads about Book Ends had become a tangle she needed to unravel. She fixed a smoked salmon and cream cheese sandwich on brown bread, poured a Coke, and grabbed a pen.

She started with her last conversation about Book Ends, with Carl, and worked backwards.

Item One: Barb's finances. There'd been nothing discovered there, Carl said. Nothing suspicious. Suspicious! She hadn't registered the word at the time. What were they looking into—money laundering? At any rate, it seemed Barb's finances were solid, taking her off the arsonist suspect list.

Two: Where was Barb on Saturday night? The police were tracing Barb's movements on Saturday. Movements. Barb would have laughed at that, said it made her sound like her last day was spent in the bathroom.

When they'd talked about it on Sunday night, she and

Kathy and Chris had all assumed that Barb went to the Equal Partners in Faith meeting. They needed to confirm that. Had Barb mentioned other members last week when they'd talked about the group? Alex ran back through their conversation: Thanksgiving, the benefit...yes! The woman with the Q-Tip hair. Amanda Wagner. She was going to the meeting that night, after the benefit. Should Alex call her? It sounded like she lived in Sherman; hopefully they were in the phone book.

But they also needed to check the bookstore hours that day. And was Book Ends busy before Barb closed up? That could be important in terms of the timing of the fire.

How the fire had started was another question, but it wasn't an item for her list. If the lab results showed something, though, Alex was counting on a call from Carl.

Three: the broken window in Barb's apartment. Again, Alex would have to rely on others for info on that: Carl or Kevin.

Four: the Wayne hunt. Alex needed to look up the Eustace telephone listings. Wherever that was. That would be a computer task.

She looked at the growing list. Damn, she should have started on that this morning, instead of lazing around the apartment. Number four was important. They needed to know what Wayne had been up to and if he and Barb had been in touch lately.

That brought her to item five: did Wayne still own the farm? But they were stalled on that until they could discover his last name.

Six was the most nebulous and probably the most difficult of all: what did Don and his friends have against Barb? They'd have to start with Don, the ringleader, and go to his lair. Huskers. Talk about creepy. Her walk through Book Ends at night would probably pale by comparison.

She tucked the list into her back pocket. Where to put it so it wouldn't get lost?

She'd think about it later.

CHAPTER SIXTEEN

They drove to Cooper Saturday morning through a landscape of checkered green and golden fields. Despite the bright October sunshine it was a blur to Alex as she gazed out the back window of Chris's Jeep Cherokee. She'd stumbled to bed at 2:30 and hoped it was a joke when she heard her alarm go off at 7:15.

Chris had taken one look at Alex and assigned her to the back seat where she could curl up and nap en route. She tried. But she never could sleep in cars and the roads were pretty bumpy. She dozed off once, while Kathy and Chris's dimly-heard conversation washed over her, a sensation that reminded her of long family car trips. Her half-nap ended jarringly, though, when they hit a pothole the size of a house foundation.

Good thing. When she sat up, a glance in the rearview mirror showed an amazing hair sculpture in progress. The imprint of the seat cushion pattern on her left cheek was a lovely finishing touch. A pretty girl is like a melody. But was that coffee she smelled?

Kathy read her mind. Alex took the travel cup she passed back with trembling gratitude. She'd packed them a big thermos and it was still hot.

"You're a goddess."

"I try."

Chris's dashboard clock read 9:20. Alex had been drifting in and out longer than she thought. They'd be there soon. She sipped her coffee and watched the fields go by. The car got quieter and quieter, the closer they got to Cooper.

A cheery "Welcome to Cooper!" billboard greeted them at the edge of town. No one was cheered. It was like the Sherman town sign, listing the churches and service organizations. Sin city. Cooper had a lot fewer things on its sign than Sherman, though, so it must be smaller. That would make sense: they didn't have a state college here.

They reached the top of a gentle hill and saw Cooper nestled below them. Maybe Sherman had once been like this, years back, before the college came and filled the town with kids from other towns, and professors from the cities and coasts. "When was Sherman State founded?" Alex asked.

"Was it like a hundred years ago?" Chris sounded uncertain.

"No, you're right," Kathy said. "They had that big celebration a few years back, remember? I'm sure that was their centennial." She looked back over her shoulder at Alex. "What made you think of that?"

"Just comparing Sherman and Cooper. Size-wise. But hey, you know what else is different? The farms." There had been something pleasurable in her semi-conscious survey of the country around Cooper. "They're pretty around here."

A big smile lit Kathy's face. "This is a Swedish area!"

Alex had to hand it to the Swedes. The round-roofed white barns with little steeples on top, the white-painted wooden fenced fields and well-maintained farmhouses were a cheerful sight. These were storybook farms, and she bet they'd inspired many an idyllic rural dream in the cars passing through. The Sherman farms had no such magic.

The town was almost as pretty as the farms: great big trees shaded streets of brightly painted homes adorned with gingerbread. They were looking for Poplar Street.

St. Andrew's was a small redbrick church, a far cry from the sandstone structure Alex had anticipated. It was about a third of the size of Fort God, for one thing. Time had weathered the bricks to a mellow luster and ivy climbed up one side. The stained-glass windows looked real, too.

Cars were parked everywhere around the church. Chris navigated slowly to the parking lot in back and eased into a space just about big enough. Alex was awake enough now to notice the beautiful cut of her black suit and how it set off her golden hair. "I was thinking," Chris said. "We should keep our eyes open today."

"Right." She shifted her eyes guiltily from Chris.

They opened the doors gingerly, trying to avoid dinging the Buick Regal on their right and the huge Ford F150 to their left. A parking lot full of American cars surrounded them. Alex was looking vainly for a foreign make anywhere but she saw something else. "You guys! Come here!"

They scurried over. "What's up?"

"Look. Sherman county plates." She pointed to the 32 prefix on the license plate of a rusted-out, cream-colored minivan.

In Nebraska, the counties are all numbered and the first digits on your license plate show where you live. Kathy said it was a law-enforcement thing. But it wasn't only the cops who took note of those numbers. Everyone here did it, automatically. When you grow up here, Kathy said, you learn the county number system around the same time you learn the alphabet.

Kathy squinted at the van in the bright sunlight. "I don't

know this vehicle. Do you?" Chris and Alex shook their heads. Then again, it wasn't one you'd ordinarily notice unless you were a rust connoisseur.

Chris walked around to the back of the van, motioning them to follow. More rust. And three bumper stickers on the back doors: "My high school student is on the Sherman High School Honor Roll," "Save the Family Farm," and a Christian fish symbol. The kind without legs.

"Christian farmers with a kid in high school," Alex deduced. "That doesn't exactly narrow things down."

"Or with a former high school student," Chris noted. "My mom still had one on her car until she sold it. Jess and I were out of college by then."

"And not necessarily farmers, either," Kathy said. "They just might support the idea of family farms."

As least they could assume the owner was Christian. "Friends of Barb's from Sherman, I guess." It was a comforting thought, that others in Sherman had cared enough to make the trek here to say goodbye.

But what about the crowds at the Book Ends fire, the excited or neutral faces watching it burn? "What if this isn't a friend? "Alex felt a flutter in her stomach. "What if the arsonist is here today?"

A small silence followed her question.

Chris looked around. "Then don't the police show up, too, to watch for suspects?"

Kathy was skeptical. "Sounds like a TV show."

"It's worth a thought," Alex countered. "Her killer might have been in that crowd at the fire—maybe he just couldn't stay away. Could be the same with the funeral. Besides," she added, "police shows aren't pure fantasy."

"Could be," Kathy conceded.

Chris glanced at her watch. "The service starts in five minutes."

As they hurried along a brick pathway bordered with flowers, they had a quick strategy session. During the service they would all keep a sharp lookout for anyone they recognized from Sherman. Including cops.

A shiny black hearse stood in front of the church. The sight of a hearse always gave her the major creeps: on the Parkway, Alex would put on a burst of speed to get away from a hearse in the lane next to her. She gave it only a brief, shuddering glance before shooting inside. They took seats in the second to last row.

Worse was to come. Kathy squeezed her arm as four men wheeled a gleaming silver coffin up the aisle. On her other side, Chris gave her a brief but powerful look of sympathy. That's all it took. The tears came. Alex couldn't stop them. She felt Kathy's arm go around her shoulders.

Twelve tissues later, she settled back against the pew, wrung out. Someone was up there reading from the Bible: a late middle aged man, balding and heavy set. He wore a cheap, shiny suit.

"That's Barb's brother-in-law," Chris whispered. Alex had missed the introduction.

Where was the rest of Barb's family? They would be up front, of course, but in this crowd it was hard to see them. The church was packed. Barb had left Cooper behind a long time ago and hardly ever mentioned it; Alex had assumed her remaining connections to her hometown were few. But maybe the Nichols' were a big clan in this area. She looked at the people around her, a seriously blond crowd that made the Aryan Nation of Sherman look like Italy. Blond and blue eyed and healthy looking. Big, too. She had no problem pegging many of the men as farmers—or farming stock, anyway.

The minister was up in the pulpit now, talking about Barb. Not very inspiring. It was obvious he'd never known her and he trickled faint and unspecific praise over her coffin.

If Alex were up there, she'd talk about what a good friend

Barb was, how she'd come to Sherman and built a wonderful bookstore out of nothing. She wished these people had seen Barb there, happy and fulfilled.

The minister droned on about eternity and peace. Peace: not likely. There lay her good friend, getting her final sacrament from a stranger. Burned. Autopsied. Gone. Barb deserved better than this. Alex couldn't get up and give her a ringing eulogy but she could try to get her some justice.

She began to look around again, scanning the crowd for anyone who looked familiar from Sherman, trying not to be obvious. But the people in her vicinity were bored and restive too, and her head was not the only one swiveling around. As her eyes swept along the next aisle she was stopped by the beady blue-eyed stare of a woman: *What are you doing? And by the way, who the hell are you?*

Alex suspended her survey.

Kathy was writing something on her program. She tilted it toward Alex: "Seen anybody from Sherman?"

Alex shook her head no and passed it over to Chris. Chris took out a pen and wrote. "Not yet." This was starting to feel like seventh grade.

"You?" Alex whispered to Kathy.

An affirmative nod. But before Kathy could fill them in, the beady-eyed blond across the aisle whipped around and gave them a gorgon stare. Alex shrank back.

Not Kathy. Like cats about to launch into combat, the two locked eyes until, about thirty seconds in, Beady Eyes finally conceded defeat. She looked away and made a little huffy noise. Kathy blazed a look into her back for a few seconds, finishing her off. Alex suppressed a laugh.

"Over there," Kathy whispered, pointing to the the pews up ahead on the opposite aisle.

"Which row?" Chris asked, but just then the organ music started up at deafening volume. The service was over. The coffin was wheeled back down the aisle. Alex looked away as it passed.

Right after it came an elderly couple—Barb's parents, Alex assumed—and behind them, a flood of people from the front rows. They lost sight of the aisle.

"I'll point her out later," Kathy promised.

And now a church bell began to ring. Bong-bong-bong, slow and steady, far more mournful even than the organ. That John Donne meditation popped into Alex's head.

Ask not for whom the bell tolls.

She sure as hell hoped not.

Chapter Seventeen

They hit Kathy with questions as soon as they were back in the semi-privacy of the car. Alex leaned forward from the back seat. "Who did you see?"

"Just one person?" Chris asked, as she maneuvered her Jeep into the long line of cars following the hearse.

"Yeah." Kathy rolled down the window, lit a cigarette, and took a big drag before continuing. Refusing to be hurried: a true Nebraska trait. "Pauline Thies. She bought a basket from me at that craft show in the auditorium last spring and ended up introducing me to some other customers. I was all ready to sell her a big Jeremiah basket! But she just bought a small market basket—said it was all she could afford."

"If that rust bucket was her van it's probably true," Chris noted. They were in the funeral procession now, crawling down Main Street.

"I guess. Then she called me a few weeks later. She'd kept my card. Her church was having a raffle and they might want to buy one of my baskets for a prize. So I went over to Our Redeemer that week—"

"Our Redeemer?" Alex cut in. "Isn't that Fort God, where the Promise Keepers meet?"

"God's Warriors," Chris corrected.

"That's the place. Anyway I went, and it turned out to be a women's group—the Ladies Auxiliary. They loved my baskets and they bought a big harvest one for the raffle. They wanted a discount, though, since it was for a church." She flicked an ash out the car window. "I cut a little off the price; that made them happy. A few of the women took my card and bought baskets from me later."

"Was Barb in that group?" Chris asked.

"No." Kathy looked back at Alex. "Barb wasn't Lutheran, was she?"

Alex thought back to their conversation. "She told me she was raised...wait, I know it was something else. Not Baptist." That was black, at least back home. "Um..."

Chris saved her. "St. Andrews is Presbyterian."

"That's it! But when she was married to Wayne she had to go to his church. And it was Lutheran." Some specific kind, though. "Montana Lutheran?"

They burst out laughing.

"What? Okay, something with M, what the hell do I know?" At least the Catholic church had the virtue of simplicity. One holy, apostolic and all that.

"Try Missouri Synod." Kathy was still chuckling.

"Yeah, Missouri. Pretty weird name for a church, by the way. But Barb never liked it. She said it was really conservative and women had no role. When she moved to Sherman she switched back to Presbyterian. Much more liberal."

"No question." Chris affirmed.

"So Pauline Thies and the basket buyers are from the retro church, huh? The Ladies Auxiliary. Wow. We had one of those at our sailing club. They made sandwiches and punch for the parties. But that's going back a while."

"You've come a long way, baby." Kathy stubbed her cigarette out.

Alex sat back in her seat and thought. There was a connection somewhere if only she could make it.

They drove into the cemetery and Chris took a hard right, towards the tall pine trees that sheltered the oldest area. It was a nice spot and a good place to park, giving them a little space from the other cars that crammed into the new area, as close as they could get to the blue canopy and chairs that marked the gravesite.

Standing in the shade of the pines, Alex watched people get out of their cars and wander towards the canopy. As they did the sexes, following some invisible law, separated into groups. Just like at a party: groups of men and groups of women. Then it clicked.

"You guys…" Alex turned to find her friends had wandered a little way off to check out the old headstones. She walked over. "I think I figured it out. How Pauline knew Barb."

"How?" Chris and Kathy said in unison.

"Equal Partners in Faith! Barb said the members were women from different churches. I bet Pauline was in it."

"That could be," Chris agreed.

Kathy nodded. "When I spotted Pauline in church I was wondering if she was a regular at Book Ends. But this sounds like a stronger connection." She looked towards the canopy. Cars were still pulling in. "I'll keep an eye out for her."

"What does she look like?" Chris asked.

"Mousy."

Alex told them about her brief, odd meeting with Amanda Wagner at Book Ends. "I need to call her, ask her about the group. But Kathy, can you ask Pauline about it too? And the meeting Saturday night?

"You got it."

She'd been called a weirdo for it, but Alex liked cemeteries: the old mossy headstones, the pathways winding under old trees. Most people want to run the other way when they see a graveyard. But the dead aren't restless. Alex never felt this more surely than when she was in the palpable silence and peace of a cemetery.

The cemetery in Cooper was small and beautiful, perched atop a hill at the edge of town. As they wandered through its oldest section the familiar tranquility stole over her. The jangle of today's emotions—the sadness and anger—faded.

Kathy and Chris stood in front of a small gravestone, talking quietly.

"1887?" Kathy sounded doubtful.

"I think you're right," Chris squatted down and traced the date towards the bottom of the stone with her finger.

"Look at this," Kathy turned to Alex. "Otto Lindfors, born 1799, died 1887. He was eighty-eight—way back then!"

"You're kidding." Alex stooped over and squinted. The dates were faded to near-invisibility on this old gray stone, its edges blackened with time. But she could just about make them out.

It turned out this section of the cemetery was full of dates like that, people who'd lived to see advanced old age during a time when life spans were cruelly short. The Swedish settlers of Cooper were tough old birds indeed. Imagine what they'd been through. Emigration. Crossing half the continent in a wagon and then living in some primitive sod hut. Breaking the ground. A little different than Alex's Irish ancestors who got off the boat in Jersey and pioneered their way to the nearest pub.

"Tough stock you come from," Alex commented to Kathy as they made their way towards the newer section of the cemetery where the graveside ceremony was about to get underway.

"Don't mess." Kathy winked.

They slipped into the back of the large crowd who'd gathered around the grave. The coffin sat on a metal contraption, the turned-up earth next to it covered by a bright green plastic sheet. Under the canopy, two rows of metal folding chairs were filled with people who looked a lot alike. Barb's family. Her parents, looking small and gray and sad, had the seats of honor in the middle of the front row. Two middle-aged women flanked them on either side.

"Those must be her sisters," Alex whispered, remembering Barb's obituary. "She has a brother, too, but I can't pick him out."

Kathy craned her neck. "The sister on the left looks like Barb."

She was right: the resemblance gave her a jolt. The woman's face was a younger version of Barb's. But the likeness was even stronger in her demeanor. There was Barb's quiet dignity all over again. The sister on the right was a different story. She was a mess. Sobbing and carrying on, eye makeup running down her face, she clung to her father's arm. Even from a distance you could see he was embarrassed. He sat stiffly in his chair, a stoic expression on his face, doing his best to ignore her. It couldn't have been easy.

The minister began praying and the crowd went silent. Alex searched the faces around them. Kathy and Chris were doing the same. They hadn't planned it this way, but their position in the back gave them a good vantage point.

"She's over there," Kathy said quietly, motioning with her head to their right. "About half-way up. See the woman with the really bad perm?"

That didn't narrow it down enough.

"The big woman with the jet black perm. Look to her left."

Alex stood on her toes but could barely catch a glimpse of

Pauline Thies. Pauline was short, which didn't help. From the back she could see her light brown hair was short, too, well above the neckline of her black dress. Pauline was talking to a woman on her left. A woman with a familiar blond Q-tip do.

"You guys," Alex whispered. "Check out the woman on her left. That's Amanda Wagner."

"Let us pray," the minister intoned, and a hundred heads dropped like a shot. Alex dipped hers down and then cautiously raised it.

Two tall young guys to the right of them in the back row had their heads raised too. Fellow pagans? But wait a minute: Alex knew them from somewhere. She looked away before they caught her staring.

Then she snuck another look at them and their faces slotted into place. Of course. They worked at Book Ends—Sherman State students. Alex had seen them there many times. The blond one, in fact, had been the kid who came to ask Barb about where to find a book when she'd been there last week. Next to them stood two college girls who also looked familiar. Yes, they'd worked at Book Ends, too. Her heart lifted at the sight of them all. Then the prayer ended and the service was over. People began drifting towards their cars.

"There they go," Kathy was already moving to head Pauline and Amanda off. "I'll meet you back at the car." They watched her as she caught up with the women and got smoothly into step beside Pauline. It looked like Kathy was feigning surprise to see her.

Chris smiled. "She's good."

"I'll say." Kathy stayed right by Pauline's side as they walked towards the line of parked cars. "Chris, I'll be right back. I just want to..." Alex gestured towards the coffin on its stand.

"Of course." Those kind eyes again.

The coffin gleamed in the sunlight. It was a beautiful day.

"Goodbye, Barb." Tears pricked the back of her eyes. She

didn't think Barb could hear her. The dead were dead and that was that. Where they live on is in our memories.

But goodbye was not enough. "We'll find out who did this to you," she said, if only to herself.

⬤

"Boy, was that weird," Kathy remarked as they drove out of the cemetery a few minutes later. "I couldn't believe how uncomfortable Pauline was!"

"What happened?" Alex asked.

"Well, she was kind of startled to see me there, but we got into small talk for a few minutes and it was fine. Then I asked her—casually— if she knew Barb from Equal Partners in Faith, and you should have seen her expression: like a scared rabbit! And that Amanda woman, she looked the same." Kathy shook her head. "It was like I'd asked about some secret society! But it wasn't secret, was it? Weren't there signs up advertising their meetings?"

"Absolutely," Alex confirmed. "I used to see them in the front window of Book Ends. And on the community bulletin board there."

Chris chewed her lip. "Maybe Pauline and Amanda don't want people to know *they're* in it."

They pondered that for a minute. "What do they do, again?" Kathy asked Alex.

"All Barb said was, they talked about gender issues in their churches. Sounded pretty harmless to me." Alex shrugged.

"Well, it would to you, Miss East Coast!" Kathy teased. "But it might sound pretty radical to a Midwestern minister. Especially in the more conservative churches."

"But," Alex pointed out, "they held their meetings at the churches. Are we talking about a real revolutionary vanguard here?"

"Probably not," Kathy conceded. "Anyway, I asked Pauline

about Saturday night. She said Barb was there, 'of course,' and the meeting ended around nine."

At last, Alex thought, something solid. "She said of course? Sounds like Barb never missed a meeting."

Chris tapped her fingers on the wheel. "Did Barb go home right away? And had the fire started yet?"

"But listen," Kathy broke into their speculations. "Right after I asked her about the meeting, we got to her van—that rusty one is Pauline's—and guess what? There was another woman waiting for them. I've seen her at the college but I can't remember her name." Kathy frowned with concentration. "Tall, nice clothes. She looks Italian or something. She teaches, I'm pretty sure."

They pulled into the parking lot behind the front of the battleship-gray town auditorium where the post-funeral lunch was being held.

"This woman must have been with them at the church," Kathy said. "But I didn't see her."

Alex tried to picture the three of them: mousy Pauline, Amanda of the Midwest hair, and the college professor. An unlikely group of friends. Unless…"You guys, maybe all three of them are in Equal Partners! And that's why they came over together today."

"That would make sense." Chris turned into a parking spot and killed the engine.

"Then I really want to know who she is." Kathy sighed. "Looks like I need to pay another visit to the Sherman State website."

❧

It was the ugliest plate of food Alex had ever seen.

They had been collared within thirty seconds of entering the building by two elderly women who'd seen them standing plate-less in the midst of the feeding frenzy now underway.

Frog-marched up to the food line, their collective demurrals had fallen on deaf ears.

It's hard to go wrong with a buffet of cold foods, but something clearly had. The potato salad glistened with giant chunks of onion and the bread on Alex's ham sandwich was slathered with butter and—insult to injury— Miracle Whip. The punch was orange with a one-inch layer of foam.

"Food snob!" Kathy's grin broke into Alex's mournful reverie.

"Oh, like you're any better!" Then she took in the pristine simplicity of Kathy's plate: a blob of clear green Jell-O and a couple of crackers.

Chris's plate was about the same. She gave Alex a poor-baby look. "When you don't want something, you just tell the old ladies you're getting something further up the line."

"Gee, thanks for the tip."

"I think I'll go get some coffee." Chris shoved her untouched plate aside. "Can I get you some?"

"Thanks," Alex said. "With cream—if it's the liquid kind. Otherwise, I'll take it black."

"Black for me, thanks," Kathy added.

The auditorium was as packed as the church had been, if not more: deafening noise and a picnic atmosphere. All the restraint of the church and graveyard was thrown aside as people talked and ate with abandon. Alex had always heard people were hungry after funerals, that it was a healthy "life goes on" response. It was a little too healthy for her.

She was grateful that at least the table next to them was quiet, but then the noise in the room abated for a few moments and it quickly became clear that they were being quiet for a reason. A low-voiced, intense argument was underway. Alex looked to catch Kathy's eye. She was listening already.

It was Barb's sisters, sitting with two men she assumed to be their husbands.

"Now honey..." the shiny-suited Bible reader from church

was saying as he laid his hand on the arm of the sister who'd been carrying on at the graveyard.

She shook it off like a fly and, ignoring him, leaned across the table towards the dignified, Barb-resembling sister. "I don't care if someone hears!" she hissed loudly. "It's shameful what she did to him, and our family. They could have worked it out, but no, she just had to 'start again!'"

Kathy and Alex exchanged a wide-eyed look. Was she talking about Barb and Wayne?

"Donna!" Her sister tried to interrupt.

"Did you see that poor man today, Claire?" Donna shrilled, her voice edging on hysteria. "He looked shattered. Just shattered! He's never gotten over it, you know."

"Oh that's nonsense!" Claire scoffed. "He looked fine to me. And I don't think he should have come, anyway."

"He had every right!" Donna practically screamed, standing up so fast she almost knocked her chair over.

Claire had had it. "Get a hold of yourself," she seethed. "Everyone's looking at you."

"Let them look!" Donna pulled a strand of hair out of her gummed-up eyelashes: Tammy Faye Baker on a bad mascara day. "I have nothing to be ashamed of!" She huffed off.

The room had gotten very quiet. Claire's chair scraped back. "I'd better go talk to Mom and Dad," she said to the men. "They look horrified." She crossed the room.

The noise started up again all around them, louder than before. New gossip: meat for the wolves. But that wasn't the most startling part. Alex leaned over to Kathy. "Wayne was here today?"

"Looking shattered, no less!" Kathy snorted. "Do you think he's still here?"

"No," Chris said, coming up behind them. "He just left."

"What?" Alex whipped around to see her face but Chris pulled up a chair and sat back down. She was keyed up, alert as a cat that's just spotted a bird.

"I saw him. I was waiting over by the coffee urns—they'd run out. A group of men were standing right next to me, talking to this one guy. Big guy, fifties. They kept calling him Wayne. I was coming over here to get you then all of a sudden he had his keys out and was leaving. I followed him outside and lost him for a minute, but then there he was, getting into a rusted-out brown Chevy truck. He's gone." She held up a piece of paper. "I got the license number, though."

"Good job!" Alex exclaimed. Then deflation followed. "But what can we do with it? It's not like we can get on the DMV database."

"Who needs those?" Kathy waved a dismissive hand. "Everybody's plate numbers are listed in these little books. You can buy them at the county courthouse for three bucks."

"That's legal?" Alex was dumbfounded. What a stalker's dream.

"They've just always been around," Chris said. "People have them at home, and if a strange car's parked on their street, they look it up."

"What county?" Kathy asked Chris.

"Forty one. Gazelle."

"So do either of you have this stalker book?" Alex asked.

Kathy ignored the jibe. "I'm sure my parents do."

"But listen," Chris leaned across the table. "As soon as I saw this guy I thought he looked familiar. When I followed him out to his truck and got a good look I knew why. I've seen him before." She paused. "In my pictures at the fire."

It took a few seconds for what she'd said to sink in. "Yes," Chris said. "Wayne was there."

CHAPTER EIGHTEEN

Barb's violent ex-husband had been at the fire. Jesus.
"Are you sure?" Kathy asked Chris. "Don't you need to see the pictures again?"

"I'm sure," Chris said levelly. "But let's go look." She led them out the door and to her Jeep.

The manila envelope was in the side pocket of Chris's door. She riffled through a familiar-looking stack of pictures. Then she stopped and looked fixedly at one shot. "That's him," Chris said, passing it to them with cool certainty.

⌖

The pretty farms around Cooper flew by the car windows, disregarded.

"Let me see that again," Kathy reached back to snag the photo Alex had been studying.

"Wait. Give me another minute." The picture showed four men standing at the barricades halfway down the block from

Book Ends. They'd seen this one before, but had passed it over. None of the faces were familiar.

Alex scrutinized the image again as the hills around Cooper rolled by. He was as Chris had described him: a big stocky man in his fifties with the fair hair Alex had imagined, wearing a heavy canvas coat. Wayne. He stood with his arms crossed, a neutral expression on his face. It was impossible to tell what he was feeling. She took a last look and handed it up to Kathy.

"Recognize anybody around him?" Chris asked Kathy.

There was a pause while Kathy looked. "No," she finally admitted. "But you know what? It doesn't look like he's with these guys he's standing next to—not part of a group, like with Don and those others."

Alex leaned forward. It was true. There was no sign of interaction at all; each of the four men had a self-contained expression. "Those guys around him are probably from Sherman. Or they could have been in town for Homecoming. I think Wayne was here on his own."

A small silence fell.

Kathy broke it. "Is there anything *else* he could have been in Sherman for? Aside from burning down Book Ends?"

"Homecoming?" Chris guessed.

Alex shook her head. "He and Barb went to Madison. And I don't think they had any connection to Sherman. Barb told me she picked Sherman because it was a college town without a bookstore. Not because she knew anyone here."

Chris met Alex's eyes in the rearview mirror. "Could he have come to see Barb?"

"It sounded like she hadn't been in contact with him in years." She looked out the window. They were about an hour into their drive back and the farms were getting shabbier looking as they approached Sherman. Barbed-wire fence ran along the boundaries between farms and highways. Farmhouses were ranch style, without an ounce of character.

Perhaps they had long been out of contact. But what if Wayne had recently called her, or appeared out of the blue? And if he had, would Barb have told her about it? Probably not. She'd been such a private person, so guarded about her past.

But wait a minute. Maybe she'd meant to. "You guys, we've been spinning our wheels, trying to think what Barb was worried about. Maybe this was it. Wayne."

"I can see that!" Kathy exclaimed. "I'd be pretty freaked if a guy like that suddenly came back into my life."

"What could he have wanted?" Alex asked.

"Who knows? Maybe he's been angry at her all this time. She did up and leave him after all! And he came back to harass her."

"After all this time?" Alex was doubtful. "Sounds a little unbalanced to me."

Kathy shrugged. "So maybe he's unbalanced. Why not?"

"Or," Chris speculated, "it could be a money thing, like we were talking about the other night. Issues about the divorce settlement."

They were all quiet for a minute. What next?

"Should we give the police this picture?" Alex asked.

"Definitely." No hesitation from Chris.

Alex held up her hands. "It's someone else's turn to deal with Sherman's finest!" She looked at Chris. "Maybe the person who took the picture should be the one."

"Good idea!" Kathy chimed in.

Chris shot Kathy a look. She clicked her right blinker on as they approached the last piece of highway, a ten-mile stretch that would take them into Sherman. "Okay," she said, reluctantly. "But who should I talk to?"

The insider's track might save time. "Why don't you call the station and ask for Kevin Oh, but wait, you don't want to go seven rounds with Dee the Dispatcher!" At least on the phone Chris wouldn't experience the malevolent stare.

Chris shrugged. "I'll just tell her I have some pictures from the night of the fire."

"Been there. That's not good enough for Dee. She'll want more."

"And people in hell want ice water," Kathy said.

Alex laughed. "I have a better idea. I'll see if I can get Kevin to call you. And I promised I'd call Carl if we found anything out." She looked at her watch. Three o'clock. She should have plenty of time.

❧

She didn't. Mid-to-late afternoons on Saturday were usually a quiet time at the pub. But half the tables were still full when she walked in and Annette turned a frazzled face her way. Damn. It was one of those days when a festive late-lunch crowd lingered on into happy hour. A beer delivery had come, too, in the middle of lunch, and a party of ten had just made a dinner reservation for tonight.

At 8:30, in a little lull between the dinner rush and the bar rush, Alex dashed upstairs to feed the girls and make her calls. Kevin's cell went right to voicemail and she left him a long message explaining why he should call Chris. Hopefully he had the patience to listen to it all.

She had better luck with Carl, who answered on the second ring and listened without interrupting as she told him about Wayne.

"You're sure it's him?"

"We didn't see him. But Chris is sure." And so would Carl be, if he'd seen the look on Chris's face when she'd pointed to Wayne in the picture. It was like a dead bolt shooting home.

"Well," he blew out a breath of air. "It is a big coincidence, him being in Sherman. If he was there," he qualified.

Alex started to protest.

"We'll find out soon enough. You don't know if Barb had

stayed in touch with him?"

"It really didn't sound like it. Sorry, Carl, I've gotta run. We're busy tonight."

"Okay. Have a beer for me!"

She laughed. "Maybe later."

But a post-shift beer was the last thing on Alex's mind as she trudged up the stairs at 2:00. Her agenda was sleep. It never crossed her mind that she wouldn't be unconscious the minute her head hit the pillow. The irony: she was too tired. With too many things to think about.

Welcome insomnia, my old friend. She hadn't had it in a while—the flat-out busy pub-opening months had held it at bay somehow—but the tired-awake feeling was deeply familiar. Every advice article said the same thing: don't lie in bed, wakeful and tossing, willing yourself to sleep. For the millionth time she ignored it, sure each new position would do the trick. Lucy meowed: all this leg-shifting was pissing her off. The red letters on the alarm clock read 3:15. She got up.

Maybe she should try a snack. Scenes from various movies played in her head, sleepless characters wandering into the kitchen to assemble a club sandwich and pour a tall glass of milk. Or maybe tuck into a big slice of chocolate cake. This, of course, was the prelude to the appearance of the second character and the obligatory heart to heart talk.

Chocolate cake at 3:15 would lie in her stomach like lead and she was alone. But one thing was sure to go down smooth: Jameson's Single Malt Twelve Year Reserve. She poured a measure into a heavy-bottomed rocks glass she'd bought years ago in Venice. The hours stretched bleakly ahead. Might as well sip and think.

At least things had moved forward on the Wayne hunt. She looked at the steady red light on the answering machine.

It had been blinking at 2:00.

Alex hit the replay button. It was Chris. "Hey Alex, Kevin just came by here in his patrol car a minute ago and took the picture of Wayne." In the background, Charlie was barking. Kevin's car must still have been in hearing range. "And he took the license plate number from the truck. Just wanted to let you know. Give me a call when you're not too busy. Jess drove by your place tonight and said it looked packed! Long day for you," Chris finished, her voice warm with sympathy. Alex felt her face flush.

She sat back in her leather armchair. Well, the ball was in their court now. Surely the police wouldn't ignore a piece of concrete evidence like that? Chris might have handed them the answer to the Book Ends fire on a silver platter.

The Jameson sent a lovely warm burn down her throat. She closed her eyes briefly. But there were more things to think about before she crawled into bed again. And in the coming days, more things to do.

Where had she put that list? She hauled herself up and scanned the kitchen counter and the magnets on the fridge. Nope. Typical: another lost list.

Resigned, she flopped back in her chair, pushing her black suit jacket aside. Bingo. She'd put it in the inner pocket last night, thinking the three of them might go over the list in the car on the way to the funeral. In her head-fog on the way there she'd forgotten it. On the way back they had other things to discuss.

Lucy settled on her slippers and the pool of light from the reading light made a circle around them. The list looked surprisingly long. It was about to get longer. But could anything be scratched out?

Yes. The Wayne hunt was surely over. Over before it started, as he'd come, in a way, right to them. No tedious searching through area phone books now. If the cops had any sense they'd follow up on the picture and license plate and bring all their resources to bear on the question of what Wayne had been doing in Sherman that night. Alex ran a line through that item. In pencil.

But Chris's identification of Wayne wasn't the only discovery they'd made that day. Now they knew Barb had indeed gone to her Equal Partners meeting on Saturday night, and that it ended at nine. She made a new note: *Pauline Thies and Italian professor—Kathy will check.* And under that, *Amanda Wagner: look up phone/address.* Pauline's reluctance to talk about the group was puzzling. Try as she might, Alex couldn't imagine a group of women meeting in a church basement as a threat to anyone.

It didn't seem relevant to the fire at Book Ends, but she wanted to know more about them. Who, aside from Barb, had started the group? What had motivated them? Maybe she could get Pauline and Amanda down to Fitzpatrick's and ply them with liquor till they spilled their secrets. Or not. A more likely source would be that professor; hopefully Kathy would find her on the Sherman State website. Alex's professor customers were never reluctant to talk about anything. The problem was getting them to stop.

Groups with an air of secrecy that met at a church. It seemed Sherman had two of them: Equal Partners in Faith and God's Warriors. Odd. Could they be related, somehow? Didn't sound like it. Nonetheless Alex made a new note at the bottom of the page: *GW and EP—Local orgs only? Look for website.*

She settled back in her armchair and reviewed the events of the morning and early afternoon. What had they learned about Barb's past, her family? Not much. Barb came from a prettier place than Sherman, that was for sure. And it seemed she had a big family around Cooper. Yet her visits home were very rare. The last time they'd talked, Barb said she wasn't going home for Thanksgiving and was evasive about why. Some family problem she didn't want to discuss.

Now she could put a face to that problem: Tammy Faye-Donna, the hysterical drama queen who blamed Barb—after her funeral, no less—for the "scandalous" breakup of her marriage. No doubt she'd made Barb's visits a misery. Probably had cried into the cranberry sauce about Wayne at every opportunity.

Or maybe she'd done worse. Had Donna stayed in contact with Wayne? Donna seemed to think Wayne was a better person than her sister, and if he still had the farm he didn't live that far away. Is that how Wayne found Barb? Alex felt a chill, evaporating the whisky's warmth.

Surely Barb's parents would never have given Wayne that information. They had protected Barb from him after she'd walked out, and feared his temper and unpredictability. And Claire obviously despised him. Of course, the internet made it easy to find anyone these days. But you didn't need to get online if you had someone volunteering the information. She added another item to the list: *Barb's sister Donna—informant for Wayne?*

She'd meant to introduce herself to Barb's parents today but somehow it hadn't happened. That was a shame. Barb had had friends in Sherman who loved her and missed her; her family should know that. They hadn't seen Pauline and Amanda and their friends at the lunch, so odds were they hadn't talked with Barb's parents, either. Barb's college student employees, too, had disappeared after the graveside ceremony. She pictured it: Pauline's rusted van and a car full of students traveling in unplanned tandem back to Sherman, the occupants speculating about who was in the other car.

The tall kid, the one she'd recognized from her last visit to Book Ends—what was his name? D-something. Dean? Dan? Drew! That was it. Come to think of it, a list of Barb's employees would come in very handy. They could find out from Drew what hours Book Ends was open on Saturday, and when they'd been busy. She made another note.

The whisky was gone and Lucy slept heavily on her feet. Alex yawned. Time for her to try for some heavy sleep herself. She picked up an unresisting Lucy and laid her on the foot of the bed.

Slipping under the covers, she reflected on her Miss Marple moment in the church parking lot, her deduction that the killer may have driven to the funeral from Sherman in a rusted cream-colored van.

She'd been looking too close to home. Odds were, he had come in a rusted brown Chevy pickup with Gazelle county plates.

CHAPTER NINETEEN

"**W**hat's that?" Kristen peered over Alex's shoulder at the vivid red page on the laptop screen. It was mid-afternoon Sunday and she was Googling God's Warriors. There'd only been one hit.

"Something weird."

Kristen leaned closer and took in the title. "Church thing, huh?" She drifted away, interest gone.

Alex was riveted. The fiery red of the background just about put her eyes out, for starters. Across the top of the page, God's Warriors was emblazoned in a heavy black gothic script. A glowing gold sword ran through a silver, eerily lit cross. Talk about creepy. But the scariest part was the text:

Christian men, take back your homes, your churches, your country!

Warriors for God, we answer His call to reassert the Natural Order of Male Leadership in America's Christian homes and communities.

We reject political correctness and a socialism. Join now!

Help be a force to bring back our nation to her glory days."

Alex took a sip of Coke to relieve the sudden dryness in her mouth and scrolled down to the next page. But that's all there was.

She scrolled back up and looked at the page more closely. The web address was strange too: not godwarriors.com (surely they didn't qualify for "org" status), but www.paulsmen.com. Paul. Paul from the Bible? Not for the first time Alex regretted her Bible illiteracy. Even back when her parents had gone to church, there'd been no Bible in the house. The priest read it for you once a week.

Strange too, was the site's total absence of links. It led to nowhere, except to an information form that you could send back with your name, address, and church affiliation. Where was the info going?

But it was another absence on the page that struck her most of all. Not a single chapter of God's Warriors was listed. No addresses, no contact information. A secret organization, then, with an unknown number of members. Men who met quietly, determined to get power back into white, male, Christian hands.

Ku Klux Klan, anyone?

They weren't a secret in Sherman, though: not if Alex's feminist, semi-pagan friends knew about them. More like an open secret, another thing they had in common with the Klan, come to think of it. The Klan had gone after blacks, Jews, Catholics. Would God's Warriors go after uppity women? Gay people?

The rain slashed against the windows, driven by the wind that had picked up steadily all afternoon. It was a perfect day for gloomy thoughts, just as this morning would have been perfect for staying snugly in bed. Brunch had been dead. Oh well. Alex was half-asleep when she stumbled downstairs late this morning, and a demanding crowd was the last thing she could have handled. Making a big pot of turnip soup was more her speed. She wandered into the kitchen to stir and sip.

She was checking supplies in the bar cooler a while later when the door opened and Kathy blew in, shaking the rain off her hair and laughing. "What a great day!" Water poured off her coat and onto the floor. Kathy's favorite thing was rain. And walking in it.

"Maybe if it wasn't so windy," Alex grumbled. "Have you noticed lately that when you come here it's always bad weather?"

"Oh right, the fog the other night!" Kathy tugged her raincoat off. "Hey, what smells so good?"

A few minutes later they were ensconced at the bar, breathing in turnip soup fumes and slurping in companionable silence. Kathy gestured to the laptop. "You doing inventory or something?"

These days, accounting tasks were about the only thing she had time for on the computer. Her days of leisurely e-mailing and net surfing seemed like the distant past.

"No, I was Googling something from my list."

"What list?"

Alex filled her in. Wedged under the bed table lamp, the list had been the first thing her eyes had focused on when she'd woken this morning. Bits and pieces from it floated through her mind as she had lain there listening to the rain, and two items—Equal Partners in Faith and God's Warriors—kept bumping together in her head.

"Good idea. Any luck?" Kathy dunked a wedge of pumpernickel in her soup.

"Not with Equal Partners in Faith. There's a whole bunch of groups with that name— all over the country. The Sherman group didn't have a site. But get a load of this." She pulled the laptop over and angled it towards them. The God's Warriors logo filled the screen.

Kathy scanned the page. "Gross. This is even worse than I thought."

Alex nodded. "If anything is going to give me another

night of insomnia, that's it."

Kathy peered closer. "They hate everybody, don't they? Women—that's implied—non Christians, PC people, socialists."

"Socialism, PC...sounds like coded racism to me," Alex observed. "And the glory days: where did I hear that recently?"

"That creep math professor, that's where! His letter in the Sherman State paper, remember?"

"That's right! Vanderberge." Vanderberge, who had stood watching the Book Ends fire with Wayne and company. She mulled it over. "They sound like some cross between Libertarians, the Klan, and Promise Keepers."

"What a sick joke. Too bad they don't get it."

"Fanatics can't afford to laugh at themselves."

"Well, at least we can get a laugh out of them," Kathy said. "Sometimes. Hey, let's have a drink."

"Irish coffee?"

"Yes, please."

"Take a look at the website again and tell me what you think looks different about it." Alex went into the kitchen to get whipped cream.

When she returned, Kathy looked up from the screen. "They're demented. That's different! And it's really stark, isn't it? They need to hire some kid to jazz it up."

"Hey, maybe they could sell advertising. Survivalist gear, that stuff."

"Or attire for the Christian family—pants for men only!"

"And bonnets and dresses for the little women. But what's the deal with the web address? Why would they call themselves Paul's men?"

"Are you kidding?" Kathy turned the laptop towards Alex. "Let's do a little search. Google Saint Paul and...misogyny."

"Oh, that Paul."

"Let's see what comes up."

A lot came up. Forty hits. St. Paul and misogyny went

together like baseball and hot dogs. Alex scrolled down the list and they looked at the summaries. Each one was a variation on the question: is he or isn't he? "Only his hairdresser knows," Alex said.

"I know his hairdresser," Kathy returned. "He is."

The door banged open and two men came in, dripping rain. A vision in orange: orange slickers and pants, orange caps. Hunters. Alex shot Kathy a look as the men settled themselves heavily at the other end of the bar, right under the blank screen of her one TV.

She had been dimly aware that some kind of hunting season was underway. Last week, she'd passed a couple of slow-moving SUVs full of men in orange hats. What they were doing hadn't registered, though, until she noticed the cheap plastic sign, in Day-Glo orange, slung across the front of Huskers: Hunters Welcome.

They both ordered Beck's Dark bottles and stared forlornly at the TV. Oh well. The unwelcome sound of an NFL football game drifted through the pub as she returned to their corner.

Suddenly, the Orange Men came to life. "Go! Go! Go!" the older one yelled at the screen, where a tiny helmet-head was running down the field. The younger one, in his twenties and with an identical round head—a father-son duo—pumped his fist in the air. "Yes! Yes!"

Amazing how much noise two men in an empty bar could make. The screaming reached a crescendo as the helmet-head scored a touchdown. They'd both been half out of their chairs. But now they subsided, faces alight with joy, and slammed down half their beers in one gulp.

"Déjà vu." Alex took a fortifying sip of Irish coffee. "This is what my house sounded like every weekend in the fall when I was growing up."

"Hope this isn't too traumatic."

"It is." Alex glanced down the bar: the bottles were empty.

That had taken five minutes. She brought them refills, bracing herself against the next barrage of shouts.

"Hold the line!"

"Defense! Come on!"

"You don't get a lot of hunters in here, do you?" Kathy asked.

"These are the first ones I've noticed. I guess they've been going to other places, like Don's. He has a sign up. It's orange."

"Speaking of Huskers, when should we go?"

"Tomorrow night might be good for me. Monday. I could see if Lauren wanted to cover for me for a while."

"I can do tomorrow night. Why don't we call Chris and see if she's free?"

Alex picked up her cell phone. "Wait a minute, though." She put it back down. "Monday might not be the best night. I mean, we want to see Don and his gang in action, right? But Monday...who's gonna be there?"

Kathy raised her eyebrows. "You must be joking. Huskers is packed on Monday nights! At least in the fall." She pointed to the TV screen. "What will your dad and brother be watching tomorrow night?"

Of course. Men all over the country would be huddled in front of their TVs at home, or watching in bars with groups of friends. The bars would smell of beer and the shouting would go on for three hours.

For Monday Night football.

CHAPTER TWENTY

What a difference a day makes. The rain and gloom of Sunday had blown east overnight; now it was Michigan's turn to suffer. Tomorrow, the rain would fall relentlessly on New Jersey. Alex would be basking in the sunshine while her family tromped through puddles, bitching and moaning. People in Jersey took the weather personally.

Monday dawned clear and sparkling. Or Alex assumed it did, because a beautiful day was underway when she lifted the blind in her bedroom at 8:30, refreshed after a night of rock-hard sleep. The sky was light blue and high clouds scudded along, pushed by a brisk wind. She took her first cup of coffee out to the back stairs. Yes, there it was: that crisp autumn snap in the air. She wanted to run around kicking leaf piles and heating up cider and making apple pies.

Everyone was feeling spry. The girls went tearing down the backstairs, starting their day with a race that Jane—lighter and younger than Lucy—won. Then Jane made the mistake of rolling around in front of Lucy, gloating. Lucy took umbrage and hit her upside the head with a massive paw.

The energy came in handy later, when the pub was hit with a huge lunch crowd that made it look and sound more like Friday than Monday. Office workers and college people skipped the boring lunch they'd planned at home and piled into cars to come out to Fitzpatrick's for fish and chips or bangers and mash. Farmers sat at the bar, sipping beer.

Then it was time to run some errands. Alex had just left the post office and was driving down Main Street, noting for the hundredth time its stubborn ugliness, when blue and red lights flashed in blindingly her rearview. Her blood pressure shot up. What was she doing—thirty-two in a thirty zone? She slowed to a crawl, pulled over just past the blackened shell of Book Ends, and awaited her fate.

Kevin's grinning face appeared at the window. Alex blew out a breath and then took a deep one to slow her heart rate down. "Very funny."

"Well ma'am," he straightened up and rested his hands on his gun belt. "Do you know why I pulled you over?" The sun glinted off his Ray Bans.

"I'm sorry officer, was I going under the speed limit?" Several cars crawled by them, the drivers taking in every detail of the big bust.

He leaned back in at the window. "I was gonna swing by your place later but then I saw you just now and figured I could save myself the trip."

"How efficient."

"I almost put the siren on too, but then you pulled over nice and fast."

"Is it against the law to call you an asshole?"

"Yeah, but I'll let it slide this time. Your friend with the picture was right."

Her heart sped up again. There'd been no word about Wayne since Chris had handed over her picture on Saturday night. "Chris."

"Right. We ran the plate number and got his driver's license. It matched her picture. He was at the fire, all right."

Yes! "So what happens now?"

"They're running some checks on him today."

"Like what?"

A familiar-looking pickup truck approached and slowed down. It was Sandra, her expression quickly turning from mild curiosity to incomprehension—why had he pulled Alex over? Driving by, she shot Kevin a look that could melt plastic.

Her turn to grin. "What checks?" she repeated.

Kevin—who still lived at home—dragged his eyes from the progress of his mom's truck as it turned onto Main. "To see what turns up on him."

"You mean to see if he has a record?"

"Yeah, that. And other things."

Man of mystery. This was getting tiresome. "Is anyone looking into the divorce settlement? That might be really important."

He took off his sunglasses and leaned down so they were at eye level. "Hey, it's good your friend brought us that picture—"

"Chris," Alex clarified again.

"Yeah, Chris. But we're checking into all that stuff. Don't worry about it."

Useless advice. "I won't," Alex lied. "But are you guys going to talk to him? To Wayne?"

"Probably." He started walking back to the patrol car.

"Hey!" She twisted around in her seat and called back to him. There was one more thing. "What's Wayne's last name?"

No reply. Maybe this was confidential information and she was SOL.

Kevin pulled up next to her and slid down the window. "Benson," he said, then blasted off to go hassle someone else.

The phone started ringing as Alex stood at the door trying to balance various bags and fumbling with the key. Jane, meowing out a series of demands, twisted and twined around her ankles. Alex looked down at her. "You're not helping."

The answering machine picked up just as the door swung open and Jane shot in. "Hey, Alex," Chris began, "it's around four and..."

"Chris! I was just coming in the door."

"No problem. Out enjoying the weather?"

"Kind of. Running errands. How about you?"

"I've been out taking some pictures."

Pictures. "Have you heard back from the police yet?"

Turned out she hadn't yet, so Alex filled her in.

"Good!" Chris sounded pleased. "Speaking of those pictures, my sister was looking at them and she recognized somebody else at the fire. Gerry Arens. He was standing with those guys, too. In the back, next to Ken Miller."

"Barb's contractor!"

"Interesting, huh? We can fill in a couple more names, too. I talked to Kathy a while ago and she found two people on the Sherman State website—the professor who was at the funeral, and that guy who works in the Administration building, the one who was hassling my student."

"Who are they?"

"She said she'd print the pages off and show us tonight at Huskers. Are you all psyched up for Monday night football?"

"Can't wait. And I'm saving lots of room for Don's yummy food. You should, too."

Chris laughed. "I'll remember to do that. Oh yeah, I told Jess about our plan and she wants to come along. Is that okay?"

"Of course. The more eyes and ears the better."

Errands done and phone calls to suppliers made, Alex made a big mug of tea and plopped down in her armchair. Break time. Miss Marple beckoned from the coffee table, but St. Mary Meade was no competition for Sherman these days. Her thoughts kept circling back to Wayne. Wayne Benson.

From the moment Chris's eyes had locked on that picture Alex knew he'd been at the Book Ends fire. Now they had official confirmation. And a police department officially interested. Well, boys, it's in your hands. Don't blow it.

Did Wayne have a criminal record—for assault? He would if Barb had reported him after he attacked her that last morning at their farm. She hadn't said so, but it was possible.

Alex took a big slurp of tea and mulled over what they'd discussed on the drive home from the funeral. Money or love, Chris had said, was behind most murders. Was this a long-held grudge? Barb had described Wayne as obsessed with respectability, a conservative man hardened by the farm crisis. He refused to accept their separation and had haunted her parents' house for weeks. During those weeks had Barb ever applied for a restraining order?

Alex knew even less about the money angle. Were there still financial ties between Wayne and Barb? They'd been divorced for some years when she came to Sherman, so that didn't seem probable. But you never knew. Sometimes divorce settlements dragged on for years and rancor about them for years after that. Would the police have access to the settlement agreement?

Time to cross off one thing on the list, though—item four: *Wayne Hunt*. This time she'd do it in pen.

But there was other hunting to do and other men who had resented Barb. Men who, like Wayne, had stood and watched Book Ends burn, the flames of the fire reflected on their laughing faces.

CHAPTER TWENTY ONE

What a dump. Huskers was even grosser than Alex remembered. At least in August, when she'd last been there, you could put your elbows on a table and not stick to it. Underneath a fine layer of cigarette ash, their table was festooned with a hundred or so gummy drink rings. "Does he never clean?" Alex asked Kathy as they settled into a booth.

"Maybe this is Don's idea of decoration." Kathy tried to snag the eye of a skinny little waitress who'd just streaked past their table, ignoring them for the third time in a row. This time she got her attention.

"WhatcanIgetcha?" The waitress radiated impatience.

"Can you wipe this table down for us?" Kathy gestured to the ash. "Then we'll order a drink." The girl gave them an affronted look and scurried over to the bar.

"What are the odds she's going to locate a clean bar rag?" Alex wondered.

"Well," Kathy said, "she's coming back with something, but I wouldn't bet my life savings that it's clean."

Her money was safe. A clean anything, let alone towel, would have stood out like a lighthouse beacon in Huskers. It was as dark as it was dirty. The three windows were shrouded, day and night, with heavy gray drapes that gave off a greasy shine—and smell, no doubt. Alex wasn't going to investigate that.

Almost all the light in the room came from the TVs. Don had crammed four of them over the bar and one over every booth. Sports, sports, sports. A stiff drink was clearly in order but their waitress had disappeared again.

Alex knew what was going on. "We've been put on the low-priority list." She stood to go the up to the bar when Chris and Jess showed up and their waitress darted into view. They just managed to order drinks before she vanished again.

"You're lucky you caught her," Alex told them. "Her visits are pretty fleeting."

Jess gazed after the girl as she shrugged off her coat. "I'd be fleeting too, if I was wearing that get-up! She must be freezing."

Indeed. The two waitresses wore Don's approximation of Hooterwear for Huskers. Hookerware, more like.

"Oh, that's not right." Chris stared at the table next to them, where a mini-skirted waitress was reaching over to collect beer mugs to the ogling shouts of the men at the table.

"Bend over, baby!" a fat slob roared over the noise of the TVs.

Alex's temper rose another notch. If it were her pub, she'd be over there like a shot and that nonsense would stop in a hurry. Of course at Fitzpatrick's the help wasn't required to walk around bare-assed.

The girl collected all the beer mugs onto her tray. Then she flashed the men a big smile.

"Lost cause." Kathy lit a cigarette. Speed Waitress flew by and dumped their drinks.

"Well, here's to getting drinks." Chris smiled, her eyes sparkling through the dim, murky atmosphere. Jess leaned back in her chair and took a big sip of beer. "It's so great to be out, I don't care where I am!"

"Your husband didn't want to join us?" Kathy asked. "It's not exactly girls' night out in here."

Alex surveyed the room. Kathy was right: the only estrogen in the room was at their table. "It's raining men."

"Yes," Kathy agreed, "but can we honestly say, 'Hallelujah'?"

They laughed. Alex, not for the first time, thanked her lucky stars she wasn't straight.

Chris was looking around too, but in a more systematic way, canvassing the room section by section. Like a photographer, moving her camera carefully from one subject to the next. "Recognize anyone?" Alex asked.

"Yup." She gestured with her head towards the bar and they all followed her gaze.

It was like looking at Chris's pictures again. There stood Don with Paul Nielson and Dick Wagner. Their comfortable at-home body language as they laughed and drank confirmed Alex's hunch that this was their hangout.

"Seems we came to the right spot," Chris said.

The second mini-skirted waitress was making her way through the crowd of men at the bar. She'd almost reached the oasis of the service area and was squeezing past Don when she suddenly shrieked and jumped. Paul laughed and slapped a gloating Don on the back. They probably hadn't had this much fun since Book Ends burned down.

Then Don looked their way. He detached himself from his friends and came towards them, creepy smile plastered to his face. The TV lights shone off his enormous belt buckle as he back-slapped his way through the football crowd, the king in his castle.

"Oh, for God's sake." Alex threw a despairing glance around the table. Was he coming over to play the fake friendly innkeeper? After he and his buddies' little hostility dance at Fitzpatrick's, she'd anticipated only two options for tonight: either he would ignore them, or it would be more of the same.

He went with the fake option. "Hi ladies!" his voice boomed over the cacophonous TV noise.

Alex wanted to make the retching sound that signaled an imminent Jane throw- up. She gave Don a faint smile.

He leered at Kathy and Chris, then turned to Alex. "Didn't know you were a Monday Night football fan! But wait," he smirked, "Isn't it a big night down at your place?" What a joke.

"Oh, you can have the football nights, Don." She pointed to the big-screen TV. A helmet-head was patting another on the ass. Any excuse. "If I want that kind of action, I know some fun bars where I can see it live." She paused. "And the guys are better looking, too."

Oops. Jess and Kathy laughed. Alex glanced at Chris but she was looking at Don, stone-faced.

"There are some good ones in Omaha," Kathy added, helpfully.

Don's little piggy eyes bored into Kathy for a second before switching the bogus charm back on. "You're Todd Hoffman's wife, aren't you?" he asked, peering at Jess through the gloom.

She nodded.

"Thought so! Where's Todd tonight?" He was the jolly inn-keeper again.

"Home with the kids, of course," Jess said, deadpan.

The more they messed with his head, the brighter beamed the wattage on his Mr. Charm smile. "Well," Don boomed, backing away from the table, "the next one's on the house! Bring a round of drinks to these ladies!" he shouted to no one in particular.

Chris gave herself a shake as they watched him retreat to the bar. "I feel like I have to go take a shower."

"He never acts like that when I'm here with Todd," Jess observed.

A miraculous vision now appeared at their table: speed waitress, with a tray of drinks. The right kind, even. "Compliments of Don!" She banged them down on the table before de-materializing again.

"I bet it rattled him to see us in here," Kathy said.

"Yeah, and that friendly act?" Alex tapped her glass. "These were to one-up me. I didn't offer him a free drink when he and his buddies came in."

"When were you supposed to do that?" Kathy protested. "While he and his gang were hassling you—and Annette?"

"Exactly." Alex glanced over at the spot where the three men had been standing at the bar before. Now they had barstools. And company: their numbers had doubled. "Look, you guys."

More of Chris's photo gallery had come to life. Standing behind Dick was Chuck Bauer from Bag 'n Go, his face looking even unhealthier than usual in the green glow of the TVs. Next to him, his foot up on the bar rail in a he-man pose, was Ken Miller.

"I guess it's safe to rent movies tonight," Chris said.

The third newcomer was the guy who worked in the Administration building at Sherman State. He was dressed just like he had been at the fire, in a dark sweatshirt and baseball cap.

"That's Darren Braun," Kathy said, pulling a set of 8 x 11 sheets out of her bag. Her printouts from the Sherman State website. Alex had forgotten.

Kathy pulled one out and put it on top of the stack. Darren Braun's weaselly little face stared back at them, frowning seriously. He worked in the Business Office.

Professor Moon Face loomed out from the next page Kathy had printed out. Seems the little John Lennon glasses were an everyday accessory. He wore a bowtie and his skin was awful. Martin "Marty" Vanderberge's address was on a county road.

Chris read the address aloud. "He must be renting a farm house."

"He's farming?" Alex was puzzled. "A professor?"

"No," Jess clarified. "He's renting the Reese's old house. They farm the land."

"Maybe he feels closer to God out there," Kathy muttered.

"Probably," Alex agreed. "Maybe his Take Back America group has meetings out there. They can practice burning crosses."

Kathy pulled the last sheet out. "And here's the woman I recognized from campus, who was with Pauline Thies and Amanda Wagner at the funeral."

"Please tell me she's normal." Alex leaned in to look. But she was better than normal. The mystery woman from Saturday was Gina Meziere, a Philosophy professor originally from New York City.

"A home girl!" Alex exclaimed. She read the professor's website blurb before passing the sheet over to Jess. Gina Meziere loved good Italian food, Noir film, and Art Deco architecture. "I want to meet this woman!" Gina Meziere. She would have to add that name to the list, along with Darren Braun.

"Speaking of good food...should we be brave and order some Husker fare?" Kathy peered at the grubby stand-up menu in the middle of the table.

After a quick consult of the greasy choices they decided on hot wings and mozzarella sticks. No one could face the nachos.

Speed waitress had disappeared; she was probably out back, popping more pills. Alex's patience was worn out. She went up to the bar to order the food and another round of drinks.

A skinny guy with a beard and an orange hunter's cap took his drink towards one of the booths and Alex quickly wedged herself into the small space he'd left open. She put her elbows on the bar and tried to catch the bartender's eye.

Good luck with that. The bartender—another girl in Husker-Ho-ware—was seriously in the weeds. Clearly they needed another bartender on Monday nights but it looked like Don was too cheap to pay a second one. If the two men next to

Alex hadn't ordered drinks she doubted the girl would have ever noticed she was there. The invisible woman. Down the bar from her, Don's crew grunted and shouted. Finally, she placed their order.

Did Huskers even have a women's restroom? She'd soon find out, she thought, pushing her way to the back of the bar. Here it was: Bucks and Does. Alex had often pondered the mysterious compulsion that drove people to adorn restroom doors with coy plaques announcing "Guys and Dolls," "Gulls and Buoys" or worst of all, "Little Boys" and "Little Girls."

Any attempt at cuteness ended at the door, though. It was as dirty and disgusting as she'd feared: two smelly, dirty stalls—one with a broken door lock—and a blackened sink. There was not a single word of graffiti on the wall; time was of the essence, here. Alex got in and out as quickly as she could. All the while she heard Mom's voice in her head, the one she deployed for urgent situations during long family car trips. "Don't touch anything!" Mom would cry as they ran into the bathrooms of cheap motel rooms or gas stations.

Casting a last glance at the "Doe" sign as she fled the scene, Alex noticed the painted picture next to the lettering. Country kitchen all the way. Was this the work of Don's wife? She didn't even know if Don was married. And how many of his buddies were? Was Don's crowd a bachelor club? Certainly there were no wives in evidence tonight. There was one way to find out: a quick glance at ring fingers. Alex could hardly see their rings from halfway across the bar, though. She'd have to get in close.

It was still raining men as she fought her way back through the testosterone zone and looked for a place near their established patch. A shout suddenly went up: someone had scored a touchdown or gotten maimed. Hooray.

Don's gang was clumped together right next to the service station, where the waitresses came to pick up drink orders. Don's happy hunting grounds. One thing Alex had learned tonight: they were a group who got together regularly, maybe frequently. Were they just drinking buddies? There'd been the night at the pub, and she and her friends had assumed the group had walked down from Don's, the night of the Book Ends fire.

If it were just Don and Paul, Dick and Chuck, Alex wouldn't have given it too much thought. They were locals, middle-aged men who worked in Sherman and maybe grew up together. But Ken Miller and Darren Braun? How did they fit in?

Alex had told the bartender she'd come back and bring the drinks to their table, but they weren't on the bar yet. Good. That gave her an excuse to elbow into the service station— the only open spot at the bar. Lousy service was turning out to be helpful.

Dick Wagner's big broad back was turned to Alex as she slid into the opening, trying to be inconspicuous. None of them could see her. The bartender was clear down the other end.

She leaned forward to look down the bar, pretending to be searching for the girl while she scanned their hands for wedding bands. Ken Miller had no ring. No surprise there. But Darren Braun did: a big, shiny silver one. Chuck Bauer, in the midst of the group, wore a thin gold band. So there was a Mrs. Fresh Produce. Don's left hand was ring-less, but that meant nothing: some married men didn't wear a ring and he was just the type. The country kitchen doe had to come from somewhere. Paul Neilson's meaty left hand was bare. Dick Wagner was married. She peeked over his enormous shoulders to see a grubby gold band on the hand that gripped his pint of beer.

So it wasn't a singles club. Then again, it didn't need to be. The married men in the group, it seemed, were as free as the single to indulge in endless boys' nights out. But maybe their wives liked for them to be out and gone. That was better than the alternative, anyway: that their wives had no say.

Then Don spotted Alex. "Well, look who it is!" he said, at megaphone volume. Dick Wagner swung slowly around and six pairs of eyes fixed on her.

"Just trying to hunt down our drinks." She tried for a fake smile.

"Hunting!" Don cried. "Alex is a hunter! Why don't you come down here for some of my hunters' specials? Didnja see the sign out front?"

He was drunk. It looked like they all were, or well on the way. It felt like that Friday night when she'd stood at their table taking their drink orders. They were putting off the same vibe. At other times, with other people, she would have ignored it. But there was something off about this group.

Dick Wagner took a good long look at Alex—up and down, legs to boobs—eventually coming to rest on her face with a flat look that chilled her. Under his hooded lids, his eyes were dead.

Time to go. Alex scrambled for an exit strategy that would somehow save her dignity. Then another shout went up. The men's heads all swiveled to the bank of flat-screens behind the bar. The Vikings were making a touchdown.

Good. She could ask them something stupid and harmless, like if they were all Vikings fans and then get the hell out of there. But wait: better confirm their team loyalty first. Alex glanced quickly at their sweatshirts and caps for the winged logo. Darren had one on his baseball cap. Chuck had a big wing splashed across his purple sweatshirt.

Paul's navy blue sweatshirt had a logo, too, on the upper left-hand corner of the chest. But it wasn't a Vikings one. Nor was it the familiar red N of the Cornhuskers. This was more elaborate: an embroidered silver cross with a gold sword running through it.

Alex started. Then she was out of there at a velocity that would have impressed even Speed Waitress. But not before they'd gotten in a parting shot.

"One down!" Paul's voice called cheerfully above the crowd. Don's voice followed up. "And one to go."

CHAPTER TWENTY TWO

The wind moaned and tree limbs creaked overhead. It was midnight. By the glow of the lurid red screen on her laptop, Alex re-read the manifesto of God's Warriors.

She had a mug of hot chocolate in her hand and a quilt over her legs: an attempt at coziness. It wasn't working.

Tonight had unlocked a mystery: the mystery of those men's hostility to Barb. No wonder they hassled her that night at the pub. Barb had threatened everything God's Warriors stood for. A successful female business owner, she had upset the "natural order" of male leadership. She was divorced, independent. Her car even sported an Obama sticker. Perhaps worst of all, Barb had dared to found a women's group that discussed and probably challenged gender roles in the very churches where male authority was most sacrosanct.

Suddenly so many things made sense. Their joyful faces as they'd watched the fire at Book Ends—it must have seemed like a divine judgment. No doubt some had earnestly hoped

Barb was inside.

A short while later Alex lay in bed, berating herself again for not making the connection sooner. Dope slap. The silver and gold logo blazed in front of her eyes. Was the fire at Book Ends a path to bringing back the glory days? The America we once knew?

Her gut said yes. But how to prove it?

Sooner than she ever would have predicted, Alex fell into a hard sleep. A sleep full of nightmares. She only remembered one thing, one image: a huge cross, burning orange and yellow on the lawn in front of Fitzpatrick's.

One down. One to go.

Alex was draining the dregs of her first cup of coffee and peering out through the frosted windows at 9:00 when the phone rang. It was Chris. "I didn't wake you up, did I?"

"No, I'm almost conscious."

"Isn't this frost beautiful?" Chris enthused. "I've been out getting some great shots this morning."

"Since when? The crack of dawn?" Alex tried to imagine herself cheerfully casting aside her warm sheets, quilt, and cats and heading out into the frost. The picture wouldn't form.

"Almost," Chris chuckled. Her voice was warm, sexy. When Alex had made that quip to Don about the gay bars in Omaha, Kathy and Jess had laughed but Chris didn't seem to register it. What did that mean? "You know," she continued, "driving around this morning I keep thinking about last night. I'm still feeling creeped out."

"Creepy I could live with at this point. Those men are scary."

Don's crew—or rather, God's Warriors, as she should now think of them—had kept the group in their sights for the rest of the time they'd stayed at Husker's. When she'd returned to their booth, Alex's first impulse was to hustle them all out of there. But Kathy refused to budge. She sat, arms across her chest, a picture of stubborn immovability. Déjà vu. Only now, instead of returning the stare of Beady Eyes at Barb's funeral, Kathy was locking looks with God's Warriors. Alex admired her guts. But it probably wasn't the smartest move.

Chris pulled her back to the present. "You remember I said Dick Wagner used to be our neighbor? I was thinking I'd call my folks in Arizona, see if I can get the low-down on him."

Alex saw those dead eyes again. She gave herself a shake. "Good idea." Wagner. "Wait a minute. Is his wife Amanda? From the funeral, remember?"

"Amanda? Yeah, I think that was the wife's name." A blast of static hit Alex in the ear. Ouch. Chris must still be in her car.

Alex tried to picture them together: scary Dick Wagner and spacey Amanda of the Q-Tip hair. An odd couple for sure. But their differences, she suddenly realized, ran much deeper. "Chris, can you hear me?"

"I'm here!" The line was suddenly clear again.

"This is so weird. She's in Equal Partners in Faith, and he's in God's Warriors!" Alex's list-making the other night had left her wondering about possible connections between the groups. She'd never imagined they were in bed together.

"Woah." Chris's voice echoed her surprise. "Talk about a mixed marriage!"

Then something else struck Alex. "Do you remember at the graveyard how Kathy described Pauline and Amanda when she asked them about Equal Partners?"

"Like scared rabbits."

"Exactly. And remember what you said?"

The light bulb going on at Chris's end was almost audible. "Dick doesn't know she's in it! Maybe Pauline's husband doesn't either. Oh, this is good." Her rich laugh came down the line.

Alex laughed too as a deeply satisfying picture formed in her head: Amanda, stealth feminist, stirring up the pot of church gender politics while her husband, drinking beer at Huskers with God's Warriors, assumed her home and knitting by the fireside. Ha.

A barking sound erupted on Chris's end. "That's Charlie," she said. "I'm pulling up to my house."

"Hey, do you think your parents know anything about either of these groups?"

"They might have heard some stuff. I'll ask."

The phone rang again seconds later. Probably a telemarketer; she let it ring and pulled the half-and-half out of the fridge. Chris's call had delayed the morning ritual and Jane circled her ankles relentlessly; Lucy stared balefully from the couch. She was putting down the plates when Kathy's frantic voice came on the answering machine. "Alex! Pick up! Are you there?"

She was across the room in two seconds. "I'm here! What's wrong?" She'd never heard Kathy sound like that.

"Oh, thank God." Kathy let out a big breath. "You're okay."

"Of course I'm okay! What the hell's going on?"

"Have you been out to your vehicle?"

"No. I haven't been outside at all, yet."

"Just sit tight for a few minutes, okay? I'm heading over. But I need to call Chris first."

"I just got off the phone with her. She's been driving around taking pictures."

"Since when?" The frantic note was back.

"Since early this morning. She just got home, though. Kathy, what's—"

Kathy let out another big breath of relief. "My pickup was messed with sometime last night. Chris's vehicle must be okay, though. Let's take a look at yours. Meet me down at your car in five." Dial tone.

Alex pounded down the outside stairs, the girls right behind her, and rounded the corner to find her Cabrio sitting just as she'd left it last night, nothing different except for a thin layer of frost on the side windows. No broken glass, no spray paint. Alex was inspecting her headlights when Kathy's dark green Ford pickup rolled up. She hopped out carrying a tire iron.

This was getting a little too Southern. "Are we going to rough some people up?"

"Maybe." Kathy squatted down in front of the Cabrio's left rear tire. It looked okay to Alex. But Kathy wasn't inspecting the treads. She was looking at the bolts.

"This one's okay." Kathy stood up and pushed a loose strand of blond hair behind her ear. "Someone loosened the lug nuts on my tires last night. All of them." She continued around the car, quickly checking each tire.

Alex stood there stupidly wondering why someone would do that and then it hit her: loosen the nuts and the tires come off.

"They're all okay," Kathy reported. "Guess it was just my truck." The tension drained from her face as she leaned against her hood and lit up a cigarette. "I am so lucky I saw it."

"How long do you think those bolts would have stayed on?"

She shrugged and took a big drag. "Who knows? Maybe as far as the highway. I was heading to Byron this morning to pick up some willow. Imagine going sixty-five and your tires come off."

Alex did imagine it: the sudden, total loss of control, the pickup spinning, bouncing into other cars, into trucks, rolling finally into a ditch. She sagged against the Cabrio.

"How did you even notice?"

Kathy flicked an ash into the driveway. "My front tire has a really slow leak. I need to get it patched but I just haven't had time. So I look at it most mornings to see if it needs a little air. Somebody last night was having a little too much fun and he left one bolt barely on. Lucky for me."

"You think it was one of them." Alex looked down the highway, towards town and Huskers. "God's Warriors. That's why you were worried about Chris and me."

"You bet I do."

A cold breeze swept across the parking lot. "Come on upstairs for a cup of coffee," Alex said. "That willow can wait a little longer."

❧

They sat in the living room, cradling hot mugs. Some color was coming back into Kathy's face. "I know it was them," she said. "It wasn't a prank by some kids."

"A prank? You could have been killed!" Alex exclaimed. "What time did you go to bed?"

"Around eleven. I took a shower when I got home and then just crashed."

"Did you hear anything?"

"No, but I park my truck over by the studio. I might have heard glass breaking, but not this." Kathy paused. "Don't *you* think it was them?"

Alex remembered the ugly atmosphere around those men last night, the fear she'd felt, Kathy's set face as she stared them down. "Yes. They threw a scare into me and they knew it. But you didn't back down. So they went after you." She got up and poured more coffee.

"One down, one to go," Kathy said. "We thought they meant Barb and you."

"Maybe they did, until you took them on! Did you call the police?"

Kathy shook her head. "I ran inside and called you!"

"Thanks, girl." Alex reached over and squeezed her hand.

"Let's call Chris." Kathy pulled a cell phone out of her shirt pocket.

"And what about Jess? She was with us, too."

As she washed up their coffee mugs Alex could hear Kathy recounting the events of the morning to Chris. It didn't take long.

"Her Jeep is fine," Kathy reported a few minutes later. "She checked while we were talking. And she's calling Jess now."

Alex dried her hands on the dishtowel. "You never worried about Jess, huh?"

Kathy shook her head. "They wouldn't lump her in with us. Don knows her husband."

"True. But listen, are we jumping to conclusions here? Assuming it was them?"

"It was them. I can feel it."

There was a silence.

Alex's next question felt inevitable. "Do you think they set the fire at Book Ends?"

Kathy nodded. "And if they can do that, what's a few loose lug nuts?"

"I know. But then what about Wayne? Yesterday he was my prime suspect for the fire. Today, it's all changed again." Eenie meenie miny moe. "Are you gonna call the cops?"

"I don't know. They can't do much at this point."

"Maybe they'll keep an eye on your place if you report it— you know, swing by more often."

"Yeah, actually I wouldn't mind that."

"Me neither." Alex had no intention of losing another friend.

A loud meow from the back steps signaled that Lucy was ready for her morning siesta, inside. She sauntered through the kitchen and registered Kathy's presence with surprise. Morning visitors were a rarity.

"That reminds me," Kathy said, as they watched Lucy progress towards the armchair. "I'm not letting the boys out at night anymore. You should keep the girls in, too." They'd been out for half the night on Saturday. Alex felt shaky again.

The girls' midnight rambles would be over for now. Kathy was right. None of them were safe.

CHAPTER TWENTY THREE

Alex needed to get out and clear her head. The frightening events of last night and this morning had left her rattled and she'd barely been able to keep up with a busy lunch crowd. But outside it was another gorgeous day. The countryside beckoned.

She put the top down, popped Vivaldi's "Four Seasons" into the CD player, and pointed the Cabrio towards an apple orchard she'd been meaning to visit. A vivid palette of colors flew by the windows: gold and brown and even a little green, still. Fields where tall cornstalks had stood only a couple weeks ago were now stripped, some right down to the ground, some cut to the stubble.

Fall, the season of change. Alex felt the change in her bones, and her bones were telling her this was one of the last bright warm days they'd see in a while, before the snow hit the fan and everyone huddled inside, awaiting spring. Kathy, with sadistic zest, said the first snow here often came in late October.

She'd reached that Zen and the art of driving state, when a combine rumbled massively off a county road just ahead and into her lane on the highway. He was going 10 mph. Now so was Alex.

People here imagined that nothing could be scarier than driving on the NASCAR roads of the east coast. Wrong. She'd take fast-moving Turnpike traffic any day over the winding two-lane roads around Sherman. Example: the death-defying stunt of the driver in back of her as he pulled out to pass the combine. She braced for his head-on collision with the line of oncoming traffic—three cars that weren't slowing down at all.

He made it. One more idiot saved by luck or a guardian angel.

Meanwhile Farmer Bob trundled along, oblivious to the cars collecting behind him. Or maybe not. He'd probably been blocking traffic every harvest for thirty years. Why change now?

Another man resisting change: it was a theme, lately. Wayne Benson. God's Warriors. How far would any of them go to stop the tide of change, or to lash out against a change they'd fought?

She needed to think about this like a cop: means, motive, and opportunity.

What would be the motive for God's Warriors to vandalize Kathy's truck? That seemed clear: to send a message. Alex and her friends were single, independent women. Like Barb. Troublemakers, by definition. Maybe one or more of those men had heard they were asking questions about the Book Ends fire. That would certainly ratchet up the stakes.

Means? Simple. A tire iron. Opportunity would have been a piece of cake as well. Alex lived in Kathy's neighborhood last summer and they were an early-to-bed, early-to-rise crowd. Kathy had crashed at eleven and probably hers had been the last lights to go out on the block.

Too easy to imagine. Had they been listening for sirens this morning, waiting for news of an accident? Maybe it had been like that the night of the Book Ends fire: all of them drinking down at Huskers, ears pricked for what they knew was coming.

And there was something else: the broken window in Barb's apartment. Had that been a warning? And from who? It could have been any one of those men.

Or Wayne. That would mean that he'd been lurking around Sherman for a while, not just on Homecoming weekend. Did Barb know? They had wondered, on the drive back from Cooper, if he'd been in touch. Somehow Alex had assumed that meant on the phone. But not necessarily. Cooper was an hour and a half away. To Nebraskans, that's a stone's throw.

The combine was down to five mph now, turning right onto a county road. At last. But there was no time for a burst of speed: the county road she'd been looking for came up on her left. A tiny, faded, sign with a washed-out apple and "1 mile" over an arrow directed her to the orchard. The Cabrio's wheels began to slide around on the gravel surface and the car took on that floating feeling. She was in nautical mode.

Alex rode the waves uneasily until, after cresting a big hill, she spotted the orchard below her and coasted down to it. A spray-painted wooden sign in front of a barn said, Honk for Apples. She did, and then wandered into the cool dimness of the barn, breathing in the apple smell.

Alex's honk had summoned an ancient farmer in overalls and a seed cap. He didn't have much to say, but he turned a sweet, gap-toothed smile her way as he pointed out bags of gleaming Cortlands, Macintoshes, Granny Smiths and Jonathans. She drove off with a trunk full of apples, two big bags for munching and pub desserts and three little bags for gifts, plus two jugs of fresh-made cider. The car smelled like heaven.

The orchard visit had put her back in charity with things rural. Maybe farmers weren't so bad after all, she thought, driving back down the highway and exchanging one-fingered waves with the cars and trucks she met. Her route home would take

Alex right past Bill and Sandra's farm. She glanced at the clock. Three-thirty. She had time for a quick visit. It had been a while.

Her cousins' farm wasn't a pretty acreage like Chris's, nor did it look like the spruce Swedish farms around Cooper. Like the German farms around it, the barn was nicer than the house, and the house was a typical ranch style, with some additions thrown on. But it was all trim and well-maintained, fresh paint gleaming on the buildings, a bright flowerbed surrounding the house. The leaves were turning gold on the shelterbelt of tall, old trees.

Sandra was just getting off a rider mower when Alex pulled up in the driveway. Kevin's pickup was parked over by the barn.

"I come bearing apples." Alex handed her a small bag of Cortlands from the trunk.

"More pies!" Sandra laughed, taking the bag from her. "Come on in. I was just about to put up some coffee." Two pies with perfect golden crusts sat on the old oak table in her sunny kitchen. Cherry and apple. Alex held her hand above them: still warm.

She pulled out a seat as Sandra piled plates and forks on the table. She'd forgotten that coffee didn't mean just the drink. When people here sat down to the table they didn't screw around.

A clatter of boots sounded outside the door. "Boots off!" Sandra called. She made a face at Alex. "I have to say it every time!"

Then Bill and Kevin burst in, two big sock-clad Irish-looking guys, smelling of Eau de Barn. "Hear you got a ticket, Missy!" Bill boomed at Alex, grinning.

"What could I do?" Alex held up her hands, Penelope-Pitstop helpless. "Sherman's finest was on the case."

Sandra poured coffee into thick mugs and they addressed themselves to the pies, no one talking. Normally this would make Alex uncomfortable but at that moment she didn't care. The pie was a revelation. Would Sandra make some for the pub? Bill and Kevin bolted down two pieces each in the blink of an eye.

Kevin pushed his chair back and stretched his legs. "I have some information for you."

She snapped out of her pie ecstasy. "Yeah?"

"That broken window, at the bookstore?"

"Upstairs, in Barb's apartment," Alex clarified.

"Uh-huh. Well, she never reported it."

"Damn." A dead end there.

Kevin took a big slurp of coffee. "Carl wants me to keep you updated about the investigation—except for confidential stuff. I don't know that it's the greatest idea." He sighed, pondering the matter from the heights of his twenty-two-year-old wisdom. "But he thinks it'll keep you out of trouble."

"Uh-huh," Alex replied, noncommital.

A silence fell. Bill and Sandra had been watching their exchange like an audience at a tennis match. Now Sandra turned to Alex, concerned. "What's this about?"

She was about to give Sandra a very abbreviated answer but then Kevin went on. "You were asking me yesterday about Wayne Benson?"

Alex nodded, her muscles tensing with anticipation.

"Well, they're going to Gazelle County tomorrow to question him. The two detectives on the investigation."

Two detectives and an hour and half drive each way: they were definitely interested in Wayne. Good. But something puzzled her. "Why don't they ask him to come here?"

"That's not how it works." Kevin assumed a superior look. "If we asked him, he could refuse to talk to us."

"Did they ask him?" Surely that response would make Wayne look even more suspicious.

Kevin sighed again. "Um...no? We don't want to give him any warning. Get it?"

She kept her temper in check. Just. Don't get your Irish up, as Dad would say.

He continued. "And this is the confidential part, so keep

this to yourself. They're just gonna arrive there tomorrow and surprise him."

It was more strategy than she would have given the Sherman PD credit for. "Are they going to his farm?" Alex pressed. "If he still has the farm, that is."

Kevin shrugged. "That's all I know."

"Alex," Sandra asked, "why are you involved in this?"

She went for a casual tone. "I've just been looking into some things about the fire."

That wasn't good enough. "Why?"

Damn. Alex had never intended to have this conversation with Sandra or Bill. "I just have a bad feeling about that fire," she explained. "And Barb was a good friend." She glanced at her watch. "I gotta get going. "I'll call you soon and tell you all about this. Or you come by the pub, okay?"

The last forkful of cherry pie was calling her name. She heeded the call and slurped a final sip of coffee.

She turned to Kevin. "Thanks for the info." Despite his attitude he'd been helpful. "And," she couldn't help adding, "I'll be sure to keep you updated on what *we* find."

❧

Alex spent the fifteen minutes she had to spare sucking up to her cats, who met her yowling at the back door.

She didn't dare tell them that—except for neglecting them—she was glad she'd taken the drive and the time. The scenery and the apples and the pie, Sandra's welcoming face, these had all been great. But most restorative had been the contact with nice, normal men. The apple farmer's sweet smile, Bill's gruff affection, even Kevin's usual cocky antics had been a welcome respite from the likes of Wayne and God's Warriors. She'd been feeling like a real man-hater these past few days. It wasn't a feeling she wanted to nourish.

The light on her answering machine was blinking. One

message, from Kathy.

"Hey, are you there?" A pause. "Guess not. Just wanted to let you know I'll be parking my truck closer to the house, and I rigged up nice big light that'll shine on it all night. That'll fix their wagons! Oh, and I did call the police." Good. Kathy was being proactive, but not a Lone Ranger.

"Oh, and guess what?" she continued. "I met Gina Meziere today, on campus—the professor from New York. Ran into her accidentally on purpose, if you know what I mean. She's cool!"

As Alex headed for the stairs that led down to the pub, a series of pathetic meows floated out from the kitchen. Jane had squeezed herself up against the back door and with the sheer force of tortitude, was willing it open. She looked up anxiously. It was time for a post-dinner prowl.

"Honey, you're out of luck. There's some scary guys going around these days." Alex glanced out at the sky. "And they like the dark."

～

Ten o'clock found Alex on her usual corner bar stool, resting her legs. They'd had a lively happy hour and then a dinner crowd that just kept coming at a nice, steady pace.

The bar was nearly empty when two tall guys, Sherman State students, came shambling in and grabbed stools in the middle of the bar. Alex hauled herself up to draw them the inevitable draft beers.

Then she recognized them. They were Barb's employees, the students who'd driven out to Cooper for the funeral Saturday. The blond in the hooded Sherman State sweatshirt was Drew. She didn't know the name of the dark-haired guy with zits, though she'd seen him often enough at Book Ends.

They were relaxed and joking with each other when Alex took their order and they didn't seem to recognize her from the bookstore or the funeral. When she put their beers down, though, Drew gave her a quick, sharp glance. He'd placed her.

It didn't make him chatty, though. For most of Alex's customers, the sight of her behind the bar set off a Pavlovian response to talk. Maybe this was a semi-generational thing.

She needed to break the ice. Food never failed. Alex went into the kitchen and snagged some chips and a bowl of her hottest fresh salsa.

"Hey you guys." She plonked the chips and dip down in front of them. "I just made this new salsa and I'm wondering if it's too hot. Would you mind sampling it for me?"

Drew threw a challenging look at his friend and dove right in. The dark-haired guy scooped up an even bigger portion and inhaled it. Not the best plan. His face turned crimson and he drank three-quarters of his beer in one go.

Drew's eyes were tearing up and his face reddened a bit. "Good salsa." He took a normal-sized sip. "But weak. Need another beer, Rob?"

"Fuck you," Rob croaked. "I've had hotter."

Chest beating. Alex smothered laughter as she drew a beer for herself and refilled Rob's. "I used to see you guys at Book Ends a lot. I'm Alex. Drew, right? And Rob?" She pretended she'd known his name already.

Drew nodded. "Yeah. We worked there from when Barb opened it." He frowned. "It sucks."

"Were you guys at the funeral Saturday? I thought I saw some Book Ends people at the cemetery."

"We went over with a couple girls we worked with." Drew pulled a pack of cigarettes out of his sweatshirt pocket and offered Alex one.

"I don't smoke. But thanks."

"How 'bout me?" Rob whined. "I'm out."

"You're always out. Go buy your own, cheap ass." Rob made puppy-dog eyes. Drew slid the pack down to him, reluctantly. "You're getting the next pack."

Alex put a clean ashtray in front of them. "Have you heard anything about the fire?"

"Not much," Drew said. The wary look was back.

Alex plowed ahead as if she hadn't noticed. "Me neither. Were you guys working there that Saturday?" Under the bar, she crossed her fingers.

Two affirmative nods. "Man, that was a busy day," Rob volunteered.

"Big Homecoming crowd, huh? We were slammed here, too, but probably later than you were."

Drew pushed a mop of thick blond hair off his forehead. "We got hit as soon as we opened. It didn't let up till game time."

"That was when? Five?"

"Yup. Parade at two, game at five, tailgaters in between."

"Barb told me she'd be running some kind of special to pull people in from the parade. Sounds like it worked."

They looked at each other quizzically, then back at Alex. "There wasn't any special," Rob said.

Drew widened his eyes. "She didn't need one!"

"I kept having to refill that coffee pot," Rob grumbled. "Barb didn't want it sitting empty."

Alex smiled. "That sounds like her. A full house and she still wanted everyone to get their free cup! Even the browsers."

"*Especially* them," Rob griped.

"So were people mostly wandering in and browsing? Or were they buying?"

"Buying!" they said in unison.

So Barb's last day had been a good one. Alex pictured her ringing up purchases non-stop, talking and joking with the customers, introducing newcomers to Maurice as she slid him aside to make room for their books on the counter.

"Because the cops were asking me about that," Alex said. It was only a slight exaggeration.

"Us, too!" Rob said.

"Uh-huh," Drew agreed. "About our hours that day and whether we were busy, and all that."

"When did you close?"

"Six."

"But that's not all they asked," Rob added. Drew shot him a warning look. "What? It's not a big secret."

"They said not to go around talking about it, remember?"

"Yeah, our buddies, the Sherman P.D."

The love affair between Sherman's finest and Sherman State students: Alex heard it had been going on for years.

A little silence fell. She let it stretch. A table of diners, long since finished and lingering by the fire all laughed at something. The clock behind the bar ticked.

"Okay." Drew took a long sip of beer. "So the cops call us all the week after the fire. They had our names from some payroll stuff at the bank. Asked us about hours and business, like I said. But then yesterday they came around again. Brought a couple pictures of a guy and wanted to know if we recognized him."

Wayne.

"They knew Rob and I'd worked the longest hours that Saturday, so they came to us first."

"Did you recognize the guy in the picture?"

"We sure as hell did," Drew said. "He was in the store that day." He looked to Rob for confirmation.

"Late afternoon," Rob said. "That's what we told the cops. Maybe five?"

Her heart rate sped up. "Did you see him talking to Barb?"

"No. The cops asked us that too." Drew pushed his fists into his sweatshirt pouch. "Plus, they asked was he doing anything strange?" They laughed.

"Was he?"

Rob shook his head. "Nah. He was just wandering around. Mostly in the back. I saw him when I was re-filling the coffee."

Refilling coffee. "Were you still busy then?"

"No, but we were totally out. Barb said to make one more pot."

Was it possible Barb hadn't even seen Wayne? No. Her store wasn't that big. "Did Barb seem okay then?"

They both thought about that. Something the cops hadn't asked, apparently. Rob shook his head. "I was doing stuff in the back, so I didn't talk to her much."

"I was up front with her. But you know," Drew mused, "she *was* pretty quiet. Not like earlier. Casey and I were joking around but she wasn't into it."

She'd seen him. "Did Barb close up by herself that night?"

"No. Rob and I were there till she locked up."

Rob leaned forward. "Who was the guy? Do you know?"

Alex hesitated for a second. But fair's fair. They'd spilled what they knew. "Her ex-husband."

Guys their age like to pretend that nothing surprises them. There was no pretending now. "No shit?" Drew's eyebrows shot up. "I didn't even know she'd been married!"

"Yup." She paused. "He wasn't a nice guy."

"So they think...?" Rob trailed off.

"I know they're looking at him." She drew them two more beers. "On the house." Chairs scraped. The four-top by the fireplace pulled on their coats and drifted out the door.

"So why would he want to burn her store down?" Drew asked.

"They're not sure it's him," Alex pointed out.

"Yeah," Rob chimed in. "Barb had some problems with other assholes, too. Remember? Back when we opened?"

Other assholes. God's Warriors?

"It wasn't right away," Drew corrected him. "That was after we were open three, four months."

"What happened? Barb never told me about this."

Rob grabbed Drew's cigarettes and shook another out of the pack. He pointed it at Drew. "Ask him."

"Hey, help yourself!" Drew stuffed the pack into his sweat-shirt pouch, took a sip of beer and sat back. Alex counted to ten. Don't hurry the natives.

After a long minute or so, he leaned forward. "I don't know that much about it," he began. "One day this old woman is talk-ing to Barb, up at the register. When I go behind the counter I hear the woman saying something about City Council. She leaves and Barb looks like she got the wind knocked out of her. So I ask her what's up and she says, nothing. Bullshit.

Anyway, like a week later we're doing inventory one night and it was just Barb and me, and I ask her about it again. So she tells me. Some people in Sherman don't like the books we stock and they were trying to make trouble for her. But it didn't go anywhere. It's over now, she said."

Holy crap. "What didn't they like?"

"She wouldn't tell me. She was like, 'It's water under the bridge, let's let it go and move on.'"

Water under the bridge. That sounded like Barb. The mo-mentary hurt Alex felt that Barb hadn't told her, dissolved. Maybe Barb had planned to tell her once she was more settled in Sherman. She probably didn't want to freak her out.

"And you never found out who the trouble-makers were?"

"Nope. Drew pushed his barstool back. "Well, we gotta head."

"Tap Room," Rob added. One of the filthy student bars on Main Street. The night was young.

They were heading towards the door when Alex thought of something. "Hey!" She waved them back. "Have you guys found new jobs yet?"

"No," Rob said glumly.

"Well, I don't have any openings here right now, but why don't you two fill out applications sometime? Then I'll have you on file if something changes." Barb's kids working here. She liked the idea.

Alex flipped on CNN to keep them company as she wiped

down the bar and Kristen swept around the tables. But she barely heard the anchor's report of the latest international disaster. Who had gone after Barb the year she'd opened? The old woman (she was probably forty) Rob had overheard had mentioned City Council. Did these people go to the Council? Whatever they'd tried, Barb had told Drew that it had gone nowhere. Nowhere officially, maybe.

Had some frustrated zealot finally taken the matter into his own hands? Was the fire at Book Ends a book burning?

CHAPTER TWENTY FOUR

"**D**o you know anyone on City Council?" Her first cup of coffee had kicked in and Alex knew Chris would be awake at 8:30.

Chris chuckled. "Why? Are you thinking of running?"

She'd fallen asleep last night thinking about books and the kind of people who burned them—the Catholic Church and Nazis came to mind—and woken up with the same thought. "Not quite yet. But I heard something last night. Barb may have run into trouble with the Council a few months after she opened. I want to follow up on it."

"Really? I want to hear about that! But I was just on the way out the door. Why don't you look it up on the town website?"

Most of the images on the home page were what you'd expect: a little girl waving an American flag at some parade, a bandbox-perfect Victorian house, rippling golden fields. But the bottom of the page—a broad blue river, white cranes skimming its surface—was pure fantasy. The closest thing Sherman had to a river was a two-foot wide creek that dried up in the summer. Local pronunciation: crick.

She clicked the link to the City Council page. Ten names popped up, two for each ward. Alex skimmed the list, not recognizing the names until she reached the last one. Ward Five's councilman was Don Roberts. Bingo.

Well Don, let's see what kind of devious shit you were up to a few years back. She took a big slurp of coffee, clicked on "Minutes" and scrolled down.

Forty-five minutes later, her eyes glazed over, Alex was no wiser. Not a single reference to Book Ends. Whatever scheme had been afoot, it had never made it to the City Council's docket. Why not? Did Barb have allies there? Her ignorance about Sherman politics was as wide and deep as the fake river on the home page.

She had no choice but to wade in. How much more convenient it would be to gather information from the dry shore of her bed, coffee mug in hand and Lucy against her legs.

⁓

Bright sunshine washed over the butcher-block worktable, warming her hands as Alex sliced apples for strudel. It was mid-afternoon. The only sounds were the click of the knife as it hit the cutting board and the hum of the fridge. The smell of apples filled the kitchen.

"Anybody home?" a familiar voice called suddenly from the bar.

Alex started, nearly nicking her finger with the sharp knife. Hadn't she locked the front door? She pushed through the swinging kitchen doors into the bar.

It was Chris. "Whoa!" She held up her hands. "I come in peace!"

Alex was still carrying the knife. She laughed. "Sorry, I'm a little jumpy these days."

"I know what you mean," Chris agreed. "First thing this morning I checked my car."

"Me too."

"Good." Chris nodded approval. "I almost wish they'd try something again."

Not out here, please. "Hey, would you mind hanging out with me in the kitchen?"

She got back to the apples. Chris was wearing that buttery suede jacket again and faded jeans. Alex darted quick glances at her while Chris looked around the kitchen, taking in the details in that methodical way she had.

"What are you making?" Chris came over and peered at the ingredients. "Apple pie?"

"Strudel."

"Oh," she sighed. "That's one of my favorites."

Even her sighs were sexy. Alex cleared her throat to make sure her voice worked. "Me too. I got this recipe from a chef I worked with in Maine."

"Oh, Maine." Another sigh.

"I know, it's so beautiful. I actually looked at some pubs there, but they were way out of my price range. Even the ones that were inland."

"Well, I'm glad you found your pub here." There was that amazing smile again.

Alex's knees responded predictably. She managed to stay upright. "Thanks." She pointed her knife at the box of phyllo dough defrosting on the counter. "I really like this recipe. You use that dough and layer the apples with mascarpone cheese and pecans. I'll save you a piece."

"That'll be something to look forward to. Should I do a little work, to earn it?"

Was she flirting? No, don't even think it. Chris was pulling a paring knife from the butcher block. Alex handed her an apron and they sliced away quietly for a few minutes. Slowly, her heart rate returned to normal.

"Maurice is doing great." Chris said. "He's a sweetheart. And he and Smoke touched noses this morning."

"Oh, good!"

"Sometimes he's a little quiet and withdrawn. He's missing Barb. But I think he's just one of those cats who's able to adapt."

"That's so great to hear. Want to chop those?" She pushed over a bag of pecans. "It's been a busy couple of days, huh?"

"What did you find out about the City Council?"

"That something was up." She filled Chris in on Drew and Rob's revelation of the trouble at Book Ends as well as their sighting of Wayne the day of the fire, and their later ID of Wayne from her picture. "And it turns out Don is on City Council; maybe he was on it three years ago, too."

Chris listened quietly.

Alex backtracked to her visit to Bill and Sandra's and the information she'd gleaned from Kevin. She looked up at her brightly painted Key West rooster clock. The legs read 4:00. "The police have probably interviewed Wayne by now."

"I wonder how that went."

"Join the club." Alex imagined an unmarked cop car wending its way down a bumpy farm driveway, two detectives in the front seat. Wayne, maybe out in the field on his combine, watching the car as it approached his farm, his eyes narrowing with suspicion. Or widening with dread. And maybe he didn't still have the farm. But Alex couldn't picture him any other way. She pulled the dough out of its box and covered it with a damp towel.

Was there anything else she needed to update Chris about? Yes: Kathy's certainty that her tire's lug nuts had been loosened by God's Warriors.

Chris nodded. "I talked to Kathy again yesterday afternoon. She's probably right. Jess thinks so, too."

Alex threw a few sheets of phyllo into the bottom of two high-sided baking pans and began brushing them with butter. "Kathy was really challenging them that night. It made me uneasy."

"Me too."

"But Jesus Christ, she could have been killed! Talk about an extreme reaction. Somebody has a screw loose."

"Or a lug nut."

Alex laughed. "No pun intended. But is it our turn, next? Or do they figure that that was warning enough for us uppity bitches?"

Chris mused. "I'm hoping whoever it was, they were just really hammered."

"That could be. They were all well on their way when we were at Huskers."

"Speaking of which Chris said, "I talked to my parents last night. I caught them just as they were heading out to the early-bird special."

Alex groaned. "$9.99 buffets. Sounds like Florida."

"Same crowd in Arizona: retired snow birds. Anyway, Mom was saying they'd call me when they got back and I said okay, I wanted to ask them about Dick Wagner and God's Warriors. Next thing I know, Dad's on the other extension."

"And?"

"Dad said, 'What's he done?'"

"Who? Dick?"

"Dick. I told them we're not sure what he's done, but we had some ideas and we were trying to find out." She paused. "Mom and Dad got real quiet. Then Dad said, 'You remember how we always told you to keep off their property?' Then he said Dick's an angry guy. Always had a chip on his shoulder. No use as a neighbor, either. They kept themselves to themselves over there, he and Amanda"

Chris pushed a pile of chopped pecans to one side. "Mom

totally agreed. But she had a different take on it. She said when Dick and Amanda first bought the farm she tried to be friendly to Amanda. Asked her over for coffee several times. Finally, one day Amanda comes over but she's quiet and doesn't seem comfortable. After a while, though, she starts relaxing and opening up a little, and then all of a sudden she gets all tense, looks at her watch and says she had to go. Dick wouldn't like her being away for so long. Mom felt sorry for her. She worried if there was some kind of abuse going on."

"Sounds like emotional abuse, at least."

"Agree." Chris nodded. "So a few weeks later, Mom goes over there one afternoon; she'd canned some bread and butter pickles and brought a jar to Amanda. Same story. Amanda warms up. Then Dick comes in. Mom said the air got so chilly she wished had a sweater. She left. Mom hoped Amanda would get back in touch with her, but she never did. She'd see her in town and say hi, but that was it."

Alex peeled another sheet of dough off the stack. It ripped in half. Damn. No matter what you did to keep it moist, the second half of the box always dried out at warp speed. This was a job for two people.

Chris put her knife down. "Can I help?" she asked, deftly stripping a single, intact sheet off the stack. Good with her hands. Hmmmm. Don't go there.

The next few minutes passed in a blur of rapid strudel assembly. They worked quietly, side by side. It felt like they'd been doing this together for years.

A final brush of butter, three big slits scored across the top of the dough, and into the warmed oven. "That's a big piece I'm gonna owe you now." Alex smiled at Chris. "Thanks."

Chris stood at the sink, washing her hands. Alex draped a striped kitchen towel over Chris's shoulder and joined her.

"I asked my folks about God's Warriors and Equal Partners in Faith." Chris dried her hands.

"Did they know anything?"

"Nothing at all about Equal Partners." She leaned against the sink. "Dad did hear about God's Warriors a couple times, before my parents sold up and moved. That was five years ago," she added. "So it's been around a while. All he knew was, it was some kind of secret group. And really conservative."

"We know that's true!"

"He did hear Dick Wagner was one of the leaders."

This also rang true. Alex pictured Dick as he'd stood among the other men at Husker's that night, his challenging, arrogant stance.

"Then," Chris said, "I asked what they knew about the others. They know who Chuck Bauer is. He knocked up his high school girlfriend and had to marry her. They have three or four kids. The two people from the college they'd never heard of. And guess what? Don Roberts is divorced. Has been for a while. Paul Neilson, too, but his divorce is more recent. His ex-wife teaches at the elementary school. They hadn't heard a lot about Don's divorce—this was seven or eight years ago, they think—but Mom said it was sudden. Everyone heard they were separated and then one day Don's wife had left town. Seems no one ever heard from her again."

"Did anyone ever dig up the back yard at Huskers?"

Chris chuckled. "Dad said there were some jokes about it at the time. Said he wouldn't put it past Don. Then Mom asked what we were looking into. I was pretty vague about it, just told her we had some questions about the fire. But I could hear her mom-alert sensors going on."

Alex remembered it well. Her mom's sensors had been so strong they'd surely interfered with radio frequencies.

"Anyway, I said they'd better get going or they'd miss the early bird. But before we got off, Dad had a word of advice: he said to stay away from Dick Wagner." She paused. "He was serious."

"How about your mom?"

"She said, stay away from all of them. I told her we'd do our best."

"Did she buy that?"

"Don't know." Chris slipped her leather jacket on. "I got off the phone before she could make me promise."

CHAPTER TWENTY FIVE

The apple strudel was a hit: at least half the dinner crowd at the pub that night ordered a piece. Good thing she'd saved Chris a generous wedge.

A hungry and thirsty crowd had descended on Fitzpatrick's shortly after they opened, leaving Alex little time to think about recent developments. And in those rare quiet moments, she had difficulty focusing on the mental pictures of fires and angry men that had so preoccupied her for days now. Other images had replaced them: the brightness of the kitchen that afternoon, the sunlight flooding in on the worktable; Chris's hands scattering apple slices over the dough; Chris, standing next to her in a soft chambray shirt that brushed Alex's bare forearm. The internal lecture could wait, tonight.

By 10:30 the sated crowd was pretty much gone. Alex was idly watching an old *Law and Order* and yawning when Kathy breezed in. "Better wake up!" she called out.

"Hey, you. Where's your tire iron?"

"I brought this instead." Kathy placed a small basket shaped like a tall coffee mug on the bar. The honey-colored reeds were interspersed with touches of green and orange. "For all your pens and stuff at the register."

She had noticed the perpetual mess and come up with her own solution. "Thank you! It's beautiful." Alex held it in her hands, feeling the pattern of the weave. "How about a night-cap for the master weaver?"

"Master!" She laughed. "Not quite. But thanks. Maybe I'll get there someday. There was a master weaver from Wisconsin with a booth there today. You should have seen her stuff."

Alex poured two snifters of Grand Marnier. "Today?"

"At the craft fair."

She'd totally forgotten. "Of course! How'd it go?"

A big smile lit Kathy's face. "Really well." She pulled out a cigarette and Alex turned off the TV.

Lauren came out of the kitchen, jacket on and apron rolled up under her arm, Robin right behind her. "See you guys Friday," Alex said. Two tired sets of feet dragged out the door.

"So what's been up with you?" Kathy asked.

"Lots." Alex settled back on the bar stool next to Kathy and updated her on what she'd learned since Kathy's panicked visit yesterday morning.

"Barb never said anything to you about the City Council thing?"

Alex shook her head. "Not a word. I have to do some digging on that, but I don't know anybody on the Council. Chris doesn't, either."

"Heard anything about the interview with Wayne?"

"Not yet."

"What the hell was he doing in Book Ends that day?"

"That's the million dollar question."

"I wonder if this was the first time. Or if he'd been stalking her." Kathy stubbed her cigarette out. They quietly pondered this for a minute. It seemed all too possible.

"So Don and Paul are both divorced, huh?" Kathy sipped her cordial. "Bitter, party of two."

"At least they seem to be leaving our vehicles alone. For now."

"Let them come back. I'm ready." Kathy's tone was defiant.

"You sound like Chris. Personally, I hope they've had their fun and made their point."

"Oh, did you talk to Chris today?"

"She came by this afternoon. Helped me make the strudel, in fact." Alex pointed to the dinner offerings on the blackboard behind the bar. "I needed an extra pair of hands."

"So how'd that go?" Kathy grinned. "Cooking together?"

"Um," Alex fumbled, avoiding her eyes, "fine. Hey, let's split a piece!" She shot into the kitchen.

Alex took her sweet time in there, spooning the whipped cream and positioning the sugared mint slices just so, planning a clever segue to a new topic. When she swung back through the kitchen doors, she found Kathy leaning back on her barstool, arms crossed over her chest and a let's-cut-the-shit expression. Oh well. She sat back down, sliding the plate and forks between them.

"So what's going on with you two?"

This time, Alex met her eyes. "Nothing. Honest."

"You mean nothing yet, right?" Kathy smiled encouragingly. "Come on girl, I know something is up."

Alex released a big sigh. "Yeah. Something's up. But I don't want it to be."

"What do you mean?"

Alex rubbed her hands over her face. "Remember I told you about my crazy last two girlfriends? I'm girled out. I don't want to get involved with anyone. But even if I wanted to be with Chris," she shook her head, "it's hopeless."

"Why?"

"Remember those crushes you had in seventh grade? One-sided?"

"Why do you say it's one-sided?"

"Why?" She had to explain this? "Chris is straight!"

"She is?" Kathy sounded disbelieving.

"Yeah. Remember at your house, when she was talking about her old boyfriend?" Alex groaned. "God, I thought I'd outgrown attractions to straight women."

"I do remember that. The important part," Kathy said slowly, as if speaking to a not-particularly-bright child, "being *old*. How long ago was that, anyway?"

"Chris didn't say. And believe me, I was listening."

Kathy gave Alex an exasperated look. "Didn't you have boyfriends, too, once?"

"Yeah. Up till, I don't know, sometime after college."

"Right." She paused. "Think about it."

Oh. "You think Chris doesn't have boyfriends anymore?"

"I'm pretty sure she's not straight," Kathy said.

A trickle of hope surged up. Alex mashed it back down. "Well, I'm not sure at all, and I'm the one who should know!" She paused. "Why do you think that?"

The big grin was back. "Because I think she's attracted to you!"

Now it was Alex's turn to laugh. "Oh, come on! Chris? Have you noticed how fricking gorgeous she is? And smart, and funny. She could be with anybody! "

"Including you, Alex. Don't sell yourself short."

"I don't think so. But thanks for the vote of confidence."

Kathy lit a fresh cigarette, took a drag, and tilted her head back, blowing the smoke up in the air. "I know what I know."

"Hey," Alex prodded the strudel with her fork, "this whipped cream is melting."

They forked in. Alex let the flavors meld together in her mouth. Her first cooking effort with Chris. She smiled in spite of herself.

"This is fabulous. What kind of cheese is that?" Kathy asked.

"Mascarpone, it's Italian."

"Italian!" Kathy exclaimed. "I knew there was something I wanted to tell you. I met Gina Meziere yesterday."

"That's right, you said that in your message. How'd you manage that?"

"I didn't even plan it, but it was easy. You know I'm teaching my weaving class next semester? I had to take care of some paperwork for that, so I swung by campus. Every door I walked through had this bright blue poster about a lecture Monday night by some big-name philosopher. Now guess who's listed as the contact person?"

"Professor Meziere?"

"Yup. And I thought, how long has it been since I've been to a really good philosophy lecture? I should check up on that."

"Alex chuckled. "It's been a while for me, too."

"So next thing you know, there I am in the Humanities building. Right in time for her office hours."

"And?"

"She's great! Funny, and really east coast. I introduced myself and asked about the lecture and we got talking for a few minutes. But students kept coming by and it was pretty chaotic, so I left."

"We need to get her down here. Or rather, you do."

"That's the plan."

"Yeah?"

"I thought I'd go to that lecture and approach her afterwards, ask her to come out for a drink at my favorite place. Then we can grill her about Equal Partners."

"Devious."

Kathy wiggled her eyebrows. She glanced at her watch. "I need to get to bed. The craft fair starts again at 9 a.m. You know, maybe I'll ask Chris to come to the lecture with me if she's free. Then she can come back here, too." She smiled.

"Not asleep yet, and you're already dreaming."

"You need to do a little more of that, yourself." Kathy squeezed Alex's shoulder and then she was gone.

CHAPTER TWENTY SIX

The shrilling of the phone wrenched Alex from a deep and dreamless sleep. It was 7:30. The machine picked up.

"Alex?" The cheery voice sounded familiar. "Chris said you wanted to talk to someone on the City Council..."

Jess. Alex sprang out of bed. The wood floors felt like ice on her bare feet as she scrabbled for the receiver. "Hi Jess!" she croaked.

"Oh you're there, good." Jess sounded like she'd been up for hours, and she wasn't alone. Two barking dogs in the background formed a counterpoint to the nearby high-pitched voices of small children and the bass notes of a man. Alex took a thankful survey of her quiet little apartment and dragged herself into the kitchen in search of coffee beans.

"Chris told me about the Book Ends thing," Jess continued. "She said you needed to talk to someone on the City Council."

"Right." Alex hit the speaker button, put the phone on the counter, and spooned beans into the grinder. "Someone who was on it three years back. I need someone with the inside scoop because whatever was being planned, it never made it to the agenda."

"I've got the guy for you, then. Todd's grandfather, Mern. He's been on the Council for years. Mern Hoffman."

"Should I call him?"

"I already did." Probably at six o'clock, after feeding the horses and before the crack-of-dawn enormous breakfast. "That's why I'm calling you now. He'll be down at the donut shop. I thought you could catch him there."

"I'm just out bed, to tell you the truth. Do you know how much longer he'll be there?"

"No need to rush. He and his buddies are there till nine, nine-thirty every morning. Retired farmers. They gossip and drink coffee. Free refills. You want to know the low-down in Sherman, hang out there every morning." Jess's husband suddenly spoke up, nearby. "Right. And Todd says they complain about how everyone is farming."

"That sounds fun. Can I go in there if I'm not wearing a seed cap?"

She laughed. "Todd can loan you one! But Mern's looking out for you. I gave him the gist of what you wanted to know. Said you were a friend and I'd appreciate if he could help you out." Todd's voice rumbled nearby again. "Just buy him a bear claw. Those are his favorites."

❧

Mel's Donut Shop, with its original 1950s era sign and hospital-green stucco exterior, sat about halfway down Main Street. The parking spaces out front were filled with pickup trucks.

The faded dinginess of the outside was of a piece with the inside of the shop. The dusty curtains that hung across the

plate glass window were the bright spot. Dark brown lino-
leum floor peeling at the edges, mint green Formica tabletops
with flecks of brown and black, brown chairs. A quick glance
back at the kitchen and bakery case assured Alex it was clean,
though. It was safe to order a donut.

She didn't notice all this right away, however. The stares
of the ten or so men who, cued by the creak of the front door,
swiveled their heads in her direction and stopped whatever
they'd been saying, distracted her a bit. Any second now the
girl behind the counter would ask, "What'll it be, stranger?"

Torn between apprehension and laughter, Alex made her
way to the counter, careful to make no sudden moves. Then
someone broke the silence and a murmur of conversation
started up again behind her.

The college-age girl at the counter looked bored out of her
mind. She cracked her gum and breathed through her mouth
while Alex surveyed the bakery case. Slim pickings. Three bear
claws were the lone occupants of the top shelf. Their neighbors on the next shelf were a full tray of donuts oozing lurid
red jam. Pass. Underneath was a half tray of glazed. It's hard to
go wrong with a glazed donut though Alex used to think that
about cold buffets, too. She ordered a glazed and a bear claw
and a cup of coffee.

Only one of the four tables was empty. Alex sat there and
took a sip of weak coffee. The five retired farmers at the next
table turned for one more long survey then returned to their
conversation. Tick tock. The glazed donut wasn't bad.

Then a wiry specimen from the table nearest the bakery
case pushed his chair back with a screech and clomped over to
Alex's table. Heads swung in her direction again. "Miss Fitzpatrick?" A rhetorical question.

"Alex."

He placed a chipped white ceramic coffee mug on the table—Alex's coffee had been served in a to-go cup—and took

the chair next to her. In his seventies, she figured. A John Deere cap sat atop a face that had seen a lot of weather.

"I'm Mern Hoffman." He held out a gnarled hand. For someone with arthritis he had a hell of handshake. "That new place down the road, that's yours?"

"That's right, Fitzpatrick's. Have you been out yet?"

"Not yet. Figured I'd let you get the bugs out first." He winked. Clearly some flirting was in order.

Alex smiled and pushed the bear claw towards him. "Jess said these are your favorites."

"Mern, you old dog!" a reedy voice called out from the table in the corner. "Better hope this doesn't get back to Norma!" A cackling chorus of laughter followed.

He cast a roguish look at his donut shop cronies and leaned in towards her, grinning. "They're just jealous. So," he, tore off a piece of bear claw, "you heard about Don Roberts stirring up trouble a few years back?"

It had been Don. Alex nodded as if she knew this already.

"Well." Mern licked some sugar off his lips and took a sip of coffee. "He's a real troublemaker, Don is. You know him?"

"He's never been very, um, friendly. I think I've taken some business from him."

"Yup." A slow smile spread among his wrinkles, by degrees reaching his eyes.

"So what was Don's problem with Book Ends?"

He leaned forward and lowered his voice. "Pornography."

Alex gasped. "Barb didn't sell porn!" A room full of seed caps swung their way.

"Harold!" Mern called out. "Want to pull up a chair and join us? Wouldn't want you to strain your hearing aid!" A general guffaw followed this sally.

Mern leaned back in his chair, his gnarled hands cradling the coffee mug. "It was a load of horse shit." He frowned. "Emma Gibbs comes to me one day, all in flap. Don wants to get that new bookstore shut down, she tells me. Don's saying the owner—can't remember her name—"

"Barb. Barb Nichols."

"Poor woman." He shook his head. "Well, Don's going around saying she's a bad influence. That kids shouldn't go in there. Too many un-Christian books. And porn. He's chewing Emma's ear off, how the Council has to do something. Emma says to me that's nonsense. It's a nice store and the owner's a nice woman. I thought so, too. Norma dragged me in there a couple times, looking for presents and such. Emma, though, she doesn't want to get into an argument with Don. I think she's a little afraid of him."

Alex couldn't blame her.

"So she tells Don she'll go take a look, along with another woman on the Council, Gail Thompson. And off they go one day, and they look all around, pretending they were gonna buy something, I guess. They don't find damn-all, except for one thing."

Alex waited.

"Some kind of homosexual magazines." He made a face. "And a few books."

Crunch. Mern had no idea he was talking to a gay person. She remembered the first time she'd seen *The Advocate* and *Girlfriends* in the magazine section of Book Ends. It was like seeing old friends. Barb had never made a big deal about their presence, or the slender shelf of gay and lesbian fiction and non-fiction nearby. But they sold. Many a high school or college student, Barb told her, had lurked near the register till the coast was clear, sliding their purchases onto the counter with a half-guilty, half-defiant expression. Her heart had gone out to them.

"That's right," Alex told Mern, summoning up a little courage of her own. "She did stock some gay magazines. So?"

He held up his hands. "None of my business!"

Alex ploughed ahead. "I take it Emma found out that none

of this was pornographic."

He bit off a chunk of bear claw and chewed it slowly. "That's what she said. No nudie pictures!" he chuckled.

"Then what happened?"

"Emma figures it's only fair to let the owner know what's going on, so she tells her. But she tells her not to worry, it was just Don's idea, and no one else was behind it. And wouldn't be, if she had anything to say about it."

So Emma was the mystery woman who'd talked to Barb that day. After she'd left, Drew said, Barb looked like she'd had the wind knocked out of her.

"Emma goes around and talks to the other Council members, tells them what Don's got up his sleeve. When Don started to lobby people they told him to forget it." He smiled. "He never knew it was her."

Go, Emma. Alex had guessed right: Barb had had an ally on Town Council.

"Did he just drop it, then?"

"Didn't have much of a choice, did he? But if you're asking did he shut up, then no. Kept on about it for a while. He even said something to me, finally." Mern sipped his coffee. The bear claw was gone. "Knows I can't stand him. I told him leave that woman alone, she's not harming anyone. He puffs himself up and says this isn't the end of it, he has friends who care about this town if we don't."

Let's define care. "Sounds like he was kind of threatening."

Mern leaned back and crossed his arms over his chest. "It'll be a cold day in hell before I'm threatened by the likes of Don Roberts." Don probably had twenty-odd years and forty or so pounds on him, but Alex would back Mern. "Anyway, that was the last I heard of it." He squinted across the table at her. "Jess says you were friends with the owner."

Alex nodded.

"He make any more trouble for her?"

"That's what I'm trying to find out."

"And why's that?"

"It's like you said, she was my friend." Alex lowered her voice, conscious of ears all around them. "And I don't like Don Roberts, either. Or his friends."

Mern gave her a long, shrewd look. Then he slowly stood up. "Thanks for the donut."

"Thank you. You know, I don't have donuts out at my place, but I have some pretty good beer. And a fireplace."

"So I've heard."

"I'm a mile down the road," Alex cajoled.

"Well," Mern's voice was gruff but his eyes were twinkling. "I'll think about it, missy."

"Hope to see you soon, then," Alex said, pulling on her jacket. "First beer's on the house."

"He won't turn that down!" came a voice from the corner table. The chorus of laughter followed her out into the street.

CHAPTER TWENTY SEVEN

The day went downhill from there. Sometime in the night, the ice machine had died. Alex knew as soon as she came downstairs from the apartment that something was off, but only later realized that it had been the absence of its familiar hum. She stepped behind the bar and sloshed into a one-inch deep puddle of melted ice. Her canvas sneakers soaked it up like a sponge. Fuck.

She got on the phone to Gere's Heating and Cooling and begged for someone to come out right away, but the woman with the three-packs-a-day voice on the other end seemed strangely indifferent to her crisis. "Soon as he's free," she rasped. Click.

Of course, lunch was busy and the repairman arrived right at the craziest time. Alex spent an hour stepping over his prone body as he sprawled full-length on the floor behind the bar, pulling out the guts of the machine. They would order the new part, he told Alex laconically. It might be here tomorrow. Or not.

Her customers were in a typical Thursday mood, spirits lifted in anticipation of the weekend, and she tried to let their cheerfulness rub off on her. It wouldn't take, though. She was still pissed about the story Mern had told her.

Alex had at least one consolation: she was becoming a better detective. She'd guessed right about Barb having an ally on the Council, and that Don's had been the hand behind the trouble. But perhaps there was more than one hand at work. Surely when Don had made his empty threat to Mern, the friends he'd meant were his creepy buddies in God's Warriors. Had Don acted on their behalf? Alex shivered. She'd had them pegged as a lunatic fringe. What if, instead, they occupied a place at the heart of Sherman politics?

When things died down and the lunch crowd drifted reluctantly back to work, Alex poured a cup of coffee, perched on her corner barstool, and thought. What was that old saying? To understand another, try to walk a mile in his shoes. She mentally slid her feet into size twelve boots and tried to imagine the way the world looked through the self-righteous, close-minded eyes of say, Dick Wagner. When he had looked at Book Ends, what had he seen?

This: an independent woman owner, a divorcee and an outsider, standing behind the register. College kids—most of them not local—stocking the shelves. And what was on those shelves? Porn and un-Christian works, whatever that meant. Gay people staring boldly out from the covers of gay magazines, tempting the youth of Sherman to a world of sin and sodomy. What would Dick consider anti-Christian? Barb's Spirituality section, where works on New Age philosophies, Wicca, and Paganism rubbed shoulders with Christian self-help books, would certainly have fit the bill.

Alex took a sip of coffee and a new idea slid into place. There was another piece to add to Dick's view of Book Ends: his wife Amanda walking through the door. Did Dick know she was a customer there, and friendly with Barb? Or was this another of Amanda's secrets?

If it had been God's Warriors behind the censorship attempt—and Alex had no real doubt that it was—then they'd gone the legal route in their first move against Barb. How outraged they must have been when Don brought them the news that their plan had misfired. Thwarted, in *their* town.

Alex took a last slurp of coffee and went back behind the bar to start tallying receipts, only slightly less frustrated than when she'd sat down. She knew in her bones that there was a connection between God's Warriors and the Book Ends fire. But how would she ever prove it?

＠

Her eyelids were heavy as she dragged back up to the apartment a short while later. Most mornings Alex eased slowly into full consciousness, but today had started with a jerk and her internal clock was all screwed up. A lie-down was in order. But she couldn't ignore the blinking light on the answering machine.

It was Carl. "Hi, Alex. I talked to Kevin about the interview with Wayne Benson yesterday. Figured you'd like to hear about it. Give me a call; I'm at work." He'd called an hour ago.

She found Carl's card in a pile of assorted papers on the kitchen counter and after a few minutes, the state police dispatcher found him. "Alex!" he greeted her. "How are things in Sherman?"

"Pretty eventful these days. You're missing all the fun."

"That's what I hear." Wherever he was calling from sounded pretty eventful, too. A hum of conversations and crackling radios filled the air.. "I told Kevin I'd update you on Wayne Benson. He got the story this morning."

"Thanks for calling me. What happened?"

She could hear the creak of a chair and pictured Carl easing himself back. "Two Sherman detectives went out to his farm yesterday."

"So Wayne does still have the farm."

"Yup. And seems he wasn't too pleased to see them in his field."

Alex had predicted that, too. "I bet."

"Benson was out on his combine. He ignored the detectives at first. Went down a couple rows. Finally, he shut it off and climbed down. Cursing a blue streak about having to stop and what the hell did they want."

"Brave guys. I can't imagine putting myself in front of Wayne's combine."

Carl chuckled. "The detectives told Kevin they still tried for a friendly approach but that didn't last long. Guy's a real mean-eyed one, they said. So they got right down to business. Asked him where he was on the night of Saturday, October eleventh."

Alex held her breath.

"The detectives said Benson stared at them like they were insects and then asked how it was their concern."

"He refused to talk to them?"

"At first. But then he saw they weren't going away, so just to get rid of them, he said he'd tell them." Carl paused. "Benson said he was home that night."

"He lied to them!" Alex sprang out of her chair. "What did they say to Wayne, then?"

"Showed him your friend Chris's picture. Told him they have witnesses who put him at the Book Ends fire. Told him the Sherman P.D. was real interested in what he was doing there."

Alex felt a surge of excitement. "Damn, I wish I was there!" A fly on the combine.

Carl chuckled. "Me too. Well, after that Benson started singing a different tune. He must have had his dates mixed up and so forth. Now he remembered, he was visiting a friend who lives just outside Sherman that weekend. They were hunting."

"Can that be checked out?"

"It was, right away, before Wayne could get to a phone. Turns out the guy backs him up."

Alex felt a pang of disappointment. "Bummer."

"Oh don't worry," Carl reassured her. "That still gave him lots of opportunity."

"So, do they like him for it?"

Carl laughed. "Like him? You watch too many cop shows! Anyway, he's got to be their prime suspect. Ex-husband, in town that night, lied about it."

"Do you know what the next move is?"

"They asked him to come to Sherman to make a statement. He was coming in this morning."

"This morning?" All of this had been happening down the road and Alex hadn't known.

"On videotape and the whole nine yards," he continued. "Bet he didn't like that much, but they caught him in a lie and now they have grounds."

Then Alex remembered something else. "You know, the other day, Kevin said they were checking to see if Wayne had a record. Do you know if anything turned up?"

"No criminal record."

"Damn. I was hoping Barb had reported him, that time he attacked her. Right before she left him."

"Too bad," Carl agreed. "If it really starts to look like Wayne was the arsonist, that's the kind of thing that can impress a DA. Shows a pattern. They did find something, though."

"Five dead wives in the attic?"

"You've got some imagination! No. Just that Wayne's having financial problems. He's gotten into some pretty serious debt the last four-five years."

Debt. Barb said she and Wayne had stayed out of debt and that's why they'd survived the farm crisis. But years after their divorce he was still struggling. It couldn't be unconnected.

"Well," Carl said, as the volume of noise rose suddenly behind him, "I need to get going."

"Thanks for calling me."

Alex thought they were into hanging-up preliminaries when suddenly Carl asked, "Been doing any detecting of your own?"

"A little," Alex said. "If this doesn't pan out about Wayne, I can tell you some other things we found out."

"Don't try to play Nancy Drew, okay?"

"No chance. She was always getting rescued by her boyfriend!"

"Just make sure we don't need to rescue you, Alex."

She put down the phone and glanced at her clock radio. Three twenty. Wayne's interview must have long been over. Was it possible he had confessed to the arson?

Moments after hanging up with Carl, Alex's hand strayed toward the receiver. She doubted the Sherman police station had seen this much drama in years and it must have been abuzz all day with speculation and later, information. If Wayne had confessed, or even incriminated himself somehow, Kevin would know. Everyone at the station would know. Maybe she should just call Dee at the front desk.

Or not. Alex walked away from the phone. Surely Kevin would call her if there were a big breakthrough.

Time to return to that restful place she'd been heading for when before she'd spotted the blinking answering machine. She snagged Miss Marple and a blanket en route back to the couch and enticed Jane to join her. The chance to crawl under a blanket was too much for Jane to resist.

She didn't even last two pages. St. Mary Meade, briefly glimpsed, faded into the distance as she entered that narcotic place between waking and sleeping.

CHAPTER TWENTY EIGHT

A ringing phone was usually the last thing Alex wanted to hear when she was busy behind the bar. Not so tonight. She had one ear cocked for its sound all evening.

She liked Kevin, but really, what an irritating little shit he could be. He knew she would be in total suspense about the interview. But maybe there'd been no progress. Maybe Wayne had sat and stonewalled the detectives today. It wasn't hard to imagine.

Just after 8:30 Alex checked the ice supply. Low. Things had eased up and she needed some fresh air. She got Annette off the floor to watch the bar for a few minutes.

It turned out to be longer than a few minutes. A funny thing happened on the way to the truck stop/convenience store.

The usual Thursday night mayhem was underway as Alex drove down Main Street, cars parked all around the student bars, groups of Sherman State kids staggering from one bar to the next. It was around forty degrees but some of them wore t-shirts. Bundling up was deeply uncool.

The night was clear and cold and starlit. Beautiful. But, once away from the bright lights of Main Street on Thursday night, dark. The darkness made Fort God, coming up on her right, into a looming, menacing pile. Maybe it was her unsatisfied curiosity about the Wayne interview, but something stopped Alex from just driving by. And look: there were some lights. And cars.

She turned into the stadium-sized parking and slowed the car to a crawl. The sandstone brick buildings stretched right and left, connected by glass walkways. A cluster of cars was parked up by the doors of the building to the left of the church, the usual smattering of minivans, trucks and American sedans. She parked next to the last sedan.

The wind was picking up. A big gust finished opening the car door for her. Alex got out and looked around for the source of the lights she'd glimpsed before. One light shone high into the air above her: she followed its beam from the ground up to the top of a big, high flagpole. A clutch of wind-tossed flags were illuminated: Old Glory, something that looked like a state flag, and a third, smaller one, which was red.

She stood in the cold wind and squinted, trying to make it out. A moment later, she wished she hadn't. Against the red, a silver cross shone, a gold sword running through it. God's Warriors.

Alex heard Kathy's voice again, that night they'd driven by here: "That's where they meet." And hoisted a flag. Talk about taking yourself seriously.

She whipped around to face the building. A splash of light spilled into the parking lot from the lit-up glass vestibule near the parked vehicles. But everything around it was dark. Strange. The fake stained-glass windows of the church reflected no light as she crept nearer to the buildings. The half-dead shrubbery that rustled in the wind at the base of the buildings was better lit. What was that about? Then she saw. The light was coming from the basement.

Alex squatted down and, as quietly as she could, pushed the crunchy plants aside.

The window was the kind they have in basement apartments. All Alex could see through it was a big empty room—but no, it was only the back of a room. Blue plastic chairs and long fake-wood grain tables.

A noise was coming from somewhere she couldn't see. She put her ear to the glass. Rumble rumble. Male voices rose and fell, apparently from the front of the room. She couldn't tell how many. Damn. A God's Warriors meeting was underway and here she was, too far from the action to hear a word.

Alex squatted there, knees aching and ear freezing, for what felt like an eternity. It was probably ten minutes. Then some angel of common sense mercifully descended and whispered, "This is pointless."

She heeded her, knees cracking like gunshots as she got back upright. But could she just leave, no wiser than when she'd arrived? There must be something she could do. She looked over at the parked vehicles. That was it: she'd take a page from Chris's book. Get some plate numbers and check them against one of those stalker books you can get at the county courthouse for three dollars. That would be something worth having: a membership list for the Sherman chapter of God's Warriors.

Feeling stealthy, Alex pulled out her checkbook and pen and from the inner pocket of her jacket. The deposit slips at the back would have to do for a notebook. She made her way down the first row of cars and trucks—one eye on the vestibule—jotting down numbers as fast as she could in the dim light.

The pickup display reminded her of the one in front of the donut shop. The old models were dirty and rusted out, an array of tools and ropes and things she couldn't make out slung into the back. Cornhuskers and NRA stickers abounded.

Alex was reading one of her NRA favorites, "Out Of My Cold, Dead Hands," when the doors of the vestibule suddenly swung open. She slipped between a beat-up pickup and a shiny new one, crouching down and praying it wasn't their owners who'd just come out. Clack-clack-clack, here they came, closer and closer. Two pairs of footsteps—in heels. Had she been wrong about the God's Warriors meeting?

The heels stopped. Alex breathed again. They were a couple vehicles down. She waited for the sound of locks unlocking, car doors, engines. Instead, she heard two voices, whose volume increased and faded with the gusts of the wind. Women's voices.

Deploying a cautiousness she hadn't known she possessed, Alex raised her head, inch by inch, over the trunk of the truck. The light from the vestibule fell faintly on the women as they stood talking next to a white sedan, each with a big cardboard box in her arms. One woman was a Q-tip blonde; the other, a short-haired brunette. Amanda Wagner and Pauline Thies. Together again.

Alex strained to hear them but at first could only catch murmurs. Then the wind died down. Pauline set her box down on the hood of the sedan with a loud clank. "Not a scrap left!" she exclaimed. "You'd think their wives never fed them." The God's Warriors meetings were catered by the wives?

"Well," Amanda's voice was laden with prim disapproval, "some of them don't have wives." She'd be a lot more comfortable if she took that stick out of her ass.

"Eternal bachelors," Pauline agreed. "But you can't blame some of them. Like Don."

Don, whose wife had vanished. Silence from Amanda.

"Why don't you rest that for a second?" Pauline gestured to the box Amanda held tightly to her chest. Amanda shook her head and looked back at the building.

"We should have made them carry these out for us!" Pauline grumbled.

"Oh no, I don't mind," Amanda protested. "I don't like to bother them."

"Bother them?" Pauline laughed. "We're the ones doing all the work!" Go Pauline.

"Honestly," Pauline continued, "I don't know if it's worse when they meet here or at our houses. At least when it's at home we don't have to lug all of this down here."

"But then," Amanda piped up, "you never know when they'll leave. I mean, finish," she corrected herself. "One time they stayed at our place till eleven—on a weeknight!"

There was a little pause. The shrubbery around the church walls rustled. A dog barked somewhere.

"Do you ever...?" Pauline trailed off. "Never mind."

"Do I ever what?"

"Ever wonder what they actually do?"

The million-dollar question. Was Alex about to finally learn the answer?

"They promote traditional values," Amanda returned, like a school kid reciting a well-known but not particularly interesting fact.

Pauline flapped her hands impatiently. "I know, that's exactly what Reg says when I ask him about it. But why do they hold off the business part of the meetings till we leave? Just between you and me, Amanda, sometimes when they're at our house, I overhear this and that, and I'll tell you, it doesn't sound very Christian to me. Well, you remember how they used to talk about Book Ends! And they don't participate in any of the community things, like other organizations do."

Amanda made a throat-clearing noise. She set her box on the hood. "Oh, well," she said, her voice lifting with a false brightness, "boys will be boys! You know how they are. They just like to go off by themselves and have their little secret clubs."

"But they don't like it when we have our own!" Pauline retorted. "The way Reg grumbles about Equal Partners—and we don't ask him to bring casseroles!" She hauled her box off the hood and slung it into the trunk of the sedan. Thump. "Oh and speaking of that, where are we going to meet this month?"

When was who going to meet—Equal Partners in Faith? In the church basement, surely. Maybe the very room Alex had just been spying on.

Amanda opened the driver's door of the beat-up pickup Alex was crouching next to and slid the box onto the seat. It slammed into the passenger side door with a heavy thump, inches from her head. Amanda was stronger than she looked.

"Hmmm, I don't know." She jangled her keys. The shocks creaked heavily as she got in and shut the door. Alex dropped to all fours and slithered under the shiny new truck next to Amanda's, scraping her hands as she pulled herself across the gravel. Had they noticed the sound? She lay very still and listened. It seemed not.

Amanda started her engine. Then Pauline's medium-heeled boots appeared by the driver's door of the truck. "I need to call Peggy," Pauline said, "but we've got to find somewhere to meet."

"Mmm-hmm. You do that."

It was obviously a kiss-off line, but Pauline seemed oblivious. She started a new topic. "I sure miss Barb." Even over the truck engine Alex could hear the sadness in her voice. "And Book Ends."

"Yes, it's very sad…" Amanda gunned the engine, which drowned out the rest of her sentence. Then she eased off the gas and shifted into manic cheery mode. "See you at the game!" She blasted out of the parking lot.

Pauline stayed rooted to her spot, her boots pointing in the direction of Amanda's now-vanished truck. Then the boots walked away, an engine started and a white boat of a sedan slid by.

Slowly Alex crawled back out, brushing the bits of gravel off her coat and jeans and face, happy to exchange the underbelly of the truck for the starlit sky. The light from the basement, faintly illuminating the shrubs, reminded her that the God's Warriors meeting was still very much in progress. Maybe they had moved to the back of the meeting room, now that the casseroles and Jell-o had been consumed and the little women were gone. The angel of common sense tried descending again. Alex brushed her off her shoulder.

But she must have sent in reinforcements. Just as Alex was getting back into her crouching position by the window, the air exploded with the most deafening church bells she'd ever heard in her life. BONG! BONG! BONG! One shattering peal after another. Alex stood up and put her fingers in her ears, fearing her eardrums would burst. Death by church bells: hadn't she read about that in some mystery? She ran for her car.

It wasn't until she was peeling out of the parking lot that Alex took a full breath. She caught it, though, when she looked in the rearview mirror. A man—a big tall man in a cap—stood in the square of light in front of the vestibule doors. He was watching her go.

CHAPTER TWENTY NINE

Alex double-checked all the locks that night before she stumbled upstairs at one. The light on her answering machine was blinking like a demented Christmas tree.

The first message was from Kathy, just hello and she'd call in the morning. Her cheery voice reassured Alex that things were fine at her place. But Chris's message, which was next, wasn't as comforting. She, too, would call Alex in the morning, but there was an anxiety, an edge in Chris's voice that she'd never heard before. And she couldn't call her back. One o'clock was way too late for most people, let alone a real morning girl like Chris.

The next two calls were hang-ups. But not exactly. If someone hangs up quickly, like a telemarketer or a message-phobe, Alex's machine didn't record it. This caller hadn't done that; she listened to the absolute silence on the other end, which stretched, in both calls, for almost a minute. Crank calls? No. It didn't feel like teenagers on the other end. She thought of that man standing in the parking lot of Fort God tonight, eyes pinned to her car as she left the lot. Time to check the apartment's door and window locks. That night out at Chris's acreage she'd felt the silence and isolation, but was it much different here? A mile outside of Sherman you were in the country, the lights of neighbors only seen at a distance. Alex was downstairs in the pub every night, surrounded by people and noise. No one here now.

She poured a shot of Jameson's and played the final message: Kevin. His cocky voice broke through the eerie silence. "Alex, they interviewed Benson today. We haven't arrested him. Yet. I'll stop by sometime." Click. Yet. Now that sounded promising.

Torn between worry about the call from Chris and the silence-call creep, Alex brushed her teeth and took her contacts out, sure she would have a restless night. But exhaustion won out. She joined the comatose cats on her bed and slept like death on toast.

≫

The next morning Alex sat in her armchair, sipping coffee and looking out the window to the lightly frosted fields, thinking about her Fort God adventure. There had been no time to review events last night. She had returned to find a worried staff and a bar filling up with college students who'd deserted their usual downtown haunts. They'd worked flat-out till closing.

By the bright light of morning, her spying adventure looked both scary and dumb. The darkness, the chill wind, the crackle of the shrubbery, the gravel digging into her hands as she slid under that truck—it all came back to her.

Her reward had been to overhear a conversation that raised more questions than it answered. She'd learned that God's Warriors met not only at Fort God, but at members' homes, catered to by sometimes-unwilling handmaids. But why was Equal Partners searching for a meeting place? Had the ministers decided they were a bunch of troublemakers and refused to let them meet anymore in the church basements?

Alex took a big slurp of coffee and thought about Amanda Wagner. She was a strange customer, all right. Alone in the parking lot with her friend, why not let loose a little? But Amanda's body language, clutching that box, had been as stiff as her refusal to join in Pauline's banter. And it seemed Pauline wasn't the scared rabbit they'd glimpsed in the graveyard at Cooper. Clearly, she didn't enjoy playing serving wench at these mysterious meetings, and just as clearly, she didn't hide Equal Partners from her husband or care much about his opposition to it.

Alex would bet her cats, though, that Dick Wagner was clueless about Amanda's membership.

Cats. She'd better check if hers were ready to come inside. Lucy certainly was. Alex found her glaring up at the door, her fur so puffed up with the cold and damp she looked twice her size. Jane was out there somewhere, but though Alex called she remained invisible. Probably hiding under a bush somewhere in the yard.

Hiding. Did Amanda's friends know that she hid her Equal Partners membership from Dick? If they didn't know, the awkwardness of that conversation last night and Amanda's desire to escape from it suddenly made a lot more sense. How could she stand there bantering with Pauline while the husband she feared sat with his angry men's group mere yards away?

Yes, she feared him. Alex felt it in her bones: Amanda Wagner was an abused wife. She remembered Dick's menacing face, his frightening physical presence when she stood near him at Husker's Monday night, and felt a wave of sympathy for Amanda. She thought back to Barb's story, how Barb had suffered emotional abuse without fully realizing it was happening, how she'd hung on until Wayne's anger finally burst out in violence. It was too easy to imagine Dick crossing that line long ago.

God's Warriors had tried to shut Book Ends down and failed. What if, after years of simmering resentment against Barb and her store, Dick had discovered his wife was a regular customer there? Who knows what kind of rage that might have provoked? The police, it seemed, were close to arresting Wayne Benson for the arson. But someone else had just moved the top of Alex's suspect list. Dick Wagner.

The phone rang as she was pouring her second cup. She dashed into the living room and picked it up on the second ring.

It was Chris. "Hi!" She sounded a bit startled. "You're not screening?"

"I thought it might be you. I got your message last night and I wanted to call you but it was one o'clock."

"I'm usually sound asleep by then but last night was a little strange."

"What happened? Are you okay?"

"No, no, don't worry, I'm okay. We're all okay. Nothing really happened." She was protesting too much.

"So what was the strange thing?" Alex took a slurp of coffee.

"Well," Chris began, "let me go back to earlier in the night, because I think it might be connected." Alex heard a sip on her end, the creaking of leather: Chris settling into her armchair by the fire. "I got home last night around seven, did a few things around the house, then had dinner. Then I got a call from some guy who said he was a reporter on the *Telegraph*. He was calling about my pictures." She paused. "My pictures of the fire."

"What did he want?"

"He wanted me to donate them to the paper. They're running a follow-up story and he'd seen me down there shooting that night. I told him the photos were in police custody and part of the investigation."

"So how did he find out about them?"

"I don't know. Kevin told me those pictures would be secure; he said they're considered evidence, now."

Alex searched her memory. Who else had seen them? Then she remembered another conversation she'd had recently about Chris's pictures. "Hey. What about those college guys who worked at Book Ends—Drew and Rob? The cops showed them that picture you took of Wayne."

"That's right," Chris agreed. "And they probably showed it to other people too. Possible witnesses."

"Starting with other Book Ends employees, I bet," Alex said.

"I'm sure other people noticed me down there, though."

"Of course! Aren't you a local celebrity?"

Chris snorted. "Can you hold on for a sec?" Alex heard a door opening and Chris calling for Soot, Maurice, and Charlie. She took a sip of coffee. It had gone cold, like it always did when she was halfway down the cup. Sounded like she and Chris were having the same kind of morning: drinking coffee, letting pets in and out. Kathy had encouraged Alex to daydream a little more. She let herself, for a minute.

Chris came back on. "I think Charlie must be out on patrol. He's still pretty wound up."

"From what—last night? So what happened?"

"Well, you know how nice it was last night?"

Nice and cold. She heard the leather of Chris's armchair creak again. "Charlie and the cats were out, and a little bit after I got off the phone with that reporter, I tried to call them in. No sign of them."

Alex's earlier sense of apprehension returned.

"Finally, around 10:30, I got Soot and Maurice in. They came in together, by the way. I think they were having an adventure. But no Charlie." Chris paused. "I didn't worry, though. He used to be a farm dog before I got him, and every once in a while he just has to stay out all night. When I was letting the cats in, I heard a vehicle going by on the county road, pretty slow, but I didn't think anything about it. I just came back here to my chair and my book and figured I'd check on Charlie one more time before I went to bed. You know how the wind came up last night?"

"Oh yeah." It had been part of the creepy ambience in Alex's apartment.

"I have all those big trees around my place," Chris continued, "so when I started to hear things I wasn't sure if it was the wind in the trees, or what. Now, I don't usually get spooked. But then I thought I heard something at the window."

Alex shivered. Chris was all alone out there. Like her.

"And then a voice, outside. Muffled. And just then, Charlie started barking like crazy, right under my living room windows. I picked up a poker from the fireplace and ran out the door."

Alex's heart skipped a beat. Or several. "Please tell me you're kidding."

"No. I ran around the back," Chris said, "and...nothing. Then I heard Charlie barking out in front. He was running like mad up the driveway. I couldn't see anything but I made myself stand still and listen."

Alex could see it: Chris standing in front of her house, the dark, starlit night and the sound of the wind in the trees. The front door open behind her, the light pouring out.

"Then I heard it: an engine. A diesel engine, a truck, idling up at the end of my driveway. No lights, though. I just stayed where I was. Then the engine got louder, they turned onto the county road and put the lights on and took off, fast. It was a pickup. Not a big one. Charlie came running back and I dragged him inside and called Jess and Todd."

Alex let her breath out. She'd been afraid Chris was going to tell her she'd toughed it out alone and sat up all night.

"What did they say?"

"Jess said to stay inside and Todd was at my door fifteen minutes later. With his shotgun."

The theme song for "Deliverance" began playing in Alex's head. Still, at a time like that a shotgun could be a girl's best friend. "What did you do?"

"We got flashlights and went all around the house, walked up the driveway. We found tire tracks starting about three-quarters up the driveway. Looks like that's where they parked."

"And then walked down to your cabin. Jesus. Do you have any idea...?"

"No, but I can make some guesses."

Alex could, too. "Is this the connection you talked about before—with that reporter calling about your pictures?"

"Exactly. I get this call and the same night, someone's on my property? Could be a coincidence, I guess."

It didn't feel like one. "If it's all over town that you took the pictures the cops have, that doesn't help us narrow it down." And if they didn't know where Chris lived already, it wouldn't have taken much to find out. The information highway was alive and well in Sherman long before the internet arrived.

But why come out and creep around Chris's property at night? Had they intended to harm her—or just throw a scare into her? These were the same questions Alex had asked only a few days ago about Kathy's tires. She told Chris about the silent, creepy phone calls last night.

"It all seems connected with the fire," Chris said.

"And us looking into it. What if some of God's Warriors heard about your pictures?" Dick and Paul of the big boots came to mind. "I'm lucky I didn't get a visit from them last night. Wait till you hear this." Alex recounted her sleuth escapade at Fort God.

When she finished, Chris whistled. "Wish I could have seen you under that truck!"

"Yeah, that must have been a comical sight. Except I hope no one saw it."

"But someone did see you. That guy who came out. Do you think that's why you got the phone calls?"

"First calls like that I've gotten since I lived here."

"Hey, wait a minute!" Chris exclaimed. "You know who else was around yesterday? Wayne Benson!"

"My God, that's right. For his interview with the cops." All those angry men on the loose in Sherman last night.

"What if he hung around after his interview?" Chris asked. "We have no idea if he went right home."

"Or," Alex added, "how long they kept him there. Kevin left me a message, but it was pretty late. By the way, Kevin said they hadn't arrested him. Yet. And that's all he said. I wanted more, of course."

"He's a real tease!" Chris's rich laughter rang out. He wasn't the only one.

Alex looked at the clock. "Well, I better get rolling. And oh," she groaned, "I have to get my Halloween decorations up. I'm way behind on those."

"Good luck. Oh, Kathy left me a message about a philosophy lecture Monday night." Chris sounded puzzled. "Are you going to that?"

"No, I'll be behind the bar. But I bet you are." Alex chuckled. "Kathy has a plan."

CHAPTER THIRTY

The pub was slammed that weekend. Thoughts about shotguns and men creeping around in the night receded like a distant dream. During a couple brief lulls Alex called Kevin. It went right to voicemail.

Early into happy hour on Saturday, Kevin came rolling in with his friend Neil, the fireman. They were both wearing orange vests and caps. "Please don't tell me you have a dead deer slung over the roof of your car," Alex greeted them as they settled onto their barstools.

"Why don't you go look and see?" Kevin was pulling his vest off. Neil winked at her. No dead deer.

"I owe you guys a beer. What'll it be?"

Alex drew them pints of Guinness and then she was hit with a little rush. When she got back to them it was time for round two. Kevin leaned back on his stool, relaxed and expansive, reminding Alex again of his dad. He took a big sip of beer and wiped the foam mustache off. "Wayne Benson was interviewed yesterday."

"Yeah, I heard." She glanced at Neil.

"He knows all about it."

"But I don't!" She resisted the urge to put her hands around his throat.

A big, slow smile spread over Kevin's face. He'd succeeded in getting a rise out of Alex; now they could proceed. "I saw the tape of the interview," he began. "Guy's a pretty hard case."

"The whole interview?" Alex interjected. "How long was it?"

"Pretty long. I just saw the highlights. Anyway, he just sat there at first." Kevin crossed his arms over his chest. "Like this. Wasn't gonna say a word. He hadn't done anything. But he didn't call for a lawyer, either."

Probably too cheap. Or maybe too broke.

"They let him cool his heels for a while and came back. Ed told him they were getting a warrant for his house, his car, his phone records, everything. So if he'd been calling his ex-wife, there'd be a record of it.

Then they left him alone again. When they came back he was ready to talk. Ed and Mike had been going at him about how he lied to them on Tuesday, how nobody bought that he was just in Sherman to visit a buddy. Then Benson admitted he'd been calling his ex-wife. For two, three weeks before the fire. Ed asked, did he want to get back with her? Benson bust out laughing. Said no, he hated that bitch. He said it was about money. Money she owed him."

So it had been a financial thing. The love motive had never been a realistic possibility, though revenge might still be part of the mix. But Barb owing Wayne money?

"Ed and Mike asked if she'd taken a loan from him," Kevin continued. "Benson said she owed him because that divorce settlement about wiped him out. We'd gotten a hold of that."

"What was the settlement?"

Kevin took a big slurp of beer. "They went to court and

the judge split everything down the middle. Thing is, it was all tied up in the farm and machinery, and Benson wanted to keep the farm. He had to take out a loan, and your friend walked away with a nice check."

"Believe me, she earned it."

"Well," Kevin said, "Benson doesn't think so. He started cussing up a storm. Bitch this, bitch that. That farm was in his family for generations, and this bitch up and leaves and takes half of it with her! Made her sound like a major gold-digger."

Alex shook her head in disgust.

"You know how crop and livestock prices have been these past few years—or maybe not." City girl.

"I've heard a bit about it," Alex returned, declining to take the bait.

"Shit and shittier, that's about it. If you've got big loans out, you're toast. Benson has a big loan. So he starts thinking, who do I know with money? Who would float me a loan so I don't lose the farm?"

"And he thought of Barb?" Alex's jaw dropped.

Kevin shrugged. "You don't know how fucked up people are until you get into law enforcement. This is nothing."

"Did he actually have the gall to ask her for a loan? And how did he know where she was, anyway?"

"Barb's sister," Kevin replied. He screwed up his face. "Can't remember her name."

"Donna?"

"That's it! He'd run into her in town, and she'd call him now and then. Pretty weird."

"I saw her at the funeral. She's a piece of work."

"Benson said Donna kept him updated on where Barb was, what she was doing."

"Donna wanted them to get back together," Alex explained. "Thought Barb had disgraced the family by divorcing him."

"Well, this summer she runs into Benson in Cooper," Kevin continued, "and tells him all about how great Barb is doing with her bookstore in Sherman. By this time, he can't meet his loan payments. And now here's his ex-wife, rolling in money, according to the sister. He gets all cocky at this point with Ed and Mike, tells them he knows how to get around Barb. He'll just sweet-talk her, like her used to."

Talk about living in your own alternate reality. "And how did Barb respond to Wayne's sweet nothings?"

Kevin pointed a thumb down. "No go. He kept calling her, though. At the store; her home number was unlisted."

An unlisted number. Had that been a precaution taken long ago?

"Benson said Barb was pretty surprised to hear from him. Of course she said no to the loan. So Benson kept on calling, but after those first couple calls, she wouldn't talk to him. Then he decided to come to Sherman. She couldn't hang up on him then."

At last: the sequel to Barb's unfinished story. No wonder she'd been so quiet and preoccupied that night at the pub, so unable to respond to those taunts from the God's Warriors crowd. Had she lived till Sunday Alex would have heard about these calls, these nightmare visitations from the past.

"Just around then," Kevin continued, "his friend who lives outside Sherman called, asked Benson to go hunting. He jumped on it. But he didn't know it was Homecoming weekend, and that everywhere was gonna be mobbed, including Book Ends. They went hunting that Saturday and then late afternoon, he went by himself to the store—"

"After a few post-hunting beers, I'm sure," Alex added.

"And a few during-hunting ones, too," Neil grinned.

Kevin ignored them. "But he said it was packed. He couldn't talk to her, though she spotted him, all right. You should see him on the interview tape. He smiles, says she looked like she'd seen a ghost.

He'd called the day before to find out the store hours, and some girl told him they'd be open till ten on Saturday. So he figured he'd come back later, when it would be quieter."

"Huh." This was an interesting twist. "Whoever he talked to must not have been scheduled to work Saturday. But I'm surprised he didn't see signs up about the earlier closing time that day."

"Sounds like Benson's the kind of guy who sees what he wants to see," Neil commented.

"He'd seen a bar a few blocks down," Kevin continued, "and figured he'd kill some time until then. Claimed he couldn't re-member the name of it."

A bar that would attract Wayne, a few blocks down from Barb's. "Huskers."

Kevin nodded. "We took Benson's picture around to the bars yesterday, and the bartender and a waitress at Huskers ID'd him."

Probably he'd been drinking right alongside some of the God's Warriors. Separated at birth. "I'm surprised they could remember him, weeks later."

"The bartender remembered him sitting off by himself, when everyone else was in big groups. The waitress said he com-plained about the price of the beer."

Alex smiled. Poetic justice.

"Up to this point," Kevin said, "we found witnesses to back his story. Two employees at Book Ends put him there between five and six. The bartender and waitress at Huskers aren't as sure of the time frame, but they say it was early evening. After that though..." He shook his head. "We think he's lying about the rest."

At their corner of the bar, you could have heard a pin drop. Down at the other end, though, things were getting noisy. Glasses were empty, or nearly so, and a gallery of impatient faces was turned towards Alex. She gave Kevin a hold-up gesture. "I'll be back in a few minutes." He shouted an order for two more Guinnesses at her retreating back.

It took her bout ten minutes of drink pouring and chatting and ringing up checks before she could get back to them. In the interim, Kevin had commandeered the remote and had turned her lone TV over the bar to some football game. She snatched it off the bar in front of him. "If you don't finish this story, I'll turn it to PBS. I think there's an opera on."

A flicker of horror ran over Neil's face. "Keep the game on and I'll tell you the rest," Kevin bargained.

"Deal." She hit the mute button.

He gave Alex a wry look but continued. "So here's where Benson's story gets hinky. He says he left Huskers around nine, and went back to Book Ends. Says when he pulled up, the lights were on and some cars were parked out front. But then when he went up to the door he saw the Closed sign. And the door was locked.

"Closed? With the lights on? And Barb closed at six."

"Well, that's what he says. Claims it didn't make sense to him either so he knocked and thought he heard something inside, but no one came."

"Then what?"

"Then," Kevin put on his most sarcastic expression, "Benson got back in his truck and drove back to his friend's house."

"Oh, right!" Alex scoffed. "And an hour later Book Ends is on fire. And he was there, watching."

"He said his buddy heard about it on the police scanner and they drove into town to see what was up."

"Bullshit," Neil pronounced.

"They knew he was lying but they couldn't budge him after that. He stuck to his story." Kevin sighed. "We had to let him go."

"So what's the next move?" Alex asked.

"We're looking for witnesses. Anyone who might have

seen Benson downtown that night, between eight and nine."

"Hmmm," Alex mused. "That was a crazy night. Plus, you had all those out-of-towners around, too."

"Tell me about it." He shook his head gloomily. "We know he did it. It's just a question of how."

Kristen was frantically signaling Alex from the waitress station. She left the boys at their corner with fresh beers in front of them, in conditional possession of the remote. The condition was that the TV stayed on mute.

It seemed like everyone Alex knew came in to Fitzpatrick's that night: her regular crowd plus Bill and Sandra, Jess and her husband, Todd— a big, tall guy with a big laugh—and Mern and some cronies she vaguely recognized from the donut shop. When she made her way over to Bill and Sandra's table, Sandra shot her a reproachful look. Oops. Alex had forgotten to call her.

She leaned over so Sandra could hear her above the noise, while Bill was sharing a joke with a guy at the next table. "Sorry for not calling. But you don't need to worry. I think my detective days are drawing to a close."

≫

She told Kathy the same thing when she breezed in for a nightcap around eleven-thirty. Kathy was on her way home from yet another day out of town, this time in Lincoln where she'd been buying basket supplies and having dinner with friends.

Alex put her fingers to her temples and closed her eyes. "I'm getting an image. I see a glass, a glass with Cabernet in it."

"How did you know?"

"Gypsy ancestors," Alex said, setting a brimming glass down on the bar. Then she noticed Kathy hadn't taken her coat off yet. "Cold out?"

"You wouldn't believe how fast the temperature's dropping." Kathy shook a cigarette out of her pack. "Beautiful, though. Tons of stars out tonight."

"Like last night. I saw a few stars."

"Yeah." She lit up and gave Alex a sardonic look. "I heard you got a little religion."

"You talked to Chris today?"

"Yeah. And you should have heard how worried she was about you creeping around in that church parking lot!" The grin of Wednesday night was back.

"Oh." She paused to digest that. "But my night was nothing compared with Chris's!"

"They came right up to her house!" Kathy exclaimed.

"I know. Did Chris tell you Wayne was in town yesterday? So it could have been him. Along with someone else, I guess. Maybe his friend from Sherman."

Kathy gave a little shiver. "That's even scarier."

"No kidding. But it fits. Listen to what Kevin told me tonight." Alex updated her on Wayne's interview with the police. "You guys were right about the farm being involved, somehow." She poured herself a tot of whisky and took a sip. "It's really starting to sound like Wayne did it."

Kathy held up one finger. "He had a serious grudge against Barb." She held up a second. "He was at Book Ends right before the fire started." She held up a third. "He stayed to watch." Fourth finger: "And then he lied about it to the cops."

"And he's violent," Alex added, "and clearly a little out of touch with reality."

"If he was driving his truck from the farm," Kathy pointed out, "he could have had all kinds of chemicals in there, things that could easily start a fire."

"True." Alex hadn't thought of that. Farms were loaded with deadly substances. She sighed. "You know, this week I was so sure it was God's Warriors. I've had such a strong feeling they were involved. I guess I've wanted it to be them."

"You're not alone," Kathy sympathized. "And I'm sure

they were the ones who messed with my truck. But they don't come near to having Wayne's motive for burning down Book Ends."

"Can't argue with you there," Alex said. "And the other stuff last night."

"True. But why were the lights on at Book Ends between eight and nine? Barb closed at what, six that night? I never saw her store lights on after she closed."

"Me neither. But why would Wayne lie about that? I mean, how would it help him?"

Kathy shook her head. They were both stumped.

"I'd better get going." Kathy was looking at her watch. "I've got to start a bunch of baskets tomorrow. Orders for Christmas."

"Are you still planning to go that philosophy lecture Monday night?" Kathy seemed pretty stretched for time these days.

"I don't know. I guess the most appealing part would be kidnapping Gina after, and bringing her down here."

"That's appealing to me! I want to meet her. You know," Alex suggested, "you can always get to the lecture late. Just slip in the back. I bet they'll all be too deep in thought to notice."

"Great idea! I'll do that."

"Will you be kidnapping Chris, too?"

"That goes without saying." Kathy smiled.

"Please don't tell me you have an agenda."

Kathy assumed a dumb-blond expression. "Agenda? What's that?"

❧

Getting ready for bed that night, Alex felt a sense of letdown. It looked like her instincts had been wrong: almost certainly, it hadn't been God's Warriors who'd lit the match that burned down Book Ends. Her list was on the nightstand lamp next to her bed. and she scanned the crossed-out items that she'd thought would lead them to the solution. Secretly, she'd cherished the wish that they would be the ones to solve the case. The consolation would have to be that they helped the cops get there.

Her sense of let-down was premature.

CHAPTER THIRTY ONE

L ater, when she looked back on that Monday, Alex saw that it began very much like the Saturday of the Book Ends fire: peacefully, and without the slightest premonition of things to come. The luxury of two nights in a row of deep, sound sleep had left her feeling rested and reconciled to moving on from the mystery of the fire. It was up to the cops, now.

Alex certainly didn't expect any quick developments. So she was startled to hear Kevin's cheerful voice on the bar phone just as they'd started setting up for lunch.

"Good news!" he greeted her without preamble. "We found three witnesses."

Witnesses? With an effort, she shifted her attention from the boxes piling up around her. Two beer deliveries had arrived at the same time. Then she remembered. "People who saw Wayne outside of Book Ends? How'd you find them?"

"We put a notice on the community TV channel last night.

Asked anyone who'd seen activity near Book Ends between eight and nine that night to call us. A guy called this morning; he and his buddies had been going to the bars on Main Street. They saw Benson in front of the store just after nine. The guy came in and ID'd him from the picture. But it gets better."

"They saw him setting the fire?"

"They saw Benson with Barb, out on the sidewalk. Arguing. It was pretty heated. These guys walked right by them. Our witness kept looking back, thinking it might get physical. But it didn't—at least not by the time they reached the next bar and went in."

Big heroes. Alex thought about the timing. Nine-ish: Barb must have just returned from her Equal Partners meeting. Maybe she'd gone into the store to check on something, then heard knocking at the door. And there he'd stood, in the dark, drunk probably, and insisting she talk to him. She imagined Barb slipping outside, closing the door behind her, determined not to let Wayne into the empty store with her. In the end, it seems, it hadn't mattered. "So what's the plan now?

"They're picking him up this afternoon."

"At his farm?"

"Unless he skipped out."

"Are they arresting him?"

"I don't know," Kevin said though a burst of static. "They've got him on obstruction, so they can if they need to. Once we get him here, we'll bring those guys in to make an ID."

"Where are you, by the way?"

"On the way to the farm." More static. "Talk to you later."

"You're not working today?" She hated to think her mole in the Sherman PD wouldn't be around for the action when Wayne was brought in.

"I'm on at four. Gotta go."

"Call me if you hear anything!" Alex got in before the line went dead.

She was in the kitchen around three, rolling out pizza dough with John when the next piece of news came. Her hands were covered with flour but she picked up the phone anyway. It might be Kevin.

"Alex, it's Carl!" he shouted over highway noise. "Can you hear me?"

"Just about," she shouted back.

"The lab has a result on the fire..." He faded out.

"Carl, I'm losing you; can you hear me? What did they find?"

His voice came suddenly back, saying the last thing Alex would have expected. "They found a fragment of a cigarette butt."

She was speechless.

"Hey, Alex, are you still there?"

"Sorry. A cigarette butt? Where did they find it?"

"It was in material taken from the back room—the point of origin"

"Why did it take them so long?"

"Lab was backed up. Lots of fire investigations lately. Just wanted to..." The connection finally gave out. Just wanted to let her know, probably.

A cigarette? Alex grabbed the heavy marble rolling pin and went back to the piece of dough she'd been working on. She couldn't make sense of it and yet, she now remembered, it was the first thing they'd talked about as a possible cause. The night of the fire Carl, sitting at the bar with Bill, had asked her if Barb smoked.

She rolled another piece of dough into submission. By the time it looked like a pizza crust, she had come up with two explanations. Either the fire was accidental, started by someone sneaking a cigarette in the store, or it was, as they had suspected, arson, and the arsonist had somehow used a cigarette to get it going.

How did Wayne fit into either of these scenarios? He'd been in the store around five. But Barb closed at six. Her smoke alarms hadn't gone off till sometime before ten, though. No, it hadn't been Wayne with a cigarette.

The clarity Alex had felt since Saturday began to dissipate. So did that vague sense of let-down. Maybe this wasn't over yet.

❧

At 4:00 she left John prepping in the kitchen and came upstairs for a break. The girls were fast asleep but roused themselves to hassle her for attention and treats. Then she let them out.

It was so quiet she could hear the clock in her kitchen ticking. Alex wished, as she settled into her armchair with a cup of tea, that she could somehow absorb the tranquil atmosphere. No dice. There was too much to think about. She put her detective shoes back on and mulled over the possibilities but no new ones came: her mind circled round and round the same theories and suspects, over and over. Wayne. God's Warriors. Had they overlooked another possibility?

Alex pulled Miss Marple off her coffee table, dusty and neglected. If the book was a car someone would have written Clean Me on the back window. Oh well. She'd read it before, though she couldn't remember the solution.

Her break had vanished and it was time to head back downstairs. Lucy came in but there was no sign of Jane. Damn. Alex didn't want her out wandering around tonight.

She went back downstairs with a growing sense of unease.

❧

At 8:30, the bar was so quiet Alex expected tumbleweeds to come blowing through any time. Her two unsuccessful attempts to get Jane in had been the most exciting events of the early evening.

At 8:40, a river of people poured through the door. Kathy and Chris led the pack of assorted professors and students who headed to the pub en masse after the lecture. More trickled in as Kristen and Alex scrambled to get the first drink orders out. Philosophy must be thirsty work.

Alex's friends perched at their usual corner. To Kathy's right sat a tall, attractive, Italian-looking woman: Gina Meziere. To Chris's left sat Pauline Thies and Amanda Wagner. Kathy's career in kidnapping had gotten off to a spectacular start.

Her friends had the glazed look of people who'd been trapped in a lecture hall against their will. Chris was wearing that butter-colored suede jacket. Down, girl.

Kathy did the introductions; strange to realize that she'd never actually met these women. Of the three, Gina was the most relaxed, making herself at home in that New York way, talking a mile a minute, complimenting Alex on her selection of red wines. Alex soaked in her accent like a sponge.

Pauline seemed a little wary and out of place: Alex was sure she'd never been in the pub. But Chris and Kathy's banter was thawing her out. Not so Amanda. Rigid and unsmiling, she sat on her barstool looking like she would rather be anywhere else. Even her Q-tip hair radiated tension. "I'll have a Diet Coke," she said primly, not quite meeting Alex's eye.

Pauline protested. "Oh, Amanda, have a drink! This is our girls' night out!"

"Have a glass of Bordolino," Gina suggested. "It's good for you, hon." Hon. Alex hadn't heard that in a while. More resistance from Amanda. She poured her a Diet Coke.

The professors, esconsed at fireside tables, got their first drinks down in a flash and Alex was soon busy pouring and mixing a second round. When she returned to the corner they were all chatting comfortably. Except for Amanda.

Alex smiled at Gina. "Girls' night out, huh?"

Gina nodded. "It's turned into one! I asked Amanda and

Pauline to come to the lecture tonight. We haven't seen each other recently."

"Not since the fire," Pauline said quietly. Then everyone got quiet.

Chris broke the silence. "Were you friends with Barb?" The playing-dumb strategy: it was a good way to get information.

"Yes," Gina sighed, "we were. And Barb and I started a group together. Equal Partners in Faith."

Pauline nodded. No response from Amanda. She was looking down the bar, seeming to ignore the conversation. But she had become, if it were possible, even more rigid.

"And Barb," Pauline added regretfully, "gave us our nicest place to meet."

"What?" Kathy, Chris and Alex spoke almost in unison. Alex leaned in towards Pauline. "Equal Partners in Faith met at Book Ends?"

Gina and Pauline looked puzzled: what was the big deal? It was Gina who answered. "Yeah, sometimes we did, when it was convenient for Barb. Otherwise, we'd go to church meeting rooms. But they weren't as comfortable. You know?"

Alex looked from Kathy to Chris: their wheels were turning too. Kathy pulled out her cigarettes and offered the pack around. Gina snagged one right away; Pauline hesitated but then took one.

Amanda continued looking down the bar, seeming to absent herself from the conversation. Nice try. Jane and Lucy did the same thing: totally alert, taut with attention but pretending to ignore Alex. Amanda's ears weren't swiveling around but her body language was just as obvious. With the cats it was funny. With Amanda it was creepy.

Now it was Kathy's turn to act. "Alex," she said, as if she searching her memory for a vague recollection, "didn't you say Barb had a meeting the night of the fire?"

"That was us!" Gina slapped her hand down on the bar.

"I called the police the next day. A woman took the message but they never got back to me." She gave a big Italian shrug. "What are you gonna do?" Dispatcher Dee strikes again.

"What do you mean, that was you?" Alex asked.

"Equal Partners—we met there that night. And then the fire started, what—an hour later? I just couldn't believe it!"

So Barb had not been away at a meeting, returning shortly before nine: she'd been at Book Ends with her group. And the fire started shortly after. How?

"Refills?" Alex asked, hardly waiting for an answer before swooping up their glasses and heading over to the wine bottles. Why had she thought Equal Partners met at churches? Think. She poured Chris a glass of Syrah, the same house wine she'd served to Barb the night of her half-told story. But their conversation about Equal Partners had been in Book Ends that Tuesday. She closed her eyes and remembered: the food magazines she'd browsed, their conversation about a Thanksgiving dinner at the pub, the pride in Barb's voice as she talked about the group. And then it came back. Barb had indeed said they met at their churches. *Usually.* Bad word to forget.

From the corner, fragments of the women's conversation drifted down to Alex: missing Barb, missing Book Ends. Alex brought back four refills; Amanda had barely touched her Diet Coke. "I heard you took some pictures at the fire," Pauline was saying to Chris.

Chris smiled ruefully. "That got all over town pretty quickly. The police found a few of them interesting."

"We did, too," Kathy said. "You know, Chris is a professional photographer. She just got back from a trip to Africa."

"Africa!" Gina exclaimed. "I'm so jealous!"

"Where in Africa?" Pauline was clearly impressed, too. Chris must get this reaction to her work all the time.

Amanda was looking at Chris too. But her expression was blank. It reminded Alex's of someone else—last week, at Huskers. Dick Wagner, with his dead eyes. Sociopaths had dead eyes. Like husband, like wife?

Her cell phone rang and she tore her eyes away from Amanda. It was Kevin. "Hey, I'm at the station."

"What's up?"

"Thought you'd want to hear this. We've got Benson here now. They're still questioning him."

"Anything new?"

"Two of those guys—the ones who were bar-hopping on Main Street—ID'd him in a lineup. So now he admits he saw Barb. Still swears up and down he didn't set the fire, though." Kevin snorted. "But get this. Now he says when they were arguing out on the sidewalk, a woman came out of the bookstore. Slipped out is how he put it."

"Just one woman? Do the police know there was a meeting there that night?"

"A meeting? No. When was it?"

"Right before the fire started. A women's group Barb was in. I just found out, myself. Did Wayne give a description of this woman?"

"Hold on, I'll ask." Kevin put the phone down. There was a sudden burst of radio noise and people talking on his end. He came back on. "Medium height, thirties. Blond. Short hair."

Slowly and stiffly, as if she had a crick in her neck, Alex turned her head to look back down the bar at her friends. They weren't looking at Alex.

Amanda was.

Alex turned her back and hunched over the phone. "Kevin, can you come over here?"

"What—"

She cut him off. "I can't explain, but I need you to come down here. Fast."

"Come on, Alex," he began to protest. Then the line went dead.

"Kevin??" But the call had been dropped. She called his cell back; it went right to voicemail.

After that, everything happened quickly.

⌇

She was returning to her friends, a fake smile plastered to her face, when the philosophy crowd decided to decamp. All at once. The next ten minutes passed in a blur of ringing up checks and talking to the professors who came up to the bar to pay their bill and chat. She went on autopilot, making change and small talk while her brain tried to process what she'd just discovered. As the last professor turned to leave, Alex looked down to the corner of the bar, trying for a neutral face.

Amanda was gone.

She zoomed over to her friends. "Where's Amanda?" They all looked startled. So much for neutral.

What's up? Kathy mouthed. Alex ignored her. There was no time to waste with mimes.

"She went home," Pauline said. "Honestly, I wouldn't be in such a rush if I were her."

Gina nodded. "I guess we shouldn't have pressured her to come out after the lecture. I thought it would be a nice break."

"She needs it," Pauline agreed. "But Dick's just got her so…" Alex could have finished the sentence: Dick's got her so scared.

Gina tipped up her glass and took a last sip. "I'd better get going, too. I haven't seen my husband all day."

"Me too." Pauline stood.

"I'll come back here soon, with Max." Gina flashed them all a big smile and they headed out into the night.

"What's going on?" Kathy asked.

"Jesus Christ, you guys. The fire—I think Amanda Wagner started it!" She summarized Kevin's call. "And when I was on the phone with him, she was watching me. He gave me the description and I turned around and she was staring at me.

She knows that I know." Alex pulled her canvas jacket on.

Chris locked eyes with her. "You're sure?"

"I'm sure. When did she leave?"

"Right when everyone came up to the bar to pay." Kathy looked at the Guinness clock. Like ten minutes ago?"

Ten minutes. An arsonist could accomplish a lot in that time. Alex ran through the kitchen to the back door. She flung it open and ran headlong into a wall of smoke.

❧

The wall was thin. Alex came right through the other side of it and stopped.

The fire was in the dumpster. Flames leapt out of it, framed by a night sky of black velvet. In front of it, maybe six feet back, stood Amanda Wagner. Just watching. Alex would never forget the light of the fire on her frozen, empty face.

"You crazy bitch!" she screamed. No response. She ran to the dumpster, tore off her coat and began beating at the flames with it.

Kathy and Chris burst through the wall of smoke carrying fire extinguishers. Only seconds later, it seemed—time was telescoping for Alex—the flames were sizzling out under the foam.

Amanda Wagner still stood there, looking blankly at where the fire had been. Alex dropped her ruined coat and walked over to her. Did Amanda even see her? She stepped right in front of her, blocking the view of the smoldering dumpster. Kathy and Chris came over flanked her on either side.

And then Amanda finally seemed to take them in. She looked from one to the other, her pale, dead eyes finally resting on Alex. "The first time," she said, her voice a near-whisper, "it was an accident. This time, it wasn't."

CHAPTER THIRTY TWO

When Kevin pulled into the parking lot a minute later, that's how he found them. Lit by his headlights they stood in the swirling smoke facing down Amanda like some spaghetti western in hell. It took several confusing minutes to make Kevin understand that he was looking at the arsonist of Book Ends and the near-arsonist of Fitzpatrick's, not some harmless church lady who'd wandered onto the scene. This, Alex told him, was the blonde Wayne saw slipping out of Book Ends that night. The blonde just stood there, her strange eyes gazing at Kevin as if he could somehow save her.

After that, after Kevin had bundled an unresisting, handcuffed Amanda into the back of his car, it was a chaos of flashing lights and fire hoses and men shouting. Alex protested to Neil Schaeffer that the fire in the dumpster was out. Didn't matter, he said, the back wall could still catch. It didn't. But the wall would need time to cool down and the Fire Chief ordered her to close the pub for a day. It would the first time since August.

Small price to pay. Alex looked at the barely scorched walls. She'd been lucky.

She didn't feel quite as lucky the next morning; she could barely raise her head off the pillow. The girls, too, seemed unwilling to move and looked blearily at her from atop the blankets with morning-after eyes. When the firefighters finally let her upstairs she'd found Lucy squeezed into the back of her bedroom closet. Jane hadn't shown herself till Alex returned from the police station at three a.m.

Alex was brewing a pot of coffee, inhaling the fumes, when the phone rang. She needed a cup before talking to anyone. "Alex!" Carl's cheery voice boomed from the answering machine. "Kevin called me. Great news! I hear you and your friends were in the thick of it. I warned you!" He paused. "But I'm glad you're all okay. Give me a call sometime, when things settle down there."

She smiled. Hopefully he and Suzanne would be out to visit soon; dinner and drinks would be on the house. Alex would call him when her brain was functioning. And she had the full story.

It was a beautiful fall day—Indian summer—with a breeze from the south that was, for once, gentle. Alex opened all the doors and windows in the pub, hoping it would flush out the faint remains of the smoke. The room looked forlorn, empty of customers, chairs turned upside down on tables.

A little after four Kathy and Chris arrived, looking tired. Even Chris didn't have her usual glow of health. Alex had taken down the barstools at their corner.

"Has he been by yet?" Kathy asked.

"Should be any time."

When Kevin blasted in a few minutes later, she was pouring them large whiskeys. "Well, look who's here!" he hailed them, fully back into smart-ass mode. "It's the Hardy Boys!"

"And Miss Marple," Alex added, feebly. She drew Kevin a pint of Guinness and he pulled up a barstool. From his inside jacket pocket he fished out a DVD. "I have to get this back by quarter to six. My friend goes off duty then." He fixed Alex with his best stern stare.

"How late were you at the station last night?" Chris asked him. "I mean, this morning."

"Till five." He rubbed the red stubble on his cheeks.

Alex took a sip of whiskey. "What finally happened with Wayne?" The police had still been holding him when they left the station.

"We let him go this morning. After we got his statement processed. Once we told him we had a confession for the fire, he spilled the rest in a hurry."

They were all ears. Kevin sat back, reveling in their attention. Just like his dad: that ham ball love of holding an audience. It's an Irish thing.

He took a big gulp of Guinness. "Well, it turns out Benson told us the truth, up to the part about him just driving away. He didn't. They kept arguing out on the street and it escalated. Barb started to look scared. He thought she'd try to go back into the store or up to her apartment. But she must have known he'd follow her, force his way in. So she started walking down Main and went into the first bar she saw.

Kevin cracked his knuckles. "That was a smart move. Benson followed her in; she'd found a seat at the bar. There was nothing he could do. She was just gonna wait him out. So he left. Back at his friend's house a little while later, they heard about the fire on the police scanner and came down to watch. He admits he wasn't too heartbroken about it."

Here, finally, was the explanation of the timing. Barb had gone outside the store to deal with Wayne. Then when it escalated she became frightened and took shelter in a bar, knowing that in the middle of a big Homecoming crowd Wayne couldn't touch her.

"How long were they there?" Alex asked.

"At least forty five minutes, Benson said. Though it felt like hours to him."

While she'd been arguing with Wayne in the street, Amanda had set the fire. And then slipped out. When Barb came back from the bar, the fire had started. Alex was sure she ran back inside to get Maurice.

Two questions remained. How had Amanda started the fire? And, of course, the biggest one. *Why?*

"Gotta head." Kevin stood.

"Hey you," Alex got up and put her hand on his arm. "Thanks for all your help." He grumbled and shuffled and got himself out the door at top speed.

"He's not so bad, really," Chris said.

"That's the thing about my family. They're a pain in the ass, but they always come through in the end." She topped up their whiskies and popped the DVD into the TV.

Snow filled the screen for a few seconds, then there she was: Amanda Wagner, folded hands resting on top of a table. She was alone, no lawyer by her side. And still not a hair out of place.

A detective's voice recited the date and time, their names and hers. He asked her if she wanted a lawyer present. A vehement head shake no.

The voice continued, "Mrs. Wagner, please tell us your whereabouts the evening of Saturday, October eleventh."

She took a deep breath and stared straight ahead. Would she talk? Alex held her breath. But Amanda had just been getting a lungful. It all came spilling out.

"That was a busy night," she began, her hands fluttering.

"So much to do. I was one of the organizers for the benefit, you know, for Fred Clausen, and we ran out of spaghetti and we didn't have enough chairs. Some people were even rude about it!" Imagine that. She spoke as if she were gossiping with a neighbor in Bag N Go.

"That made me late for our meeting," she continued. "Equal Partners in Faith. Last spring, my friend Pauline told me about it and she made it sound like a nice women's church group. Well!" She pursed her lips. "Sometimes we talked about the Bible but really, they were just looking to make trouble. They wanted equal roles for the women in our churches!"

A detective's voice cut in. "Why did you stay in the group, then?" Good question.

Amanda shifted in her chair. "Well, I liked some of the women, and the Bible discussions were quite good. But," her eyes flashed with sudden anger, "the last few meetings, I didn't like where some of them were heading. They wanted to start a petition and circulate it to all the churches in Sherman. Except the Catholic one, of course!" she hastily amended.

Alex laughed.

Amanda's face took on a shocked expression as she leaned forward. "They wanted to demand that women be deacons! Can you believe it?" Shaking her head, she settled back. "Well, you can imagine how the ministers would have felt about that! And the men in Dick's group. And Dick..." she trailed off, her face darkening.

Amanda visibly pulled herself back together. "I never imagined they'd really go through with it. But when I got to the meeting that Saturday night at the bookstore, they were writing up the petition! And they wanted *me* to circulate it at Our Redeemer." Her eyes widened. "Then I knew I had to get out of this group. Before Dick found out, or the minister. I just didn't know how. I hate fussing and arguing, and if I told them how I felt they'd all just be against me."

"God forbid," Kathy said.

"Whenever we met at Book Ends," Amanda continued, "one of us would stay behind and help Barbara clean up the coffee mugs and plates. That night it was my turn. She didn't want me there, though, I could tell." Amanda frowned. "Seemed like she was a little high strung and I was getting on her nerves, fussing around. Fussing around, that's what Dick calls it, though if the house weren't neat as a pin he'd have a fit!" The indignant face again.

"Then someone started knocking really loud on the front door, and Barbara went to answer it, and that's the last I saw of her." Amanda shrugged. "I finished cleaning and waited, but she never came back. So rude! She just up and left me there." She leaned back in her chair.

A detective's voice. "But you didn't leave. What happened then?"

"Well," she resumed in over-the-neighbor's-fence mode, "I went to get my purse from the coffee table. And someone had left a pack of cigarettes—the matches were tucked into the cellophane. Pauline's, I bet, all ready for the ride home. Sneaky." Her lips pursed in disapproval. "Her husband doesn't know she smokes! I used to smoke. Dick made me quit though, years ago, said it was a filthy habit. But when I saw that pack of cigarettes that night...well. I couldn't resist." A naughty-girl face. Alex almost gagged. "I took one out and lit it."

"There's our cigarette butt," Chris said.

"I smoked a little of it," Amanda admitted, coyly. "It felt good. Then I thought, what am I doing—what if Dick smells the smoke on me? I looked around for an ashtray, but of course the store was no smoking. I'd have to throw it into the gutter, out front." She put her hand up to her neck.

"I was in the back of the store, having one more puff before I went outside. But then when I went to pick up my purse, over by the magazine shelves, what did I see? A magazine: a disgusting magazine! Two women were kissing on the cover! And when I looked around, there were more just like it."

"The gay and lesbian section," Alex breathed. "She must never have noticed it before."

"It was trash!" Amanda's face contorted with rage. "How dare she bring that into our community! And then," her expression changed again, miming surprise, "I heard all this shouting out in front of the store. Barbara's voice, and a man's. She sounded like she was in trouble. But I couldn't run out of there with that cigarette in my hand! So I dropped it on the floor and stepped on it. Then I went out the front door, but there was no one there. I looked up and down the street but she was gone, and the man, too. So I left."

"Holy crap," Kathy said. "What a whack job."

She'd switched into scolding-schoolmarm mode. "Now mind you, I'm sure that cigarette was out! You can't be sure it was me! And she was gone! Why did she come back?" The nerve of Barb.

"And when you heard about the fire?" a detective's voice asked.

"I couldn't believe it! I drove back downtown and walked up as close as I could. I saw Dick and his friends but they didn't see me—I stayed back. I watched the fire and I was afraid, and then…" She hesitated.

"Then I started thinking about all the trouble that woman had caused. Making the men angry when she opened the store—the kind of books she had. Starting this women's group. She even had an Obama campaign poster in her store window!"

A strange light came into her eyes. "And then I thought, maybe it was an act of God, and I….I was his instrument. Dick and his group were saying at one of their meetings that that place needed a good, Biblical fire."

There was a pause while the detectives digested this.

"Fucking freak!" Alex yelled at the TV. "So God kept the

cigarette burning?"

"And what about tonight, at Fitzpatrick's?" a detective asked.

The prim schoolmarm transformed herself again: Medea with a Q-tip do. "Those women! Drinking and carousing around and I don't know what-all. Not one of them married and not one of them goes to church."

"Right on," Chris commented.

"They'd all been poking their noses about the fire. Everyone thought it was an accident—and it was! But no, they had to go stirring up trouble. One of them had taken pictures. And the one who owns that bar..." Her eyes narrowed. "She knew. She knew it was me. I saw it in her eyes tonight. I couldn't have Dick find out. No," she said, fear sweeping over her face. "I saw those big garbage bins with all that paper sticking out." She paused. "It seemed like a sign."

"Jesus," Kathy said. "Does she carry matches around with her?"

A detective's voice: "What did you mean last night, when you said it was an accident the first time, but this time it wasn't?"

Silence from Amanda.

"Did you plan that fire last night?"

"No."

"Did you want anyone to get hurt?"

Amanda shrugged.

There was a scraping sound. Probably the detectives pushing their chairs farther away from her. Good plan.

"One last question, for now, Mrs. Wagner. We've had some incidents reported—vandalism, harassment—involving the women you were just speaking about. Are you responsible for that?"

A twitchy little laugh. "I may have made a call or two. But the tires—that wasn't me."

"Who was it?"

"You'll have to find that out yourself." She was coy again. "Let's just say alcohol was involved." Her face darkened and she pressed her lips together.

"Okay then, we're concluding this interview..." the detective began. Amanda patted her hair and looked straight ahead.

Alex hit the stop button. "Well, if she thinks we're bad, I hope she likes her new girlfriend in the state pen."

Kathy lit a cigarette. "Oh, they're gonna love her in Lincoln. Those magazine covers will seem pretty tame to her in six months."

"I wonder," Chris mused, "what a psychologist would make of that confession—or maybe will, if she goes for a psychological defense. It was so weird. She shifted all her anger to Barb—and us. Like Barb and us troublemakers were to blame for her problems!"

"Classic victim response," Kathy noted. "You never attack the oppressor, you go after the people below you. That's probably how she saw us unmarried carousers."

"God forbid she'd known I'm gay," Alex added. Oops. She'd just come out to Chris. Chris didn't respond. She knew. Duh.

Kathy sipped her whisky. "Looks like it was Amanda who called you, Alex. My tires and the people Chris's visitors—that sounds like God's Warriors. Probably Barb's broken window, too. Maybe another drunken night, after they left Huskers."

"If Amanda knows who it was," Alex said, "it had to be Dick. Probably with his buddy, Paul. She must have heard them bragging about it. And then gotten her own ideas. But they had me fooled. They must have had loved that—swaggering around, hinting they'd started the fire. But it was the little woman all long."

"But," Chris pointed out, "there *was* a God's Warrior's connection, if indirectly. That woman is so scared, so programmed, she put a cigarette out on a wood floor rather than have anyone see her with it—and maybe tell her husband. Then she has to justify it as God's mission."

Alex sighed. "So Amanda goes to prison and Dick gets away with all the years of abuse." She paused. "And Barb is dead."

"Domestic abuse. That's our dirty little secret in these small towns." Chris shook her head. "It never seems to change."

And it doesn't just harm the victim. Barb had escaped her own situation, but in a way, domestic violence had gotten her in the end.

Kathy raised her glass. "Here's to Barb." They raised theirs and took a sip. A silence fell.

Chris broke it. "I have another toast. Here's to, well, a semi-successful detective adventure."

Kathy was up and putting her jacket on. "We did one thing, for sure. We made Amanda Wagner crazy enough that she tried it again. You know, she might never have been caught, otherwise. No one was looking at her at all."

True. Seems they hadn't done such a bad job, after all.

Kathy jingled her car keys. "Well, girls, time to get back to the baskets. Let's get together soon."

"I'll be here," Alex said, "barring another crazy arsonist."

"Hope you both get a good night's sleep!" She breezed out the door. Chris didn't follow her.

Alex went behind the bar and pulled out a big box. "I must be the last business in Sherman to put up Halloween decorations."

"You've been kind of busy."

She took the paper decorations out and laid them on the bar: spiders, witches, black cats, a collection she'd bought at a garage sale last summer and then promptly forgotten about. She held a vampire aloft, three feet tall and fangs dripping.

They stood on chairs and hung them randomly throughout the pub: instant Halloween. The sunlight came in through the windows as they worked quietly side by side. It was like last week when they made the strudel together.

Chris looked up at Alex as she hung the last one, a black cat with its back arched. "Would you like to come over for dinner tonight?" She knew the pub was closed. She didn't say anything about asking Kathy.

Alex could feel a smile starting as she looked down. Chris smiled back.

And the breeze blew through, and the goblins and witches danced above them.

THE END

ACKNOWLEGEMENTS

My thanks to everyone who helped to midwife Shot Glass through its long birth process. To my Nebraska readers and partners in crime: Ed and Maureen Batistella, Ruth and Eddie Elfers, Heather Thomas, Stacy McMillen and Jan Meyer. To Lisa Hardaway and Leslie O'Ryan for filling this Jersey girl in on the the facts and realities of farming. To Lisa Sandlin for her incisive, invaluable suggestions on various drafts. To Bob Lascaro, for a beautifully designed book and the coolest cover ever. To Charles Salzberg for his advice on the opening, and Fire Chief Phil Monahan for feedback on arson investigation procedures in Nebraska. To Cagney, Tess, Fiona, and Moo, who rode shotgun on Shot Glass and live on these pages.

And greatest thanks of all to Katja: best friend, cheerleader, editor extraordinaire and love of my life, without whose encouragement and belief in me this book would not have been possible.

About the Author

Siobhan Kelly is a Jersey girl who taught for thirteen years in Nebraska, where she wrote a food column for the Norfolk Daily News. She lives at the Jersey Shore with her partner and three demanding cats, and is at work on a sequel to Shot Glass.